MY SISTER'S BABY

SUSAN EDMUNDS

Copyright © 2026 Susan Edmunds

Layout design and Copyright © 2026 by Next Chapter

Published 2026 by Next Chapter

Edited by Mary Novak

Cover art by Charlyn Llanos

This book is a work of fiction. Names, characters, places, and incidents are the product of the author's imagination or are used fictitiously. Any resemblance to actual events, locales, or persons, living or dead, is purely coincidental.

All rights reserved. No part of this book may be reproduced or transmitted in any form or by any means, electronic or mechanical, including photocopying, recording, or by any information storage and retrieval system, without the author's permission.

CHAPTER ONE
AMY

This might seem obvious, but there's something singularly undignified about having a cold, plastic probe inserted into your vagina so that pulsing images of your insides can be projected on to a screen next to your head.

Every time it happened, it made me think of those expensive thermometers people stick inside a chicken going on the barbecue.

As a glob of lubricating jelly made its presence felt on my inner thigh, I was hit with a flashback of the first time I'd been in this position, lying on the crinkly plastic sheet, staring at the ceiling, crossing every finger and toe in hope.

Back then, my husband, Andy – now ex, for which I was thankful - had given me a wink as the technician readied for the procedure, as if he thought I was going to get some sort of physical enjoyment out of it.

I'd given him the iciest glare I could muster but it sailed past him. All I'd wanted to know was why I wasn't conceiving. We were having enough sex – even though it had become akin to forcing myself to go to the gym, which I also did on the advice of the fertility gurus. But while it seemed that everyone around me only had to look at their partner and they had an array of children, there was a baby-shaped gap in my life that thumped like a heartbeat.

Now, several years and countless procedures later, and one husband fewer, I just wanted the latest scan over with. The wish for a child still rattled in my bones but the process so far had been one crushing disappointment after another.

The image pulsed. I still could never tell what I was looking at when the technician took her snapshots of the moving screen.

It looked like those ultrasound photos you see from people announcing their pregnancies. But it was safe to assume there was no baby anywhere in the murky shapes, just something that might have been a fallopian tube. Or maybe a bit of cervix. Who could tell? They could point out a left phalange and I'd have believed it. I shot a look at the technician, whose name badge said she was Maria. She probably wasn't even alive when that Friends finale aired.

The baby-making process had been so long, and I had been in this spot so many times, that I was – almost – used to hearing bad news. Still, I bristled at Maria's thin smile as she started to retrieve the wand. Was it in her contract that she had to smile, whatever happened?

The instrument emerged from my body with a sort of faint vacuum sucking, then an inelegant "pop".

"I'll let you get tidied up, then head on through to the consultation room across the hall, the doctor's waiting for you."

She pushed a box of tissues my way as if anything less than a shower would get rid of the wash of lubricant rapidly pooling under me. I yanked at the paper sheet that was still lying across my midriff in a flimsy imitation of privacy. "Thanks."

I was still slimy as I perched on the edge of the chair opposite my doctor a few minutes later. I anchored my toes into my sandals, pushing them into the floor as if to stop me sliding off.

The glimpse of my shoes was a welcome distraction for half a second. If I focused on the shiny yellow leather, I could temporarily quiet the anxiety that pinged through me whenever I was in this room.

There aren't a lot of perks when it comes to being in fashion retail – particularly not in smallish-town New Zealand where most people are either Kmart devotees, disciples of Temu or are still wearing the clothes that served them well in the 1990s. But occasionally adding to my own wardrobe at wholesale prices can be one of them.

The doctor, Amelia Scott, had pulled up the images taken from the scan on her computer screen.

She tucked one side of her caramel bob behind her ear and turned to face me. Her face was gentle. "How are you feeling?"

I sighed, twisting my fingers around each other in my lap. Here we go again. "I'm fine."

She meant well, but I needed her to just get on with it. So much of my life had been spent waiting for this woman to give me the next update. Waiting for the call to let me know when my ovaries were ready to have eggs retrieved. Not fun, that procedure.

Calling to let me know how many embryos had been fertilised. Calling to let me know how many could be transferred. Calling to give me the results of the pregnancy tests.

She travelled up from Auckland to her clinics in Whangarei and probably saw me almost every other time she made the two-hour trek north. I knew the pictures on her walls – prints of inoffensive beach scenes that were no coastline that I was familiar with, although we were surrounded by beaches on all sides – and the softly vanilla scent pumped out by the air freshener cartridges plugged into the walls.

It hadn't all been bad news. Three times, she had called to report a positive result. But none had stuck. Some had lasted just long enough to get everyone's hopes up, but none had ever made it to the finish line. It was wildly frustrating that the one thing I wanted most in the world was also completely out of my hands, and maybe not even entirely in Amelia's extremely qualified ones.

Surely, she didn't need to ask how I was. Worry was running laps of my stomach; it must be evident on my face.

My phone buzzed, momentarily popping the tension. A text from my younger sister Breanna, reminding me of her daughter's upcoming swimming sports. I'd already told her I would be there, ready to put my game face on for her and her group of Botoxed, shiny-haired private school mum friends. We used to play "guess who's just had too much filler" when her son, Charlie, first started at the school but over time Breanna had ended up getting to know most of the women, which made it more awkward. They also started making it so obvious that most of the fun went out of it. I turned my phone over.

Amelia was waiting for me when I looked up.

"I'm afraid we don't have great news here," she cleared her throat. "I requested the scan today, as you know, because I wanted to see whether there might be something else going on that's stopping us getting the outcome we want.

"It looks as if the problem with your pregnancies may relate to an issue with your uterine wall."

I looked at her. What did that mean?

She gestured to the monitor next to her. "You can see here and here, there's a bit of a lighter shade. I think that could be your issue."

I leant back in my chair. "So, what do we do?"

She tapped her fingers on the desk. "I know you only have the one embryo left and I think you said you're not interested in pursuing another round with donor sperm."

I cringed. I couldn't put my body through that. Between the temperature fluctuations and the bloating, I'd felt like a sweaty Michelin man with an attitude problem.

"I believe it could be time for you to consider other options."

It was like I was floating above myself, looking down. When

was this going to end? What else could this process throw at me? "Other options?"

Amelia nodded. "Is surrogacy something that you would consider? It can be a useful solution for people like you who have healthy embryos but are having trouble carrying to term."

The word smacked me in the face. Wasn't surrogacy something that celebrities did, so they could produce a baby and a movie in the same year? Not women like me who had $35 in their bank account – just enough for a bottle of wine and a takeout - and planned to kit out the baby's room with a thrift shop haul or three?

Of all the things I might want to have in common with Kim Kardashian or Nicole Kidman, the use of someone else's uterus was not near the top of my list.

My stomach did a slow somersault and I had to fight an urge to bolt from the room.

How could I ask anyone to do that for me? There was also something about the idea of someone else being pregnant with and giving birth to my baby that made me feel sick with envy.

Yes, I know. Pregnancy isn't exactly something you do for the fun of it. I listened to Breanna complain through the nine months of both of hers about heart burn and smell aversion and swollen ankles and brain fog. But – as with many things in our lives, weird friends excepted – she had what I wanted. Two healthy children at the end of it. I wanted my turn at all of it.

I had it all planned out – the people I would have with me when I gave birth, the way I'd bring my child home to a beautifully decorated nursery, with a gorgeous decal of peonies I'd found online if it was a girl and a beautiful khaki shade if it was a boy.

But then what was the alternative? Just no baby? My green, satin t-shirt had begun to cling to my skin where a sheen of sweat had broken out. That couldn't be an option. I didn't spend a whole lifetime dreaming of giving a kid the little cocoon of unconditional love I'd never had, only to give up.

Amelia was still looking at me.

"It's a big decision, you'll want to take your time over it. Why don't we regroup in a month or so and see what you're thinking about for your next step?"

I nodded mutely. "How long does it take, the surrogacy thing?"

She screwed up one side of her face, thinking. "If you have someone who's willing, it might not take too long. There's not as much prep in it if we're not harvesting."

I swallowed hard. "Okay, I'll give it some thought."

She gathered a stack of paper together and tapped one edge against the desk, indicating our meeting was over.

I pretended to look for something in my handbag to give me a minute to collect myself. There wasn't a whole lot of thinking to do. I still needed this to happen.

Over the past few years, it had become all-consuming.

Without getting all psychoanalytical about it, I'd decided it stemmed from my childhood. You'd look at the photos and think it was idyllic – two little girls living in a house by the beach with our gorgeous mother and doting father. And maybe you'd be right, I mean it certainly wasn't awful.

But my father left when I was two and Mum married Breanna's dad shortly after. Brian was loving and kind but, particularly when I was a teenager, I felt like an outsider. The three of them in their little biological bubble, and then weird old me over there. It didn't help that I was the one always getting in trouble for having parties and stupid things like trying to clean up a drunk friend's vomit with the vacuum cleaner. Breanna was the quiet, annoying achiever, who was interested in all the things Brian was into and got up early on Sundays to cycle with him when Mum was well enough to be left at home with me.

The trickier my fantasy family proved to achieve, the more I wanted it. It pulsed in my brain all the time, pulling me into the kind of metaphysical questions you normally associated with weed-smoking university students. What was the point of my life if I was just going to be me? Where did all my love go if I couldn't give it a kid?

People who wrote to Breanna's advice column would suggest adoption. As if that were so easy. Vanishingly few children are really put up for adoption here and a messy almost-middle-aged single woman isn't likely to feature highly on any list of potential parents.

As I walked from the doctor's office out towards my car, I scanned through a mental directory of people who might have willing wombs.

There was Simone, probably my closest friend, who owned the music shop across the road from my dress store in town. There was my cousin, Dita, but she was flaky about turning up for Christmas. No way could she be trusted.

People asked strangers all the time, didn't they? But even though you weren't strictly legally allowed to pay surrogates, the amount of money that would no doubt be involved in one way or the other in "covering costs" would be prohibitive. And there was something about it that made me uncomfortable in a sort of bad sci-fi, bodies-for-rent way. Not that asking a friend was much easier.

I opened the car door and slid behind the steering wheel, adjusting my rear-view mirror to check my face. I hadn't actually cried during the appointment this time, so my appearance remained passable. I ran a hand through my hair, trying to push it back into place. It could do with a colour – for the past five years I'd been having to top up my natural red with a bit of synthetic assistance, but it had slipped down the priority list as my baby quest became more fraught. Andy once told me I looked like Julianne Moore if you squinted. Now you'd probably need a serious case of astigmatism to appreciate the similarity.

I pulled my car out of the carpark and turned right on to the main road into town. The first traffic light turned red as I approached. I pulled to a stop behind a horse float. The long black tail and brown back legs of the horse were just visible through the open top half of the back end. It must have been someone travelling from one of the farms on the far end of the city through to the equestrian club near Breanna's house. The trailer had a bumper sticker with a picture of a horse's head and a plea: "Please be patient, I find this stressful."

I drummed my fingers on the steering wheel. "Me too, horse. Me too."

Eventually the light turned green, and I edged my car forward, trying not to get too close to the float. There was my sister, of course.

Could I ask her? Perfect Breanna with her husband earning oodles of money and her gorgeous house and the job at the online magazine that everyone in the country read. Would she be willing to go through a pregnancy one more time, for me?

It was only a couple of weeks since I'd asked if I could come and stay in her spare room for a few months so I could Airbnb my place to make a bit of money while the shop was in a quiet patch. I'd thought it might be a win-win. They had more than enough space – far more rooms than one family needed, anyway. I could have helped with housework, looked after the kids. She wasn't always impressed with me sneaking them treats when I came to visit, but I would have behaved myself.

The plan backfired, though. Her husband, Brad, had acted like I was asking him to pay my mortgage for me.

Maybe I could write to her advice column to broach the topic. "Dear Breanna, AITA if I ask my sister whether I can borrow her body for nine months. I would be forever indebted…"

It took me 10 minutes to drive from Amelia's office into town, even though every one of the three traffic lights I had to pass through turned against me.

I congratulated myself again on the purchase of my bright red Suzuki Swift, with the personalised number plate 01AMY01, when I was able to nose it into the tightest carpark on the road outside my shop, Sage.

The small shop, entirely glass on the front wall, was one of a short row on one side of the main street through the centre of town. The first part of the road is open to cars, before later turning into a pedestrian mall. The location of my shop meant we were perfectly positioned to see drivers who hadn't encountered this layout before being taken by surprise when they could drive no further and had to turn off down a side street.

I wiggled the car into the parallel park until it was perfectly in alignment with the footpath.

A woman was standing about three metres from me, playing a guitar and singing something that sounded like it could have been Bob Marley. I hauled my bag on to my shoulder and stepped on to the footpath, squinting in the glare of sunshine reflecting off the ground. The pedestrian portions of the road are paved in tiles that are slippery when it rains and both barbecue-hot and mirror-reflective when it's sunny.

I pressed the button on my keys to chirp the car locked.

The little car had been my first post-separation purchase and the fact I could squeeze in just about anywhere was still a novelty, two years on.

When Andy and I were together, he always insisted on the most ridiculously big cars – and because they were funded by his business, I just went along with it. That was a bit of a metaphor for our marriage, now that I thought about it.

As marriages went, it hadn't been a bad one. We just hadn't made it through the stress of infertility, which now seems boringly predictable. There's something really specifically difficult about trying to hold a relationship together while injected hormones addle your brain, you develop swelling in all sorts of weird places and generally feel as though you've been chewed up and vomited out by the IVF process.

Maybe because it was to do with something that I'd always assumed would come easily, the fact we struggled felt like a personal insult. When Andy tried to cheer me up, I'd think he wasn't taking it seriously enough. When he was upset, it was as though he was blaming me for the trouble. There was no way through, so the only solution was to part.

Even from this far away, I could see that my shop was empty. A relatively steady – at least for our town - stream of foot traffic was passing the doors, but no one was heading in. The window that my assistant manager, Natalie, had spent hours finessing was colourful and inviting with three mannequins dressed in summery florals. They caught the eye of a couple of women passing who paused for half a second. One checked her watch before they continued down the road.

I was at the shop door in less than a dozen steps. As I turned to push it open, Simone, doing something at the doorway of her shop across the street, raised her hand in greeting. She was wearing bright orange lipstick and her long dark hair was pulled back into a messy bun right on the top of her head, with her growing-out fringe plaited around the side. One strand of hair had fallen from the bun and almost reached the middle of her back. Her white tank top showed her lightly muscled back and right-arm tattoo, a traditional ta moko design she'd had done for her 35th birthday a year earlier.

I waved back. Simone was the only reason that shop did well. There was something about her that pulled people in. Even if they were shopping for something entirely different, she somehow convinced them that what was really missing from their lives was an expensive clarinet – not a good night's sleep or a cup of coffee or whatever they thought was ailing them.

I took a deep breath of Sage's air-conditioned air, faintly scented with an expensive candle Breanna had bought me for good luck. If only good smells were enough to bring in the customers. Of course, she could afford to spend money on things like bougie candles. Her husband earned possibly half-a-million dollars a year working on an oil rig. Talk about selling your soul. I just looked at her candles and saw a decent chunk of the shop's rent payment literally going up in smoke.

Natalie peered out from the back office at the sound of the door opening.

"How's it been?" I spoke quickly before she had a chance to ask about the appointment. I still hadn't properly processed it and there was no way I would be able to put it into words for anyone else yet. Particularly someone who relied on me keeping things together.

I unfolded and then refolded a pile of cowl-neck tops on one of the four display tables in the middle of the shop. There was a rack of dresses on either side, and rails along each of the walls holding evening gowns, tops, skirts, and trousers. A display of shoes sat on top of each rack, as well as on the front of the table closest to the door.

Natalie bit her lip. "It's been quiet."

I tried to keep my voice light. It had been quiet for what – three years? "Not your fault. Maybe everyone's got more important things to do today."

When I'd started this shop, I'd imagined it being a kind of hub for the women of my town, a place where I'd know what all my regulars liked, where I might send an email to someone when I spotted a dress in her favourite colour and cut, or where we'd have evenings with wine and cheese and check out new collections from local designers. There was a serious lack of anything like that anywhere nearby.

We had started okay, with a big launch party and some good sales in the first year. But then the economy hit a tough patch, the farmers were getting less of a payout and the promised cruise ships that were meant to be coming into the port didn't turn up. I'd started to wonder whether the "tough patch" was actually real life, and it was the busier period that had been the aberration.

If I was honest, my attention started to be spread thinner as time went on, too. What had been a fun and sometimes profitable enterprise when I was a married woman with a husband with a stable job had become another thing to keep me up at night as a single person trying to fall pregnant.

The bell at the door bleeped as someone pushed it open, her gaze focused on the floor. She wasn't a regular, but I knew her face from behind the counter a café down the road. Her eyes flicked up to meet mine as I greeted her, then her gaze returned to the floor.

Natalie took a couple of steps towards her. "Can we help you?"

I pretended to read something on a shelf. The last thing this woman needed was two of us focusing on her.

Something twigged in the back of my mind. Maura. Her name was Maura.

Maura gestured at a row of dresses by a floor-to-ceiling mirror. As she reached for one, she seemed to recoil a bit from her reflection as it loomed up opposite her. "I need something for my niece's wedding."

Natalie smiled. "How lovely. Do you have anything in mind?"

Maura shook her head quickly. "I haven't bought any clothes for years. I had a look online, but I just don't know... How do you dress this?"

She gestured at her body.

Natalie turned to me. "It sounds like you need the Amy touch."

It sounded like some weird disease. I wriggled back from the counter and took a couple of steps towards her, as if I was approaching a wild animal. "How do you dress a totally normal body, you mean?"

She didn't smile. She clearly had strong summer colouring but was dressed in an off-white jumper that was doing nothing for her skin, and her trousers had lost their elasticity, making her look unnecessarily frumpy.

I reached for a deep, emerald-green shift dress with cute cap sleeves, which had been tucked behind a bigger black one.

"Let me show you something," I held it under her chin and directed her to look in the mirror. "See how this colour brings out your eyes, and makes your skin glow? I think you just need to find the right shade."

She let herself smile slightly. "That does look better."

I nodded. "Dress for your colouring. It makes all the difference."

She turned slightly to see the colour reflecting on her cheek. "I always thought I was just pasty."

I laughed. "Not at all, look at those rose undertones coming out. Now, you hop into the changing room, and I'll show you some options. You'll be amazed."

She did as she was told and I conducted a circuit of the shop, loading my right arm with dresses in green, royal blue and pink.

People think fashion is all fun and frivolity and terrible impacts on the environment but sometimes a trip to a clothes shop where they know what they're doing can be as good for your mental health as a counselling session. And I should know.

I was locking the front door of the shop when someone tapped me on the shoulder. I turned and found I was face-to-face with Simone. She grinned, the smile radiating from her still-glossy lips to her sparkling hazel eyes. How did she keep her lipstick on all day? When I tried a bright shade – on the advice of someone who said it would help my dopamine – it just ended up on my teeth and smudged over my chin by mid-morning.

She put her hand on my arm, sending a warm tingle through

me. "I was walking past earlier and spotted your face. Thought you looked like you could do some cheering up."

There was something about her that made me jittery. It reminded me of being at school trying to impress the cool girls a couple of years older than me, feeling self-conscious about everything from my clothes to the way I spoke.

Was it just that she was so much cooler than me? I had hoped it would dissipate as we got to know each other better, but even a couple of years after we became close, it was actually getting worse. I'd hoped that nearing 40. I might be past the days of crushes but evidently not.

I jangled my keys in my hand. "Sorry to be your neighbourhood storm cloud. There's a bit going on."

She raised her eyebrows. "You had your appointment today, right?"

"Yep. Just more waiting at this stage." The prospect of surrogacy still felt too foreign to put it into words.

Simone put her hand on my forearm, her skin warm against mine. "I told you – take up drumming. It'll get all your frustrations out."

I snorted, picturing myself sitting in my tiny, two-bedroom house with its paper-thin walls. The old couple who lived next door and went to bed at 6.30pm would not be impressed. Nor would the family with a baby across the street, or the young couple who I suspected both worked night shift on the other side. It was bad enough when I tried to have a few friends over for a barbecue in my handkerchief-sized back garden.

Simone gestured up the road. "Come on, come for a drink? I have half an hour until I have to pick Audrey up from ballet."

Audrey was Simone's eight-year-old, who was exactly the kind of girl I had idolised when I was younger.

She was so much more sophisticated than I could have hoped to be at her age. But if I thought about it, Breanna might not have been too dissimilar. Breanna was the pretty brunette with cute freckles – even though she hated them at the time, who got her father's sky-blue eyes. I was the gangly redhead with the haircut that was meant to be styled like 1990s Princess Diana but was a bit more 2020-era Prince Harry.

A drink did sound like a nice idea, though it had been a long time since I had anything other than diet cokes when we went out. "You lead on."

There was a pub a bit further up the road into the pedestrian area that we visited at least once a week, where the staff would get our drinks ready between the time we walked in the door and when we arrived at the bar. It had some tables outside on the pavement, and booths that were perfect for hiding away in, inside. It was just dimly lit enough that it was sort of cosy and wintry even on a middle-of-summer day when the air seemed to pulse with humidity.

As we walked the 500 metres, I could feel Simone flicking glances at me. "I don't want to make you talk about it if you don't want to, but you know I'm here for you if you ever need to chat about what you're going through."

I caught her eye and attempted a smile. "I'm okay. Those jeans are amazing, by the way. Are they the ones we found for you?"

She poked her bum at me. "Yep, your magic jeans. Can't believe how good they make my butt look."

I laughed. "You don't need the help. All your ancient rockers must be spellbound, though."

Simone did a twirl and walked backwards in front of me, her eyes bright. "You won't actually believe who came in..."

She launched into a story about a pensioner who had been in a band in his 20s that was apparently quite a big deal in this specific part of the North Island of New Zealand. It was unclear whether this influence was felt more widely. I was clearly meant to know who he was and be able to sing at least one of their songs. Simone hummed a bit of something that maybe sounded a little bit like a jingle from a commercial of 10 years earlier.

"I'm not sure I know it," I winced.

No matter how many times I told her that my musical knowledge extended to R&B of the 1990s and early 2000s, and maybe two or three songs that were on the top 50 playlist that Natalie put on in the shop, she still expected me to have a working knowledge of the town's indie music scene in the 1970s. I wasn't even alive in the 1970s. Nor was she, to be fair.

Simone held open the pub door. "And what about you? Sell any expensive dresses today?"

I smiled. She lived in jeans but pretended to care about the designers we were stocking. "Just one, to a woman who is going to look absolutely stunning at her niece's wedding. We did move a couple of pairs of silk trousers that was had on 30 percent off."

I'd really thought they were going to fly out the door – gorgeous grey silk and so flattering, they would go with anything. But they sat on the shelf for too long and I found I couldn't keep looking at them. Maybe it was the need to iron them. Just a quick glance around our town would confirm that few people owned an iron. I'd been expecting too much.

Simone tapped me lightly on the shoulder. "Things will improve soon. Just a tough patch. What are the economists saying? Middle of the year everyone will be feeling better."

I half-rolled my eyes. "I think I trust them about as much as the weather forecasters."

There were a couple of groups of people nearer the bar, but the pub was quieter than normal. I was glad of it – I had enough noise buzzing in my head to crowd out a conversation anyway. I averted my eyes as a woman with a pushchair walked past us to the door.

We headed for our normal booth in the far-left corner. From there, we could see everything happening in the pub and also get a view of the small lane that ran down the side of the building.

"I'll go and get us a drink," Simone tapped her pocket, checking for her phone. "Then you can tell me what you need me to do to cheer you up."

I shot her a look. If a man had said those words, I'd have

thought it was innuendo. She just winked and was already on her way to the bar.

People actually moved out of her way. The one time I'd tried that test that they told women to do – not moving out of men's way on the footpath – I'd had three crash into me before I gave up.

I leant back against the cold leather of the bench seat.

I turned her words over in my mind. Things would improve. It couldn't stay this tough forever. Something had to go my way, somehow.

What would Breanna tell me to do? Probably set some goals and targets and start making small steps towards them. She could be so annoying. There was a sequin bomber jacket set aside for her at the shop – I just had to convince her that the sparkles would keep her mood up, not just make her the centre of attention.

Simone returned and handed a glass to me. The liquid sloshed slightly as I placed it on the table.

"Ever know anyone who's been a surrogate?" I blurted as she slid in next to me. I regretted saying the words as soon as they were there, gestating in the air between us.

She frowned. "Like, a baby? God no. Can you imagine?"

I cleared my throat and stared hard at the table. I should have known better than to bring it up.

"I mean, going through all that and it's not even your child? You'd have to be a saint," Simone almost visibly shuddered at the idea.

She was right, of course. You would have to be an enormously selfless person to even consider it. Breanna was just that sort of selfless person – but was asking her even fair?

Simone took a deep sip of her beer and looked at me over the rim of the glass. Colour flooded into her cheeks. "Shit. You're going to tell me that you are looking into it, aren't you? I'm an idiot. You know me, all mouth and no brain sometimes."

I stared at the table in front of me but shook my head quickly.

"Don't worry, I was just thinking aloud. You're totally right. It's a massive thing."

She reached out and rested her hand on top of mine. "Are you okay?"

I nodded, forcing myself to meet her eyes. "Totally fine."

The truth was, I wasn't, and until I worked out what I was going to do, I probably wasn't going to be.

CHAPTER TWO
BREANNA

I stared at my computer screen, the image of a blank page doubling up in the reflection in my new thick-rimmed glasses, as if reinforcing just how empty it really was. The white space vibrated in front of me, taunting me with its lack of words. A breeze ruffled the cream curtains on my office window, drawing my attention out to the swimming pool beyond, where sunshine scattered across the water. The wind had set my poolside white egg chair rocking.

At the bottom right of the screen, a notification popped up from my calendar – a reminder to book the dog in for a groom. She was curled at my feet, and I wriggled my toes into her fur. There was the start of something that could be a mat under her right front leg. My calendar notification timing was clearly down to a fine art. As it should be – I allocated part of every Sunday afternoon to checking that I had the week ahead well scheduled.

My daily tasks popped up every morning at 6am to be checked off. Weekly chores, like changing the sheets or washing all the towels, were scheduled in on evenly spaced days each week. Monthly and less frequent tasks were scheduled at appropriate intervals for about the next 50 years. Food planning was set up on a monthly rotation, so we had the same 30-odd meals on rotate, pre-loaded into my online supermarket shopping accounts.

There was every chance that my calendar system would end up outliving all the animals that I had checks in there for, and probably me, too, if I was honest.

But as a mother of two children usually parenting solo while juggling a full-time job, there was no room for failure. If one domino of my finely organised life fell, there was no telling how many more would go with it. I imagined it like I was standing at the bottom of a huge sand dune – if the structure holding it up collapsed, I'd be buried and never find my way out.

I pulled up my email app and fired off a note to the groomer. Poppy had the same appointment every three months so Lara would know what to do.

It was 2pm – just under an hour until I had to go and get the kids from school.

I balled my hands into my fists and drummed them on my thighs. This was not like me. Among my weekly workload I had to provide one advice column for our website that was also syndicated to a number of newspapers around the country. I'd recently been promoted to lifestyle section editor but in effect that just meant that along with my own job, I also had to try to make sure that other people were doing theirs, too.

The column was usually the easiest part of the week because it satisfied my urge to be nosey about strangers' lives. Most of the time, my column was written and submitted hours in advance of the deadline, and I was back to writing features about the health benefits of ice plunges or why bathing in black coffee is good for your skin, or emailing freelancers to find out how far beyond the due date they were planning to file their pieces.

But the words weren't flowing so easily today. A woman had written in about her attempts to have a baby, how she'd tried for years and watched all her friends have their own families. She was upset because she had been left off the invitation list for a kids' birthday party that they'd all been at. "How do I tell them that I wanted to be invited to Inflatable World, too, without sounding like a total weirdo?"

I bit my lip. Amy would have advice for her. But the whole baby thing was an increasingly sensitive subject for my sister. I should instead have picked the letter where a woman had mistaken her partner's interest in Mediterranean cooking for questions about his sexuality, instead.

I jiggled my leg, balancing some of my weight on the balls of my feet, just enough to get that involuntary shudder in my knee. Sometimes, when I read an email, I'd know immediately what I would say in response. Other times I immediately thought of an expert who would be able to give a pithy and hopefully witty insight for me to build an answer around.

"Maybe you need new friends," was too harsh a response. This was thoughtlessness at worse, from parents who probably hadn't had a full night's sleep between them in years. They maybe mistakenly assumed that the writer just wouldn't be interested in a kids' party, too. I'd been to enough of them to understand that. At least with adult parties, you'd usually have a few glasses of wine before you worried about anyone throwing a tantrum, lying on the floor or throwing drinks and food at each other. At kids' parties, you'd be expected to referee all of the above before 11am on a Saturday morning.

"Your feelings are totally valid," I typed the words carefully. "I'm sorry you feel left out and I'm sure your friends don't mean you to. It's easy to become a bit narrowly focused when you have small children, just because the effort of keeping yourself afloat can take so much of your brain."

Did I leave Amy out? She'd always complained about feeling like a bit of an outsider, even before the kids were born. She claimed it was because Dad and I were close growing up and she felt she somehow wasn't as much a part of the circle. It was rubbish, as far as I could see. Dad loved her just the same. She and Mum were so alike that if you told me mum had created her through parthenogenesis I would have believed you.

She was a great aunt, always in touch with what was happening in Ruby's Minecraft world or which weird UK rapper Charlie was following. But I knew it wasn't enough for her. I'd stopped trying to complain about the juggle of motherhood in her presence. Even when it came to my worst days of being pulled in a million directions and feeling like a failure at all of them, she wanted her own chance at it.

"It might not hurt to expand your circle a little," I told the letter writer. "Your friends could be boring for a couple of years before they emerge out the other side of this phase and it wouldn't hurt to have some other interests – even if it's just to take your mind off your own journey to parenthood. In the meantime, try to remember that no one means to hurt you."

How I wished I was brave enough to say any of that to Amy.

I tidied up the response and returned to my folder of questions to pick one more. A man was upset that his girlfriend would rather save a hypothetical puppy from a hypothetical burning building than a hypothetical original copy of a Shakespearean play. That would be a straightforward one. Some people just had too much time to think up imaginary problems.

The biggest potential pitfall with my job was that, with any letter, there was a significant chance that they were the product of someone's particularly fervent imagination or sent by someone who wanted to "test" me with a well-known plot.

I had so far only been fooled once that I knew of, when someone wrote a question that was the outline of the movie Fight Club. Was it my fault that movie had completely passed me by? From memory, Amy's ex-husband, Andy, had been a fan.

My journalism degree hung on the wall above my desk because my daughter, Ruby, had demanded I find a spot for it when she found it in the attic earlier in the year.

It sometimes felt a bit like a judgement. When I'd been taking those classes, studiously learning how to cover the court system or delve into companies' records, I never would have imagined my job would basically revolve around mining the internet for the latest lifestyle trends and delving into people's messy family lives and poor parenting decisions.

The advice column part of my role had happened by accident. When I started my first internship, at least 15 years ago, the newspaper had just lost its columnist and the editor assumed the sociology papers I did before I worked out I wanted to be a journalist would give me some sort of insight. Or perhaps it was the fact that I was young and willing to work for nothing that had sealed the deal. I didn't blink as more work was added to my shopping list of tasks.

New Zealand hadn't had many advice columnists at that point – the most notable ones were Australians who popped up as imports in the women's magazines, outed by their almost-but-not-quite local slang. For my generation, it was a bit of a novelty to have the opportunity to indulge in schadenfreude reading about other people's problems, with the bonus of an answer from someone who ostensibly had some idea what they were talking about.

As I went along it became more rewarding. I started to hear more from people who had received advice from me and reported back on how things had worked out. People recognised my name and sent me messages on social media about my columns. I wasn't sure whether to be amused or embarrassed when I saw a comedian tweet that a politician who'd behaved badly with a staff member should write to me for advice.

Sometimes those who didn't take my advice were as grateful for the process as those who did. Something about writing your problem down and seeing it from another point of view could make all the difference.

It was something I tried to remind myself when I battled parenting challenges alone while my husband, Brad, lived what appeared to me to be the life of a single man, working on oil rigs in the Indian Ocean. Journal it out, I told myself. Maybe it'll help.

Brad's face grinned at me from a photo on the corner of my desk. I frowned at it. This fly-in-fly-out work arrangement had only been meant to be for a couple of years, but it was pushing eight. He was an engineer and was being paid about three times what he could get in one of New Zealand's biggest cities. Given that we weren't even living in one of those areas, it was hard to argue that he should come back to shore for financial reasons.

People still quoted one of my early catchphrases at me when they realised who I was: "That man should already be an ex."

Sometimes I wondered for a split second whether I should take that advice myself - particularly when one of the kids, fuelled by pent-up school frustration, shouted at me about having packed the wrong brand of nut-free muesli bars as I tried to get everyone into the car to take Poppy to the vet when she had swallowed someone's sock. Or when I was sick with a stomach bug and had to wake in the night to clean the sheets of one of the kids who'd come down with it, too.

And even, I had to admit, to a lesser extent when he arrived back for a month at home and got in the way of all my routines and rules with his best impression of Cool Dad.

But I loved him. He was my best friend and biggest supporter, even from afar. It was still worth the months apart to have the few weeks together every so often. I just wished it wasn't so rare. Imagine what I could do, if I had a husband who was here most of the time.

When I picked the kids up from school, I needed to run Charlie to a football practice, which was 13 minutes away, provided the traffic behaved. Then I would need to get Ruby to the dance studio to go over the contemporary routine for the exam she had coming up in 16 days.

Then we'd need to head back to get Charlie, drop in to pick up my click-and-collect order from the supermarket and get back in time to make dinner and get the house in order ready for the cleaner to come through in the morning. Amy told me that I should pay someone to help with more of the childcare but then I'd have to decide who the babysitter went with, and there was a streak of mum guilt that forced me to at least attempt to do everything – childcare, cooking, laundry - myself. If it was anyone else writing to me in the same predicament, I'd tell them not to be daft but sometimes your own advice is the hardest to take.

Amy helped when she could but she was often stuck in her shop.

Right now, though, I needed to get the column filed so I had time to pick up the dry-cleaning on the way to school and check that the man who came to check the pool once a fortnight hadn't used the last of the chemicals.

"You don't say how long you've been together," I tapped out the words on my screen, imagining the man with his hypothetical problems, my fingers rattling the keys. My nails were getting just to that length where they were a little too long and slipped from the keys causing typos every other word. I flicked a glance at my paper diary, which was a handy backup for the one on my phone. Nails were booked in during school hours tomorrow. I didn't even need to worry about what colour I'd get – the nail tech knew the shade of nude I'd been wearing for the past two years.

"You and your partner are obviously having wide-ranging discussions, which is wonderful. I wouldn't get hung up on hypotheticals – this is a situation you're not going to encounter. Focus on the things you do have in common, the differences you enjoy and the problems that need to be dealt with. Don't worry so much about the unhelpful what-ifs. Maybe start a debate club, if that's the sort of stimulation you're after."

Overall, the column wasn't the best advice I'd ever given, but it would do. I checked my clock again. Time to chuck on one more load of washing before I headed for the door.

There is nothing like an unexpected illness to throw off even the best laid plans.

Later that afternoon, Ruby was tucked into the corner of the L-shaped couch in our biggest living room, her face pale and slightly clammy.

We had to leave dancing early when she lay on the floor in the middle of the routine. Usually, she was the one cartwheeling across the floor when the class was meant to be practising plies at the barre. At least it was probably only a virus.

Ruby was extremely allergic to nuts and dairy, and any time she felt unwell I was immediately running a mental catalogue of everything she had eaten, touched, or even breathed recently. I don't know whether I had ever completely unclenched my jaw since she was first admitted to the hospital with an allergic reaction before she even turned one.

We had an app where she was meant to log her food, but you never knew what an eight-year-old might encounter at school. At least she was mercifully past the age where her friends might smear peanut butter on her by accident.

I pressed the back of my hand to her forehead. "How's your head feeling now?"

She winced. "It's still a bit sore. My chest's feeling a bit better, though."

Charlie huffed past, his gaze fixed on the iPad in his hand. "Does she get to stay home tomorrow?'

I looked at him, a mini version of his father, down to his floppy, sandy brown hair and light brown eyes. "Depends how she's feeling."

He frowned. "That's not fair. I don't feel well either."

I frowned at him. Charlie was never one to miss a moment where he might be able to get something for himself. "You'll be absolutely fine."

He shifted his body weight in a way that I knew meant he would have stamped his feet if he'd been a few years younger than his 10. "How do you know? My stomach hurts too."

I pointed to the bag that he had clutched in his non-iPad hand. "That jumbo pack of Cheetos says otherwise."

"I can be sick and hungry."

Charlie was firmly in that awkward age where he was too young to accept the responsibilities that might come with being a teenager but too old – at least in his eyes – to have the restrictions of younger kids. Just in the last couple of months, he had had a significant growth spurt. He had gone to bed complaining about aching legs many nights and shorts that used to reach his knees now looked like something my dad's brother might have turned up to Christmas in, in the 1980s – just slightly too much thigh for polite company.

He was always a chubby baby – I think the nurse referred to him as robust at one point – but now he had become so lean you could see the muscles in his arms and legs working just walking across the room.

When he was tiny, his eyes would follow me around the room and sometimes I almost bristled at his constant need to be connected to me. But now it was my eyes following him and me trying to hold on to him while I felt him slowly slipping away.

I reached for him to pull him towards me, but he wriggled out of my grasp. I turned back to Ruby. "Let me know if you need anything."

Ruby swallowed. "Can I talk to Dad?"

I checked my watch. With the time difference, it would be early morning for him, somewhere out in the ocean off India. The time difference was about as large from New Zealand as you could find. Late afternoon for us would be very early in the morning for him.

It was always a bit of a risk, calling him. Sometimes the kids were more upset if we tried, and he didn't answer, than if we didn't try at all. But he worked odd hours, so there was a chance.

Ruby was waiting for me to respond. "We can try, okay? If he doesn't answer, he might be asleep."

I pulled out my phone and Ruby reached for it. As she took it from my hands, she looked up at me. "When's Dad coming home?"

I tried to think. This was where my meticulous planning tended to let me down because it was almost easier to stop thinking about it. When the kids were smaller, we'd marked the days off on a calendar, but I worried it made it worse for them, particularly at the start when there were so many still to go. Being reminded that he wasn't there made us all miss him more.

Brad was also generally not forthcoming about his schedules, partly because he knew how much his continued absence upset me. His various contracts tended to require him for different lengths of time for each stint and I'd given up trying to keep track.

The call was taking longer to connect that normal and was just slow enough that I took a step towards Ruby to try to deflect her attention. Eventually I heard his voice and a smile lit up Ruby's face.

That was another reason why any thoughts of really making him an ex were banished as soon as they flicked into my head. He was a good dad. I just wanted more of him around, not less.

"Do you want to come and talk to Dad, too?" she looked at me over the top of the phone.

I ducked beside her and waved at Brad on the screen. He looked tired, dark shadows pooling under his eyes. But he grinned at us both.

I blew him a kiss. "You probably don't have long to talk, focus on Ruby and I'll message you later on."

He winked at me. We had a routine – I'd message him before I went to sleep and if he was somewhere he could talk, he'd call me. Sometimes I fell asleep on the phone to him and he would act offended, but I knew he secretly liked it.

As I was making dinner, my tablet buzzed with a notification. It was sitting on the benchtop next to the stove, while I attempted a new Thermomix recipe – one of those ones that promises to have your kids eating seven serves of vegetables without even noticing. I had put it into our rotation with trepidation.

I hooked a hank of my long brown hair behind an ear and reached over to swipe the screen alive as I poured some frozen peas into the bowl of the machine.

It was an email from someone whose name I didn't recognise. That was not unusual – my email found its way on to countless lists and I was constantly getting marketing emails from businesses desperate for coverage or press releases from PR people who had some sort of KPI to meet. There was one in particular who kept sending me releases about pet insurance for British dogs, no matter how many times I told her I was not her target audience.

I tapped open the message and had to read the first line twice.

"Breanna. You think you're so amazing. You ruined my life."

I frowned. I definitely did not think I was amazing, so that was their first mistake. But ruined a life? I spent all day trying to help people, not cause anyone any harm. The idea was preposterous. The next line was no more revealing: "You and your terrible advice should go to hell."

Could it be someone who had sent a question I'd answered in the column? Who? I ran through as many recent questions as I could remember. Most were the sort of thing you would never admit to anyone that you had written to an advice column about. But I couldn't think of any that had led to advice that could be described as life-ruining.

Could it be the woman who could not work out how to tell her mother that she didn't want her babysitting any more after she forgot to clip her child into his car seat? I had been so torn about that one. On one hand, of course you don't want your child spending time with someone who might make such a careless mistake. On the other, I had made just that error on one afternoon when I had been deeply sleep-deprived with Ruby and taking Charlie to a friend's house. He had survived completely unharmed, but I had told no one, not even Brad. The fact that woman's mother had told her was worth something.

There was the guy who wanted an open relationship then found his wife was more successful at it than he was. That was a common one, though – any advice therapist in the world could have had a question like that, probably more than once a week.

There was no name on the bottom of the email, and now I looked at it, the name in the sender field was probably a pseudonym. Mary Jones. Sounded fake.

I looked up from the screen. Ruby was watching me from the nearby dining table, where she was drawing cartoon cats on bits of paper that sparkled in the reflected light of the chandelier above her.

I forwarded it to my colleague, Megan. She was a general reporter – the sort who went to court and to council meetings – so we didn't have a lot of crossover in terms of our work, but she was the only other staff member in this part of the country, so we had become close-ish by default. She was almost at retirement age, and I admired how she stuck with it, even though she probably could have shifted to a much better paid and comfortable corporate role. I added one line at the top: "Do you ever get much abuse from readers?"

The bubble icon indicated she was typing almost immediately. "A bit. Nothing like that, though. You okay?"

"I'm fine," I typed back. "It's just weird. I guess it's par for the course, right?"

She responded immediately. "I suppose so. Seems to be getting more common. Look out for yourself. You're a household name these days."

I stared at the screen. How was I meant to look after myself? I had to keep doing my job.

Ruby coughed, breaking my concentration.

"How's it going over there?" As the words came out, I realised my voice was shaky. It had been a while since I had any negative feedback at all, and this was at the next level.

This was yet another time when it would have been really good to have Brad at home, so he could step in and take over while I went away to collect myself. As it was, I just had to put a brave face on and press on. I could call Amy, but I was fairly sure she said she was going to a movie with her friend, Simone. I wouldn't interrupt - she needed something like that to take her mind off everything else she was dealing with.

Ruby shrugged. "Okay. What's for dinner?"

I gestured to the saucepan in front of me. "Pasta."

She scrunched up her nose. "Yuck."

I felt my shoulder sag. "Give it a go, okay? You never know, you might like it."

She hunched over her paper. "Can we have chips?"

Charlie craned his head around the corner of the door, from where he was positioned on the couch in the lounge, with his tablet in his lap. "Yeah, chips would be good."

"Definitely not. But I'm glad you're feeling better." I could feel my pulse picking up. How much of this was due to the email, and what was a pavlovian response to the return of the dreaded dinner battle? The kids would exist on chicken nuggets and chips if I let them, but I would go mad – and there was no point cooking separate meals when I was the only adult around to eat them.

"If you eat now, you won't have any appetite for dinner, and I've spent the last half an hour trying to sort this out."

Ruby rolled her eyes, instantly looking at least five years older than her eight years. "Yes, we will."

"We will, promise," Charlie was already on his feet, making his way to the cupboard.

"No, you won't," I tried to position myself between him and the door. I could imagine what this looked like, a grown woman taking up a defensive position against a 10-year-old dead set on snacks.

If his father were there, he wouldn't even push it. But with me every boundary was more like an invitation. Sometimes, as I was going to sleep, I had to take myself through some mental exercises to stop myself catastrophising about what his teen years would be like if we were still without his father most of the time.

"Please wait until dinner."

Charlie reached over my head and grabbed a packet of cassava chips from the middle shelf of the pantry. He threw one to his sister. At least he hadn't found the family-sized block of berry biscuit chocolate I had hidden at the back of the top shelf for after they went to bed.

I felt my mouth drop open. "Charlie. I said..."

He shrugged and patted my arm. "We'll eat dinner, I promise."

I stared at him as he made his way back to the couch. Was it even worth being angry?

My phone buzzed again. Amy. Maybe I was wrong about the movie. I picked up the call. "I was just thinking about you."

"Good timing?"

"I wondered whether you wanted to come over."

There was a pause. "I'd love to, but Simone and I have that thing..."

I cut her off. "Of course, no problem."

"I was calling because I want to see you, though. Lunch? Tomorrow?"

My gaze flicked to my inbox, where the other would-be mum's email had been. Maybe Amy had baby news.

"I think I can do lunch. I'm just tied up with a few things here but send me a text and let me know what time. Assume the usual place?"

She was rustling with something in the background. "Yep, great. I have something important to ask you."

I frowned. "You can just ask me now?"

"It's better face-to-face. I'll see you tomorrow. Love-you-and-kids-have-a-good-night." The last words came out in a jumbled rush as she hung up the phone.

I stared at the screen. What could she need to talk about in person? If Brad were here, he'd already be rolling his eyes and warning me to take care. Amy was prone to grand, impractical plans that she embarked upon with little thought to how much work or effort would be involved – usually for other people, particularly me.

I could see it wasn't intended to be as disruptive as it was – this was the same girl who dropped flyers for a craft fair at our house around the neighbourhood on the promise that she was going to teach herself pottery in a week. Dad had had to explain to the two people who turned up that it had all been a misunderstanding.

Brad was always grumbling that both Amy and Mum leant on me too much. But with what Amy was going through as she tried to become a mother, and since Dad died and left Mum alone, I felt a bit obligated. And anyway, he wasn't one to talk.

CHAPTER THREE

AMY

Simone held up a bright orange sheath dress under her chin and regarded herself in the mirror. She turned side on, smoothing the material over her abdomen.

"How do I look? Are you going to be able to see everything I eat at these awards?" She caught my eye. I was leaning on the shop counter, idly sorting through a stack of paper bags that had got wet when they were delivered. At 10c a piece, I was not letting them go to waste.

She looked beautiful. The colour brought out the warm tones in her skin and made her hazel eyes sparkle.

"You look gorgeous. And no, look at you – you've nothing to worry about anywhere. You could eat everyone's dinner and it would make no difference."

I could see my reflection behind her, and it only served to make the contrast between us starker – my glasses needed to be tightened and kept slipping down my nose and I had dark circles under my eyes. My mother used to tell me off for staying up late worrying because it never achieved anything. She had a fridge magnet that implored us to "be where your feet are" and another that proclaimed "don't let the worries of tomorrow cloud your enjoyment of today". That was easy for her when she had Brian to take care of the details and the worrying for her. I did my share, too.

Back then, my constant worry was that she would have to go into hospital or that I would come home from school and find her collapsed on the floor, as happened one winter afternoon when I was about 10. I'd kept Breanna, then just six, outside until I could get a neighbour to phone Brian.

Now, Mum was thriving, heading towards 70 and seemed almost healthier than she had ever been. Since Brian died, she'd also had a couple of boyfriends, though nothing serious she would admit to.

I, on the other hand, was being kept awake these days by the torturous baby-making process, and by money worries that couldn't be relegated to another day, because they would just join the money worries of the future and compound into some kind of superpowered worry that I would have no hope of tackling. Breanna's life operated like a well-oiled machine. Mine was a contraption no one knew how to use that had bits flying off in all directions. Mum would never understand.

Simone held up another dress. "Maybe green is more my colour?"

It was an almost-50s style dress with a puffy skirt. "That one would make your legs look stunning. Maybe try them both on and see what you think."

She nodded and ducked into a changing room. I could see in the gap under the curtain that her jeans hit the floor and her t-shirt fell into a pile. She pulled back the curtain and emerged in the orange dress first. I stared at her. "Almost enough to make me change teams. What a stunner."

Simone cackled and threw her head back. "I keep telling you. One day you'll come to your senses. Men are only good for one thing and even then, most of them aren't any good at it."

I laughed but couldn't meet her gaze. "What's that, the lawn mowing?"

"Yep! Have I told you about the competition I've been having with my neighbour? He's out there every evening doing something or other to his lawn. Meanwhile mine is perfection thanks to my trusty robot," she held up her fingers in a chef's kiss gesture.

I'd spotted a robot lawnmower at Breanna's neighbour's place and sent a photo to Simone after she complained about a weekend spent battling the incessant growth of grass that was getting just the right mix of rain and warmth this summer. She'd gone out and bought one.

I smiled at her. "You're an example to us all."

Simone gave a mock bow. "Happy to act as spokesperson for the flourishing single mother contingent any time it's needed. Now, should I try on the other?"

I smiled and forced myself to break our eye contact. "Yes, please do."

If she hadn't been such an obvious success as a parent, it might have made me more nervous about pushing ahead on my own quest for single parenthood. Simone's former wife, Hana, had left just before we met when Audrey was four and from what I could see it had not interrupted her flow much at all. It helped that she had an array of willing babysitters, including me. It also helped that Audrey was the easiest child I had ever looked after. One evening when I was watching her for Simone's stocktake, she'd actually asked if she could go and read in bed.

She returned to the changing room and reappeared in the other.

I cocked my head on the side. "It's cute but I think the orange one is more your style."

I was right, it did make her legs look great, but it didn't have the elegance and power of the orange option. Simone looked at herself in the mirror and nodded. "You're right."

She returned to the changing room and pulled the curtain behind her.

I cleared my throat. "Can I ask you something?"

"Sure." I could see from the clothes being picked up from the ground that she was almost dressed again in what she was wearing before.

"Remember how I mentioned surrogates the other day."

"Uh huh," she opened the curtain and took a step towards me, the dresses over each arm. "Are you ready to tell me what's going on?"

"You were right that I asked because I think I'm going to need one."

She reached out and put her hand on my forearm. "I thought that might be the case. I'm so sorry I was so dismissive. How are you feeling about it?"

I waved it away. "I honestly don't know. But I think I'm going to ask my sister."

I took the dresses from her, and we walked towards the counter. I still wasn't completely sure, but saying the words out loud made it feel a bit more real.

Simone nodded slowly. "That makes sense."

"Does it?" I scanned the tag on the dress, and quickly applied a discount to reduce the price. "She wouldn't say it in quite the same way, but I worry that she'd have the same reaction you did to the idea of it all. She didn't have an easy time with her pregnancies."

Simone chewed her lip. "But she's your sister and she loves you. I'd do it for my sister, I think. If I had one."

I smoothed the fabric of the dress. "It's me asking her to come to my rescue again. And maybe she'll feel she has to say yes, you know? I don't like the idea of that."

Simone shrugged. "Isn't helping each other what family does?"

An image of Brad's face flashed into my mind. He would no doubt think this was beyond the scope of a normal family request for assistance. I lowered my voice as an older woman and teenage girl walked into the shop. "A stranger would be easier but I don't even know where to start with that, and there's also the genetic thing – I think it's best if it's someone closely related because they're genetically more similar? Does that sound right?"

Simone shrugged. "It sounds feasible to me. I expect you know more about it than I do."

"I have been doing some reading."

She laughed. "I have no doubt about that." She brandished her credit card at me. "How much do I owe you?"

I looked at the total on the cash register, then waved it away and tucked the dress into a bag. I couldn't charge her. If she wasn't worried about my shop as some sort of charity case, she probably would never have thought to buy a new dress for a night out. "Don't be silly, you don't even really want to buy it."

She sighed. "Who says? If I bought it anywhere else, I'd pay. Don't be silly. Can't turn up to the awards in my jeans really, can I?"

The business awards were probably the only real "dress up" event that our town still had. The only time you'd ever see more than two men in one place wearing suits, and when some women literally blew dust off their high heels for the night out.

I loved that kind of thing – who cared that it was held in what was basically part of the council building? The food could be a bit marginal – one year we had been served hunks of lettuce drizzled with an unidentifiable dressing. But the room always glittered with fairy lights, a band would play at least six covers you knew from high school, and it was something different to break up the monotony of small-town life.

I always told my friends who had moved away that our bars and restaurants were as good as Auckland's, but the problem was there were really only three or four of them.

I'd only not entered my business in the awards because I couldn't justify spending the $100 on the entry fee and then stumping up for the tickets that you basically had to buy for the gala dinner. But Simone was up for the sought-after customer award and was going under duress. She would prefer a night at home on the couch with Thai delivery.

She pulled the bag over the counter with one hand as she reached for the card machine with the other and entered the full amount on the price tag. The transaction zipped through in seconds.

It would probably double the takings for the day.

"Now, what are you going to wear?" She gestured around the shop. She was leaning on the counter next to me, her spicy perfume mingling with the airconditioned air.

I hesitated. "For what?"

She turned towards me so that we were almost touching. "You're still willing to be my date, right?"

I blinked. She'd mentioned it a few days earlier but I had assumed she was joking. There would be people lining up to go with her – people who could actually afford the $250 that it cost to get in the door. "I haven't got a ticket…"

She frowned. "You're not trying to get out of it are you? I've got one for you."

I put my hand on her arm and her face brightened. "You know I'd love to go with you. But are you sure? You didn't buy a ticket just for me, did you?"

She dropped her shoulders in exasperation. "Does it matter if I did? I want you to come with me."

I opened my mouth and then closed it again. Natalie was in the far corner of the shop, hanging a couple of blouses that had been discarded in the changing rooms back on to the rack and pretending not to listen. She caught my eye and smiled.

Simone grinned. "Pick your outfit. Let's match – or something. I dunno. You have a better eye for it than I do." She glanced at her watch. "I've got to go. Jeff's been alone in the shop far too long. I'll catch up with you later, okay?"

I watched as she headed for the door, the bag swinging on her arm. She briefly inspected a display of platforms on her way past. She winked at me as she turned to close the door behind her. "You'll look great in anything, I'm sure."

Natalie erupted in giggles when the door closed behind. "A date at last, is it?"

I rolled my eyes but felt myself blush. "Don't be ridiculous. We're just good friends. She's probably just taking pity on me."

"Mmmhmm," Natalie nodded as if she did not believe me.

"We are!"

She grinned. "I've watched you two pretend not to fancy the pants off each other for far too long."

I balled up a piece of paper that was lying on the counter and threw it at her. "You stop. I'm straight, remember?"

Natalie raised an eyebrow. "Are you sure?"

I'd once kissed a woman, when I was at university. But who hadn't? Since then, there had really only been Andy. There was something about Simone though, if I allowed myself to think about it. A couple of years ago, Natalie's question would have been an easy one to answer. But now it gave me pause.

A parade of anxious butterflies were marching a loop of my stomach, but I pushed the thought away. I didn't have time for those sorts of worries because I had to work out how I was going to get the words out for Breanna.

We were meant to be meeting her for lunch at the café down the road opposite the police station in – I checked my watch – about 30 seconds. That was a problem, given it would take me at least five minutes to get there.

I pulled out my phone and opened a message to her. "I'm running late but I'm on my way. Grab a table."

Breanna was at a table out the front on the street when I got there just under 10 minutes later. The sunshine was broken by the shade of two bright pink umbrellas. The seal of the road was giving off a distinctive height-of-summer smell, something almost decayingly sweet mixed with car tyres and melting tar.

She was hunched over in what looked almost like a defensive

position, as if shielding herself from anyone walking by, her eyes scanning something on her phone. It wasn't like her – she'd normally look like she was running a place like this rather than hiding from it.

She looked up as I placed a hand on her shoulder and smiled when our eyes met. She gestured towards a bottle of water on the table. "You look like you could do with one of those. It's hot, right?"

Her brown hair was glossy and her skin dewy in the way that most people think is only possible in the movies. As a teenager, I'd spent hours showing her how to layer mousse foundation and cakey concealer to get a look that could have come out of an Avril Lavigne music video. She'd retaliated by drawing what her kids would call angry bird eyebrows on me. Now, I had a routine involving layering serums, oils, gels and primers. From what I could tell, Breanna just washed her face, chucked on some sunscreen and still looked perfect.

I swiped at a drop of sweat on my forehead. "Thanks," I settled on the bench on the opposite side of the picnic table and poured water into a tumbler. Her linen pants and plain white t-shirt were perfect for the weather. "You look lovely."

She waved me away. "I doubt it." She pushed a lunch menu towards me, then clasped one hand in the other, twisting the ring on her index finger. It was a habit I remembered from when we worried about exams together. "Want something to eat?"

My stomach did a slow somersault. Would there be any room for any food in there, among the nerves?

"I'll just get something small. You want your usual?"

She nodded. She had a Caesar salad and I had a vegetarian burger every time we went for lunch, even though we both paid lip service to the idea of trying something new and sometimes pretended to peruse the specials.

The contrast of the interior of the cafe with the bright sunshine momentarily blinded me. When my eyes adjusted, the owner was waiting for me. She smiled as I started to order. "Got it. I'll get it under way, I'll bring it out to you soon."

I smiled. "Too predictable, right? Thanks."

Back outside, Breanna was staring down the street, as if waiting for someone to walk by. I put my hand over hers on the table. "I wanted to apologise again for pushing the Airbnb thing. I know you said we'd put it behind us, but I've been dwelling on it."

She nodded. "Thanks. It's really okay. I'm used to your ideas."

I grimaced. "I know. Sorry."

She half-laughed, twisting a paper napkin between her fingers. "Honestly, it's fine. Brad just gets a bit grumpy, I think he feels left out, being over there."

I studied her face. "Is everything okay? You seem nervous."

This was more than just frustration with me. Was it Brad? She was a saint putting up with his work schedule. If it were me, I'd have gone on strike the first time he took off for months, expecting everything at home to continue seamlessly in his absence.

Or maybe something was wrong with the kids?

"You first, you said you had something you needed to talk about," she gestured at me.

I shook my head. "Please, I'm worried. Is Ruby okay?"

She sighed. "Ruby's fine, we all are. It's... well, it's probably nothing."

I cocked my head. "Okay..."

Her voice was shaking. "I had a weird email from someone who didn't like something I'd written, maybe in reply to one of their letters asking for advice."

I frowned. "That's odd. Do you still have it? Can I see?"

She pulled her phone out of her bag, opened her emails, and thrust it towards me. "It's not very long."

I scanned the short message. "Makes me want to reply."

She snorted. "Please don't. Let's not make it worse."

A car roared past behind us, a little too fast for the street.

"You get that sometimes, though, right? People who aren't happy with you. I remember you talking about abuse online."

She nodded slowly. "I do... this one felt a bit different, though. Angrier. Maybe I'm just extra sensitive at the moment."

I shook my head. "I doubt it. You've got good intuition. It is an angry message. Can you raise it with someone at work? They might have an idea of how to deal with it?"

She brushed her hair off her face, adjusting her sunglasses. "Yeah, I will. I talked to Megan about it, but she didn't really have any idea."

I squeezed her hand. "I'm sorry, that's not cool."

She shrugged. "I think maybe with Brad having been gone so long and there have been those reports of break-ins on our street, I'm feeling a bit over-alert and anxious anyway."

When she looked up at me, her face crumpled with worry. I couldn't remember the last time I'd seen her look so concerned. "I can imagine. Definitely talk to your work people and you know, if you're ever worried, I'm happy to come over and hang out any time."

She smiled and put her phone in her bag, as if trying to draw an end to the discussion. "Thanks. I know you have your own stuff, though. Did you need my card to pay for lunch?"

I shook my head. "She didn't ask me to pay, actually. I guess she's expecting us to get it when we leave."

Breanna half-smiled. "I guess we're trustworthy enough. Now, what did you want to talk to me about?"

My thoughts picked up speed and my water glass slipped in my sweaty palm.

I stared at the table. "I have something to ask you. You can say no. But I have to ask you. I'd kick myself forever if I didn't."

The words came out far too quickly, as if I might lose the courage to say them unless I got them out immediately.

Breanna looked at me. "What is it? Not a money thing?"

I drained my water glass. "It's not money. It's more personal than that."

Brianna frowned. I wriggled in my seat. Why was it so hard to form the words?

She leaned away, as if she could work it out if only she could get a better view of me. "What are you talking about?"

"A surrogate," I spat the words out before I could swallow them. "I need to find someone who could be a surrogate for me if I'm going to be able to have a baby. I wanted to ask you because you're the closest person to me."

I cursed myself silently. It sounded clunky and rude, and the words hung there, as if we were both staring at them. Could I not have phrased that better? Eased into it a little more?

She exhaled, quickly cutting eye contact with me and pulling her hand away from mine. She swallowed. Neither of us said anything for what felt like a very long time.

"Tell me what you're thinking," my voice sounded strangled. Breanna's face was uncharacteristically blank. Usually, I could read her so well that I knew what she was thinking even before she did. But now there was nothing.

"I..." she started then trailed off, biting her lip, and still avoiding my eyes. "Is that really the only way?"

I nodded, picking up a sugar sachet from the glass jar on the table and turning it end on end. "The doctor says I've got something wrong with my uterus that means I can't carry a baby to term. And I've only got the one embryo left. I'm running out of chances."

Breanna looked at me. "What does Andy think? Does he know about this?"

I hadn't actually thought to ask him – I'd just assumed that since he had given his blessing for me to continue the process, he'd signed on to however that happened. Either way, I wasn't going to let Breanna worry about him. "I'll need to talk to him about it, too, eventually, but you know what he's like..."

Breanna crossed her arms. "I'll need some time to think about it. What does it involve?"

I started to reply but she kept talking. "Would I have to take a lot of drugs? Would I have to have time off work?"

My reading had provided the answer to some of these questions. "You have to take some drugs because your body isn't primed for it like if it's your own baby. You wouldn't need to take a lot of time off work, though, the procedure is pretty quick and then it's just like a normal pregnancy, really, just a bit more monitoring."

Her eyes were wide. "Remember I'm not one of those women who finds even a normal pregnancy particularly easy."

"I know. I'm sorry that I have to ask. You know I'd rather be doing this the normal way, myself."

She drummed her fingers on the table. "I'm not too old?"

"You're younger than I am. We can always ask my specialist about that if we get that far."

She took a sip of her water. We sat in silence for a few seconds before she looked up. "There's another thing."

"Yes?"

"You wouldn't be able to go getting into moods with me like you do if I'm carrying your baby."

My heart leapt at the words. She was actually picturing it happening. "I'm sorry. I don't always handle stress very well."

I knew I could be grumpy with her sometimes. It was hard to watch her having the things I wanted so much, and not feel some jealousy.

"That's my concern," she rolled the paper napkin into a tube and tapped it on the table. "Let me think, okay? I'll need to talk to Brad about it too. This is a huge thing to ask."

I nodded too vigorously and pressed my lips together. Thinking about it was better than refusing it outright. The less I said now to interrupt that thinking, the better. "Of course."

There was a weight on my chest that made it hard to breathe. What would Brad say? He and I put up with each other – he was away enough that it wasn't hard to do. But he had rung me up and told me off when I'd asked whether she wanted to invest in the shop.

I shook my shoulders to pull myself back into the moment. Breanna took my hands between hers, her palms smooth and cool on my skin. Her chunky solitaire diamond engagement ring had spun around on her finger and was pressing into my skin. "I can't imagine how hard this is for you, Ames. I know how much you want to be a mother."

I nodded, not trusting my words.

She stood and walked to my side of the table, lowering herself on to the bench seat next to me. She pulled me towards her, and I exhaled hard on her shoulder. I spoke into her shoulder. "I'm so gutted it's got to this. I really thought it was going to work the last time."

I felt Breanna nod. "It's so unfair."

I blew a strand of hair out of my face and leant back to look at her. "Thanks for even considering it. You don't know how much it means to me."

A waitress appeared at Breanna's shoulder, holding two plates.

"Here's your lunch ladies," she placed them in front of us. I tried to thank her with my eyes, not trusting my voice to behave.

We ate in near silence – or rather, I pushed the food around on my plate with my fork and waited for Breanna to finish pretending to eat hers.

"What time is Ruby's first race on Friday?" I would put it in my diary. Pretending things were somewhat normal would get us through, whatever happened. "Is she just smashing them in freestyle again?"

She swallowed. "Just after 10, I think. She'd be happy to see you there."

I pulled my bag on to my shoulder. "I'll see you then. I'd better get back to work."

She shot me a look. "Are you okay? I promise I will think about it. Just let me chat it over with Brad, I should be speaking to him tonight."

I nodded. Breanna didn't owe me anything, but there was a tiny part of me, that I didn't even really want to acknowledge, which was a little disappointed that she hadn't immediately said yes.

She stood up, pulling her shirt around herself as if she was cold. "I'll just go and settle up."

It was lucky she had remembered; I'd been about to wander off without settling the bill. "I'll come with you."

We fell into step as we headed for the cafe's main door. I reached for it but before I could push it open, a man had appeared on the other side of the glass. His face took up most of the frame as he scowled through.

Breanna inhaled sharply and recoiled. I looked at her out of the side of my eye. She had taken a step to the side and was standing with her hand on her chest to calm herself. She was really rattled. Was it because of the email? Maybe I had let the conversation drop too quickly earlier.

He pushed open the door and ploughed through, his eyes already past us searching for someone on the street. I was aware of Breanna exhaling hard and moving closer to me again. She half-laughed. "Gave me a fright."

I held the door for her.

Inside, I scanned her face. "You're really worried."

She smiled but it did not reach her eyes. "It's silly. I'm sure it's just the stress getting to me. Sorry."

We headed for the counter, and she thrust her card at the owner before I had a chance to object. Although, if I was being honest with myself, it was a relief that she was paying because my credit card was hovering near its maximum, as usual.

When the bill was settled, she reached for me and pulled me in to a slightly stiff hug. "I'll call you soon, okay? Everything is going to work out."

We headed back outside again and I watched her walk away from me down the road towards where she'd parked her car, carrying the most important decision about my last attempt at motherhood with her. Now I just had to trust the process, whatever it turned out to be.

～

My cat, Crumpet, was lying on the front porch when I got home later that afternoon. My house is one of a row of bungalows from the early 1900s with large, covered porches out the front, and kitchens and bathrooms tacked on to the back as an afterthought. As the road had widened over the years, our houses had become too close it, really. The front bedrooms could get car noise at any time of night and the streetlights streamed in unless you had very thick curtains. When I was setting up this place by myself that had been something that struck me – who would have thought how expensive good curtains would be?

But Crumpet thought it was an excellent approach to house design and would chase the sunshine from one side of the porch to the other all day, shifting slightly every half hour or so through an afternoon. If it was raining hard, he might move to the sill of my bedroom window so he could glare out.

Sometimes all I wanted to do was stay home with a book and a cup of tea and join him. He ducked away from my hand as I reached for his tail as I climbed the step on to the porch. I slid the key into the front door lock.

"Why are you being a grump?" I pushed the door open with my hip, watching him groom himself huffily. "Oh that's right, you're short of food. Supermarket shopping will be here soon."

He gave me a withering stare. "You're right," I told him. "Someone better prepared wouldn't have run out."

The house was cool but still smelt a little bit like burnt toast from that morning. What did it say about my ability to be a parent, that I kept running out of cat food? In my defence, it was unlikely that a neighbouring child would sneak in the door and eat all of my child's dinner, as I suspected was the case with Crumpet.

"Hey," a voice from the street behind me stopped me. I turned around. A man in too-tight, bright green lycra, a black helmet and those sporty sunglasses that no one really looks good in had stopped astride his bicycle by my letterbox.

It took me half a second to recognize him. "Andy! What are you doing here?"

It had been months since we had seen each other and more than two years since we split. In such a small town, it was a surprise that we hadn't crossed paths until now. But he was probably still going out every Friday and Saturday night to bars to hear bands play while I stayed home trying to save money. I'd half expected him to leave when he was no longer required to be here for me to be near Breanna and Mum. But he had once told me he liked being a big fish in a small pond and maybe that was hard to give up.

As I watched him approach, I did a quick stock take. There definitely weren't any feelings left – I wasn't overly pleased to see him, but I wasn't unhappy about it, either. It was the emotional equivalent of white noise. I didn't wish him ill, and if I had to have someone turn up unexpectedly at my doorstep, there were far worse people I could imagine. My bank manager, for one.

He gestured to his bike as if it should be obvious. "Just out for a ride, I forgot you moved down here. I'm heading up to that new bike track."

I nodded. The bike track had been an economic development idea of an earlier Government, designed to link the entire country. Our bit was one of the last portions added to the chain. Why it ran through my part of town, I had no idea, though. The best sights around here were the park down the street, a huge featureless commercial building that the locals called the monolith and might have been won "the ugliest building of 1985", and the guy who put an array of junk that he seemed to fish out of his garage on to the street for free pickup every Sunday.

We had lived in a much more expensive part of town, down by the waterfront, when we had been married. He'd got to keep the apartment with its marina view and two-and-a-half bathrooms, mainly because he could afford to service the mortgage on his own. I'd heard he had a yacht on a mooring out the front now.

His unexpected arrival was relatively well timed. I was going to have to hunt him out at some point to give him an update about the surrogacy situation, anyway, and here he was presenting himself. No doubt he would be unsurprised that the problem with our baby project had turned out to be me. He had always been extremely sceptical about any suggestion that he could be playing a part. "Do you want to come in? Drink break?"

He looked at his bike, then back at me. "Sure, that would be great."

Andy stretched out on one of the two chairs at my dining table, his legs splayed and extending a quarter of the way across my small kitchen with its slightly sloping floor. I'd never thought of him as being particularly tall, but he seemed too big for any part of my house.

He was looking around the room, taking in my plants (needed water), photo frames (needed dusting) and the breakfast dishes I hadn't put on before I'd left because the dishwasher was still running. There was a painting on the wall that I had done when we first married, back when I had time for those sorts of things. He might have recognized it, but he didn't mention it.

He wouldn't say anything, but I knew he was probably doing a mental tally of all the things he was glad not to have to deal with anymore. I, in turn, was pleased not to have to worry about his judgement. There were only so many pointed sighs one person should have to hear in their own home in one lifetime. His apartment could be as showroom-tidy as he wanted it now.

A small bird, maybe a fantail, was hopping along the kowhai tree branch that tapped on my kitchen window when the wind blew the right direction. It looked as though she might be making a nest.

"So, what's news?" He was showing no signs of the awkwardness you might expect from someone having a surprise cup of tea with an ex-wife.

He took a sip of the matcha I'd placed in front of him, in a mug that I realized too late I'd bought on one of our holidays together. He hadn't given any indication that he had noticed. I retreated to the kitchen half of the room.

I swallowed. "Got some bad news on the baby front."

A wave of memories crested and crashed in my brain of us having this conversation in the past, as each month crawled by without any luck. At the time, it had felt like he was pulling away from me a little bit more with each update, as if my grief was too much for him to handle.

Now, he just nodded. "I was wondering what was happening with that."

I bit my lip, leaning back against the kitchen bench to put a bit of extra space between us. "I might need a surrogate, the doctor doesn't think I can carry to term."

He blew an exhale through pursed lips. "I thought it might be something along those lines."

He could still be infuriating, clearly. Why did he always have to act as if he knew everything about every single thing? He had taken years to agree to have his sperm count checked because he had been so sure it was nothing to do with him.

He leant back on the couch and looked me up and down. "You won't really go through all that, though, will you?"

I stared at him. Had he forgotten how much it meant to me? The stream of pregnancy tests I'd taken each month, always hoping for a different answer? The days I'd not been able to get out of bed when the few successful attempts finally failed? The way it felt as though my reason for carrying on seeped away each time the goal got a little bit further away?

But he'd never got it before, and he obviously wasn't any closer to understanding now. I let my eyes scan his body, taking him in. He wasn't going to argue, was he? If he was happy for me to do it alone, surely he couldn't be too upset about how I made that happen.

I watched his face carefully as I replied. How this could be the same person I had once – a very long time ago, to be fair – thought knew me better than anyone else in the world? It was hard to comprehend. At the beginning, I'd liked him for his arrogance and ability to rise above the sorts of problems that might concern normal people. His blasé attitude to – well, basically anything – had been a good offset to my tendency to dwell on things that didn't go to plan. But while I thought initially it was all a bit of an act and he would actually have real feelings about things if he was really honest, as time had gone by, I had been forced to confront the fact that he really was often not particularly deep. While he could be a great friend and huge fun for a night out or a week away, he wasn't a good fit for someone who was trying to find her place in the world.

I took a breath. "It's really important to me to try everything I can. After everything I've invested in this journey – financially and emotionally, you know..." I trailed off to allow him time to speak but he was silent.

"I've asked Breanna whether she would consider it."

He paused. "So, would it be like I was having a baby with your sister?"

I screwed up my face. What an insane thing to say. But typical of him, really. The first thing that came into his head was what he said, in almost every situation.

I had always suspected he had a bit of a thing for her, the younger, prettier, and much richer version of me. She wouldn't have given him a passing glance, though he would have been around a bit more than the gorgeous but elusive Brad. "Gross. No. She would just be helping to make our baby – my baby, you don't have to have anything to do with us if you don't want to, remember?"

He shrugged. "I wouldn't mind having a kid. But you know..."

If it felt like too much effort, he would be out. That would have been our entire lives together.

I watched him slurp from his teacup. He was always far noisier than was necessary with pretty much all of his bodily functions.

If we were successful, I would still be tied to Andy for the rest of my life through a baby that he only ever had a passing interest in making happen. How much like him would they be? My house was only small, and a teenage version of Andy would take up a rather large amount of room. I shunted the thought to the side.

I turned and stared out the window again, where the small brown bird was bopping her way up the branch with something that might have been moss in her beak.

Andy was tapping his foot on the floor. "Seeing anyone?"

I turned back to him; one eyebrow raised. "That's a weird thing to ask."

He raised his hands in mock surrender. "Sorry, just being nosy."

I shook my head. "No. I'm not." An image of Simone flashed into my mind. What was I going to wear to the awards?

He rolled his cup between his hands. "I've been trying out the apps a bit, but nothing too serious, just a bit of fun."

I nodded, trying not to encourage the conversation. I had wondered what it would be like when he met someone new. When we had first separated, I'd briefly toyed with the idea that it might make me question whether I'd done the right thing to end the relationship.

Hearing that he was putting himself on the market again, all I felt was a deep relief that he had definitely ruled a line under our marriage. Just as long as he kept it not-too-serious for the time being. The last thing I needed was a new girlfriend for Andy coming in and taking an interest in my plan.

The bird was pulling something out of a flower. "Well, I hope it goes well for you. I know you like to have fun."

He laughed. "Thanks, I think."

He took a swig that owned the rest of his tea, brushed something imaginary off his lycra-clad thighs, which had noticeably more muscle definition than I remembered, and pushed himself to his feet. "I'll be off."

As he got to the front door, he turned and looked at me. "Just take it easy, okay? Don't wreck yourself over the baby thing."

I ducked my head. As if I had a choice. "Sure."

We looked at each other for a second too long. There was something both familiar and completely alien about being in the same room as him again. He looked like the man I had married, albeit a few years older with a little more grey in his hair. But the spark of connection that had been there was just a memory.

"Take care of yourself," he kissed me on the cheek in the way I'd seen him do with female acquaintances so many times over the years, his lips barely touching my skin. It was a bit like receiving a kiss from a kind but not particularly interested uncle. "Let me know how you get on."

I settled on to the sofa, a cup of tea on the coffee table by my feet. The table was a purchase from a white elephant stall at a fair held by Ruby and Charlie's school. I'd bought it just after I'd moved into my own place. The cup was part of a set my grandmother – mum's mum - had left for me in her will, dainty china with soft pink rosebuds curling around it. It was cute and made the tea feel like something a bit special. It had been years since I'd allowed myself a glass of wine, always worried about the potential impact on a small person who might want to make use of my body at some point soon. So instead of a nice pinot noir or riesling in the evening to wind down, I had swapped for teas – whether you wanted green or black or rooibos or herbal or matcha, I had a selection.

Crumpet had appeared beside my right thigh and stretched across my body, so his front paws were reaching over my left leg. He bumped his head into my hand as I tried to smooth the frown-like wrinkle between his eyes.

I reached for my cup with my other hand, then hesitated. I'd cut myself off from drinking wine during the baby-making process but that rule clearly didn't need to be in place anymore, did it? Any eggs that were being used had already left my body and I wasn't going to be the one who would nurture them through to life, anyway. What was stopping me from enjoying a glass of sauvignon blanc, or a merlot?

There was a bottle of wine in the fridge that Simone had left there when she came for dinner a few weeks ago, and I had some nice pinots that I'd picked up from a trip to Queenstown when Andy and I first split.

Before I could get out from under the cat and to my feet to investigate what I might like to sample as my first drink in a very long time, my phone rang at the far end of the sofa. I wriggled my foot around to shunt it closer to me without dislodging Crumpet. My heartbeat picked up pace when I saw the name on the screen. Breanna. Was this the call I'd been waiting for?

"Hello?" I tried to keep my voice upbeat, to sound the same as I had on every other of the thousands of occasions in which she had called me in the evening as I sat in this exact spot.

"Amy, I've decided," she spoke quickly, as if she too were nervous. "I'll do it."

CHAPTER FOUR
BREANNA

When I hung up the phone, I had bitten the fingernail of my right index finger almost down to the quick. What had I done? Memories of my two pregnancies lurched queasily into my brain. I squeezed my eyes shut at the thought of living on ginger beer and dry crackers again.

It was the only time Brad had taken any real leave that I could remember. He supplied a steady stream of popsicles to me as I lay in bed when I was pregnant with Charlie. Back then, he was working in town, so even when he wasn't off work, he could pop back on a lunch break to check on me.

The second time around, I couldn't find time to lie in bed and had to devise games for Charlie that involved me spending as much time as possible prone on the couch. Brad was preparing to leave for the job overseas and in a post-partum haze I'd wondered if the sight of me lurking around in two-day old leggings, not able to wear my shoes because of how puffy my feet were, had encouraged him to go.

If I'd thought looking after a two-year-old while pregnant was tough, what would it be like now? I hadn't been trying to manage a full workload then, there were no extracurriculars to juggle and I wasn't chair of the school board. I wouldn't be able to take a meeting while vomiting.

But it was Amy. She was my sister and I loved her. How could I be the one to stop her from achieving her dream? I'd seen enough of the process she had put herself through in the past few years to know that what she wanted most in the world was to have her own children. I couldn't be the person who stood in the way of that for her, even if I sometimes couldn't quite understand her the extent of her motivation. Of course, I knew from answering the country's problems that you couldn't ever truly get inside other people's heads.

Maybe I felt that I still owed her a little bit. My big sister. She took a lot of the brunt of Mum being unwell when we were kids. She also bailed me out of problems before our parents realised what was happening, so it was easier for me to be the "good one".

When I was pregnant with Charlie and cried about having to go to Dad's funeral in a t-shirt and trackpants because I didn't fit any of my normal clothes, she had driven to Auckland and back in one morning to buy me a stunning black maternity dress.

But I was dreading telling Brad. If he baulked at the idea of her shifting into my office for a few months, what was he going to think about me being pregnant with her child? My inner advice-giver took over. He needed to understand it was my decision, even if it seemed the wrong one to him. I'd idly wondered whether I could get through the entire pregnancy without him even noticing, but even if he did not come home for nine months, the children would no doubt say something.

The only thing for it was to get it over with. The kids were outside making a fort on the trampoline, so I had a clear 10 minutes, at least, and I might be able to catch him before he started work.

I pressed the button on my phone to call his number. The tone indicated it was trying to connect for about half a minute.

He grinned when our cameras finally showed each other's faces. "Hi, beautiful. This is a nice surprise."

I smiled despite myself. "Can you talk?"

He leant back against what looked like a blank white wall. "Sure. What's up?"

I cupped my face in my chin and looked at the phone screen, which I had propped against the wall on the edge of the couch. "Amy needs me."

He shifted in his seat. "What's going on now? I really don't think we should be giving her money. If the business is in a bad state, she needs to make some decisions about that."

I shook my head. "She doesn't want money."

I let a pause stretch out between us. "She's been told she won't be able to have a baby herself."

He blew air out through his teeth. "That's tough, I'm sorry."

He was looking at me, waiting for me to go on. "What does she need from you, though? Does she want to borrow one of the kids?"

I frowned at him. "That's not funny."

He bowed his head. "Sorry." He looked up again, grinning. "But you know, the next time one of them really annoys you..."

I smiled at him despite myself. "She's asked whether I'll be her surrogate."

He coughed. "Sorry, what?"

I felt my shoulders sag. It was a huge thing to be asked. It would turn our lives upside down. And when would it end? How would I feel afterwards? Would things go straight back to normal? Probably not.

But as I found the words to respond to him, it only cemented my resolve that I needed to help. "She needs someone to carry her baby for her. I'm all she's got. You know she'd do it for me."

He looked at me but said nothing for a minute.

I kept talking to fill the space. "I'm not asking anything of you."

He screwed up his face. "Yet."

It was vaguely infuriating. It wasn't like he was around

enough to be entitled to an opinion, really. "I can't see how I could ask you for anything."

"You know I'm here for you. What will the kids think?"

I shrugged. "They won't be too fazed. They might like the idea of a little cousin."

He folded his arms and leant towards the camera. "So, you're going to be pregnant with her baby… Are you sure you can cope with that? What will it do to your body?"

With Ruby, I'd developed gestational diabetes, so I was on a diet of Special K, salad wraps and steamed chicken.

"I'll get through it. At least at the end of it, she'll be the one doing the night feeds, so I'll be able to recover faster."

He grimaced. "This a big thing, babe. Are you sure you've thought it through?"

I studied a painting hanging on the wall opposite. It was an abstract piece that Brad had bought for me from a local artist for my 30th birthday. It normally gave off a sense of calm, but as I looked at it, it grew increasingly hectic. "You understand why I have to do it."

He was looking over his camera, staring into the distance. "It's your decision. It's your body, obviously. I just want to you to take care of yourself, okay? You don't have to do everything for everyone. And you don't have to keep bailing your sister out every time. Don't feel guilty that you've got things she wants."

I bit my lip. "I love her, I want to help her."

It would be all over in less than a year. And he was right, it was my body, and I could use it however I wanted.

He nodded, looking at something a little off to the right of the camera. "Just give me a minute to get my head around it. But I've got to go. Miss you all. I'll send you a message a bit later on, see how you're going."

"We miss you too."

He blew me a kiss and disconnected the call.

I put my phone down and turned back to my laptop. An email from my editor caught my eye in my inbox.

I clicked on it, and it filled my screen. "Now don't panic..." she began. That was a sure-fire way to ensure that I did, indeed, panic. I scanned down the following paragraph.

Readership was patchy. That wasn't hugely unusual. The advice column was one of the better-read parts of the site. Revenue was down. That was nothing new – revenue had been falling for the past five years and management had been trying a range of different things to turn it around. We had implemented a paywall a few years earlier and one of my targets each month was to turn a set number of casual clickers into paying subscribers.

Krista's email informed me that the target was going up, by about 20 percent. We were also launching a new newsletter for subscribers that would feature five of our best lifestyle features each week. It looked like that was going on to my to-do list.

"Give some thought to how you can funnel more people through this channel," she signed off her email.

I stared at it. Beyond writing columns that were generally interesting and keeping the juicy bits of my advice beyond the point where people had to pay to read, I struggled to work out how I could increase my conversion rate. Our features were all well read – other media often copied our ideas after we had run our stories, which I took to be validation that we were doing the right thing.

"Can we talk about how I might do this?" I fired off a note in reply. "That's quite an ambitious target."

Her response was in my inbox within 30 seconds. "You're the best in the country on this – some analysis on the sorts of topics that resonate with readers could help. I'll get our audience development team to send through some recent stats to give you an idea of what's been flying – but you know it all yourself, anyway."

I sighed. People better start having readable problems, then. I was almost tempted to make some up myself. People always suspected I did, anyway. I sent Megan a message. "Are you getting new readership targets, too?"

She replied a minute later. "No, I'm just the one who writes the public service stuff that gets us our government funding, remember? No one cares about what I'm up to."

She was exaggerating but there was an element of truth to what she said. If they could show that she was getting to the council meetings and reporting on the important court cases, the website had a better chance of qualifying for funding each round – it was up to people like me to make sure we had enough other stuff that people would want to read to draw in the advertisers and subscribers.

My gaze travelled to the diary that was open on my desk. Depending on how quickly things progressed with Amy's doctor, and how my body coped with it, I might need to let Krista know about the pregnancy within the next few months. Hopefully everyone would be feeling calmer by then.

I had been hoping to ease my work pressure for a while rather than increase it. But at least I'd probably only need a couple of weeks off work when the birth finally happened, as opposed to the months I'd taken when it had produced a baby I needed to look after.

I could probably get an extra column and a few features in the bag throughout the pregnancy so no one would even need to know I was gone.

I pushed the idea out of my mind. Expelling a child from my body was still not my idea of a great way to spend a morning. I closed my inbox. I had resolved to check my emails only at designated times, on the half hour and hour. Checking in between had become a nervous tic and was not achieving much except stressing me out. What was it about 80 percent of your time being taken up by the 20 percent of tasks you got the least enjoyment from?

I picked up my phone to call a child psychologist I had been recommended to help me answer a question about a kid who was refusing to eat anything that was not blue. It was sometimes tempting to throw in questions of my own in cases like this. Like how can I explain to my children that I'm renting out the womb they grew in to their aunt for the best part of the year?

Roughly an hour later, I had shifted with my laptop from my home office to the kitchen counter, so I could position myself in the shaft of sunlight that was beaming through the window as the sun prepared to set. Summer filled my house with all sorts of spots of warmth and light that we forgot about over winter, when the sun seemed to pass us by for much of the day.

Ruby and Charlie were playing on their iPads in the second lounge of our house. It was intended to be an entertaining space but, since I rarely felt like throwing a party on my own, most of the time it was used by the kids. Once a week I'd grumble at them and ask them to clean up chip wrappers and drink bottles that were strewn all over the cream leather couches.

On the stove, a chicken casserole was boiling gently.

I opened my emails. It was on the half-hour and should be my last check of the working day. There were five new ones at the top. Three were instant deletes: A promotion of a mid-level manager at a company I hadn't heard of. A new type of fertiliser. A deeply boring survey about attitudes to petrol stations.

But the other made me stop. Mary Jones again. I opened it, deliberately holding my hand still to stop it trembling.

"No reply?" The email began. "I would have thought someone as perfect as you would have had something to say. How many people take your advice and destroy everything? It's not just me you've hurt, it's my entire family. How can you live with yourself? I certainly couldn't."

I let my hands fall away from the keyboard. I hadn't replied to the email because I thought it wouldn't achieve anything. These sorts of things were usually just a troubled person looking for a reaction and if you didn't give one, they would give up and go away. I hadn't even raised it with Krista because I knew others received emails that were more threatening every day. Abusive emails were so common that I had heard young journalism students were given advice on how they might deal with them.

But maybe I had misjudged the situation and I did need to do something more.

I clicked on the button to forward the message to her. "This is the second of these I've received, do you have time to let me know what I should do with them? I don't have a clue who this could be."

A hissing from the stove drew my attention. The casserole was threatening to boil over, spitting splotches of liquid on to the hob and splashback. Poppy scampered from her spot under the dining table into the kitchen.

"Always hopeful," I gave her a pat. "No disasters to clean up this time, though."

We pulled up in the car outside Ruby's gymnastics class with two minutes to spare the next afternoon. It was in a refurbished warehouse at the far end of town and had limited parking, but we had our commute down to a fine art. Charlie had his tablet already tucked under his arm as we clambered out of the car.

Ruby skipped ahead of us into the building. Her leotard was just a little too small and I could see the line where it created an indent on her hip through her bike shorts. Another month, another growth spurt. It must be discombobulating for Brad to come back each time to kids who were centimetres taller each time. This would be our second new gymnastics kit for the year. For all my grumbling about Brad being away so much, his salary did give me the luxury of not having to worry. He earnt enough that I never had to question whether we could afford any of the things the kids needed, and I never had to worry about how much our groceries cost as they started to eat their bodyweight in snacks each day.

It was quite a different upbring to mine and Amy's, where she had tried to teach me to play the guitar using elastic bands stretched over a ruler when I admitted a desire to be a pop star.

Not that either of us had the first idea about how such an instrument might be played.

Dad had earned decent money running a car dealership, but Mum barely worked because of her health. I had hero worshipped Amy as we grew up. It had taken me going away to university to really be able to find my own feet and see her as a full person – and to realise that some of the creativity and impulsiveness I'd loved about her as a teenager wouldn't always serve her well in life.

There was seating for spectators on the upper level of the gym. Charlie and I found seats near the steps. His eyes were already fixed on his screen, where he was deep in a Minecraft world.

On the floor below, Ruby adjusted her straps and readied for a run-up on the floor. My breath still caught in my chest as she propelled herself across, the springs underneath the surface giving extra lift as she hurled her body into the air, flipped and somehow landed perfectly on her feet.

A squeak of plastic seat confirmed the arrival of someone next to me. It was Cara, the mother of one of Ruby's teammates. We'd got to know each other over years of sitting on the sideline together, both crossing our fingers as our girls catapulted across the gym. With only a broken toe and a sprained finger between them, we figured we were doing well – so far.

She placed her hand on my knee in greeting. "Ruby's doing so well."

I smiled. "She has definitely come on a lot. How's Xanthe feeling about the competition?"

The girls were preparing for a competition at the weekend that counted towards their points for their overall rankings. Ruby didn't pay a lot of attention but some of the others took it extremely seriously and it was not unusual to see tears – from parents and children.

Cara shrugged. "She'll be fine. Always gets stressed beforehand but comes right on the day. I wonder if the judges will be harder on them this year."

"They're harder on them here than at dancing," I watched Ruby adjust her leotard.

"She's still doing both? That's tiring."

I smiled. "Yep, I always think she'll wear herself out and want an early night but it never happens."

Cara raised an eyebrow. "I meant for you, actually."

She was absent-mindedly stroking her midsection. Her stomach strained against the fabric of her dress. I looked away quickly. Seeing her manoeuvring her weight, beads of sweat on her upper lip, made me feel a little queasy. My bump had been bigger with Ruby than it had been with Charlie. How enormous could I get with a third baby? And to think when Cara had told me she was pregnant I'd felt a surge of relief that it was her, not me. Now I was lining up for another shot.

I swallowed. "How's it all going? Feeling okay?"

She shrugged and leant back in her seat. "Haven't been able to tie my shoelaces for a week and I have haemorrhoids like grapes. Otherwise grand."

I shuddered involuntarily and she caught my eye. "Sorry. I'm surrounded by pregnant women at the moment, I forget things like that aren't polite conversation."

I forced a laugh. "Don't worry, I remember it well. That was an empathetic cringe not a judgey one."

Cara appeared to force herself to rally. "Still, only a month to go. Max's birth was a horror show, so this one can only be better, right?"

"Surely. You're getting good care, and all that?"

She tilted her head. "My midwife is great. When I can get hold of her. Overworked like the rest of the health system, I guess."

I nodded. What they said about the pain of childbirth was true, in my experience. I knew that it had hurt. A lot. But I couldn't describe it or even properly remember it. The same was true before I had Ruby, though – I'd forgotten what Charlie's birth had felt like until the moment the first clamp of contraction hit again. I'd told Brad I'd changed my mind about having a second baby.

With Ruby, it had not only been too late to back out, but I had put off asking for help too long and I was stuck having an unmedicated birth because there was no time for anything to take effect. I wouldn't make that mistake again. This time I'd be getting everything that was available, as soon as possible.

Would Brad be there at the birth? I hadn't thought about it, probably just assumed he would be. But why would he? The baby wasn't going to be handed to him. Instead, it would be Amy – a less reassuring prospect.

As Cara turned away, I reached for my phone and positioned myself so she couldn't see the screen. I opened a message to Brad. "What have I got myself into?"

I hesitated, my finger hovering over the "send" button, then deleted it. At the tiniest suggestion I was having doubts, he'd probably try to talk me out of it, and I'd end up with a new problem. Instead, I cleared the message and started fresh. "Got any bright ideas about how I can boost my section readership? The boss wants results. Maybe your workmates have got problems."

He replied within seconds. "My workmates have lots of problems, but not the sort of thing you could publish."

I smiled, feeling the burbling in my stomach start to subside a little. "Call you when I get home?"

"Yep," he sent a heart. Then an eggplant emoji. I rolled my eyes. "You'll have to wait for the kids to be in bed if you want any of that."

Hopefully he'd forget – I had been at pains to tell the kids that we must always use the correct words for all parts of our anatomy. But it meant when we attempted phone sex I couldn't revert to any sexier vocabulary and felt like a doctor explaining a medical procedure.

Within minutes of me agreeing, Amy had sent me a list of everything that would be expected from me before the surrogacy process could begin. First up, I had to prove that I was sufficiently mentally sound to be embarking on such an unusual endeavour.

So it was that about 10.30 the next morning, I locked the door of my home in the suburbs on the fringe of town and drove to a small house in a central city street that had once been residential but had slowly been taken over by more and more businesses moving in, converting bedrooms into offices. The counsellor's little house was between an engineering firm and a mortgage broker.

The limited signage on the front of the building gave what appeared to be two women's names. I checked the calendar on my phone. This was definitely where I was supposed to be for the pre-transfer counselling appointment.

I couldn't imagine what we would talk about for half an hour, and it was scheduled at the perfect time to mess up the flow of my morning's work. But Amy said if I didn't take this spot there wasn't another one for six weeks and I could just picture her face if I told her we had to wait that long.

She sent me a message as I pulled my car into the empty carpark. "Good luck!"

She would have come with me if I had let her, but I could imagine her sitting in the waiting room, tapping her foot. Or more likely, pacing the room – or even bursting in and trying to hurry the counsellor into signing us off. It was like she wanted to get the baby into me before I had a chance to change my mind.

I pushed the front door open and stepped into what was clearly a waiting room. It was empty, and there was no one at the reception desk. A vase of red tropical flowers sat on a table in the centre. I settled on one of the scooped white chairs. The air-conditioner hummed in the corner, battling the heat of the sun that was radiating through the large front windows. The house might have been built in the late 1800s. What would the women who moved in here when this was a tiny agricultural town, hours from anywhere, think about what we were doing here now?

I waited just long enough to start to worry that I'd arrived in the wrong place, or the appointment had been misbooked. But finally one of the doors down the hallway ahead of me opened. A woman with a mass of curly brunette hair peered around the doorframe. "Breanna?"

I pushed myself to my feet and walked towards her. My hands shook slightly as I extended one to shake hers. Was I nervous about the procedure? Or of not living up to this woman's judgement?

"Nice to meet you. I'm Helen."

She ushered me into the room, craning her head to look into the waiting room. "Your partner isn't with you?"

I shook my head but said nothing. After a beat, I realised she was waiting for me to explain.

I waved it away. "He works overseas, so he's not at home at the moment."

I watched her face as she took this in.

"We're used to it," I tried to smile but it sounded feeble.

She tapped her mouth with a pen. "But he's supportive? We could do a phone consult with him, perhaps. We do like to hear from both partners in a situation like this."

I shook my head. "That's not necessary. He's supportive, just from afar. I'm not sure it'll have all that much impact on him, to be honest."

It was probably truer that he knew trying to argue now would be pointless.

She pursed her lips. "People sometimes find they're affected in unexpected ways. We can leave the option open for him to speak to someone, if he'd like to."

I focused on smoothing my skirt over my legs. There was no way Brad would turn up somewhere like this unless he was marched in under threat to his life. "Thanks, I'll let him know."

She settled into a chair and gestured for me to sit on another.

A coffee table between us that matched the one in the waiting room held a box of tissues and a couple of glasses of water. "Okay. Let's talk a bit about the choice that you're making."

For half an hour, she peppered me with questions. Did I understand the process? Mostly. Did I have concerns? Anyone who didn't have concerns about the prospect of growing a human and then expelling it from your body would be a worry, wouldn't they? Had I considered the impact on my family and plans for any future children? We hadn't got to the point of telling the kids yet, and there were certainly no plans for any future children.

Finally, Helen placed her pen down on the coffee table in front of us. "Do you have any questions of your own?"

I clasped my hands in my lap, and then unclasped them. I really just wanted to get on with it. All these steps just felt like a box-ticking exercise. Amy would make it happen through the sheer force of her own will, if nothing else. I shot Helen a closed-mouth smile. It seemed safer to say nothing than to say the wrong thing.

Helen returned the smile, except hers was a real one that reached her eyes. "You seem like a sensible woman, Breanna. And you obviously love your sister. The only question I have left for you is this – you're absolutely sure you're making this decision with your own free will? You aren't being forced into it?"

I nodded. "I am. She wants me to do this but I'm here because I want to help my sister."

She made a note on her pad. "Okay."

"So, I passed?"

She smiled. "I'm satisfied that you know what you're doing. I'll let the clinic know that you can move to the next stage of the process."

Her office smelt like jasmine air freshener. I cleared my throat. "Do you know off the top of your head what that is?"

"Just a screening, checking for any health conditions that could be an issue. I'm sure it'll be fine."

I gathered my things. It would be just the first test of many in my future. I had watched far too many videos of embryo transfers online at night when I couldn't sleep, so I had an idea of what I was in for. It would certainly be different getting pregnant thanks to a doctor while my legs were in stirrups, instead of when I'd had half a bottle of chardonnay and the rare opportunity of Brad in my bed. The number of people who peered into my nether regions could easily hit double-digits in the next couple of months.

A familiar vehicle was parked outside the house when I pulled into my driveway at home. It was Amy, and she was sitting in the car. I pressed a button on the remote to open the garage.

Climbing out of the car, I raised a hand in greeting to her as I fumbled around in my handbag for my keys to open the adjoining door to get into the house. A push-to-start car was great until you then needed to find the keys for something else. I kept moving to bigger and bigger handbags in an attempt to hold everything I needed to cart around with me, but it was just harder to find things like my keys and my phone when I needed them.

Amy's car door slammed shut and she hurried down the driveway towards me, two large paper bags in her arms. She tried to put her arms around me anyway, and aimed a kiss that landed somewhere near my ear. "My wonderful sister."

I pushed open the door with my hip and gestured for her to go ahead of me. We traipsed past the laundry and the kids' rooms to the living areas beyond. Poppy strolled out of Ruby's bedroom, where she had been sleeping on the bed, leaving a furry indentation in the duvet.

The house was quiet apart from the hum of the fridge in the kitchen. The kids would not be home for two more hours. I shot Amy a glance. I had already given up the morning for the counsellor, and I had to put together a new readership strategy to offer some ideas at the next all-staff meeting at the end of the week. What did she need me to add to that list?

She sensed my impatience and put her bags on the dining table. "I won't stick around, I know you're busy."

She started pulling things out, an array of small white bottles and a couple of cardboard boxes with bright labels.

I frowned. "What's all this?"

She smiled, almost sheepishly. "I know it's been a while since you were pregnant, so I've been looking at all the research, and I think these are the supplements you need to be taking. If you start now, you should be totally primed and ready for the transfer when it happens. I know you've also got the birth control pills to moderate your cycle, and we'll do your progestogen injection a few days before the transfer. Do you want me to do that one for you?"

I screwed up my face. "I don't think that's necessary. I'm sure I can handle it."

I picked up a bottle and turned it over in my hands. "What's this meant to do? When I had Ruby all I had to do was take folic acid and iodine."

She gestured to a couple of the smaller bottles. "Those are over there, you definitely need those."

She pointed to the others in turn. "But here we've got iron, I know you don't eat a lot of red meat so you might need that, and something for energy because we don't want you to get rundown. I've got you some calcium, some vitamin d, some zinc, some fish oil…"

"If I take all of these I don't know if I'll have any room in my stomach for my food." I tried to keep my voice light.

She turned to me. "Don't worry, I've thought about that, too," she gestured to a box. "Those are some meal replacement shakes in case you have trouble finding time to make a meal, or you don't feel like eating."

She was vibrating with energy. "Okay, well thanks." I patted her back. "I appreciate you looking out for me."

Only I had a niggly feeling she wasn't, really. She was looking out for the environment in which she wanted her baby to grow. Amy was already seeing me as the baby-making machine that needed to be kept in top condition, rather than her sister, who might have preferred a delivery of one last bottle of champagne or soft cheese.

She kissed my cheek. "I'll let you get on with your work now. Are you booked in for the test?"

I nodded. "Yep, all ready to prove I'm disease-free."

She was walking backwards down the other hallway towards the front door, still firing questions at me. "Do you want me to come with you?"

I shook my head.

"Will you let me know when it's done?'

"Of course."

She was at the front door and reached behind her to open it. "Okay. I'll wait to hear from the clinic about our next steps."

Our eyes connected. Her voice became quieter. "I really appreciate what you're doing."

I ducked my head. She had never been good with expressing emotions, particularly around me. She hid her tears so I wouldn't feel sadder about Mum being sick. She told me later she'd kept her unhappiness about her birth father not being in the picture to herself so that Mum didn't get upset.

"It's okay, Ames."

I followed her down the hall and pulled her into a hug. "I know. Everything will be okay. It'll work out."

She leant against me. All I could do was hope I was right.

CHAPTER FIVE
AMY

Two women were standing at the far side of the shop, each holding dresses to the light. One was a long shimmery evening dress and the other a sort of weekend casual piece that had been a strong seller. Well, a strong seller by my shop's standards, anyway.

"Let me know if I can help you at all," I called over to them.

They didn't meet my eyes but one of them muttered something that I assumed was telling me that they didn't need me. People rarely did, but then sometimes you'd get someone was almost deliberately keeping as far away from any of the staff as possible but then would complain that they hadn't had any assistance.

My shop intuition wasn't perfect, but it was telling me pretty clearly that only one of the women was likely to buy anything and it was probably going to be the one holding the cheaper dress.

The bell jingled at the door, indicating someone else coming in. I looked up.

"Andy, what are you doing here?"

There was no lycra this time, mercifully. He was dressed for work in a grey suit.

"I was just passing and I thought I'd pop in, it's been a while since I've seen the shop."

He looked around, as if assessing it for a report card. I watched him. The first visit was by chance, but still it was weird to see him twice in a relatively short space of time. And why would he have seen the shop? His work was on the other side of town and he wasn't exactly my target market. "Is something up?"

He picked up a pen from the counter and twirled it between his fingers. "Not really…"

I tapped my fingernails against each other. "Out with it."

He cleared his throat again and pushed himself off the counter, so he was standing looking at me. "I don't know if I told you about Lucia?"

I sighed. Andy had always had a thing for women with exotic names, particularly if they came with exotic accents and lots of thick dark exotic hair. That was at least part of the reason why his family had been somewhat surprised when he had come home with me.

"You didn't, no."

"It's not super serious," he said, "but I've been seeing her for a few months."

I nodded. "You did mention you were using the apps. I didn't realise you meant that you'd actually met someone."

He chuckled awkwardly. I knew he would secretly be enjoying being the first one of us to find someone else. "Sorry," he played with a piece of paper on the counter. "I didn't think it was going to be anything to worry about. But I mentioned that I'd seen you and that you're still pushing ahead with all that…." He gestured in a way that I assumed was meant to symbolise a pregnancy that made him uncomfortable. "She wants to meet you."

"Really?"

Keeping an eye on the browsing women, who had moved on to the jeans in the middle of the shop, I looked at him sideways. This relationship might be more serious than he was letting on.

It was typical of him, to try to give as little information as possible in any situation and then leave it up to me to fill in the gaps or take care of any problems. He'd been hoping to let me in on just a bit when he saw me at my house, but now he had been forced to tell me more.

I avoided his eyes and looked at the floor. On one hand, I could understand it. If your boyfriend – if that was what he was to this mysterious Lucia - was in the process of having a baby with someone else, you'd probably want to know about it. But on the other hand, how well did she actually know him? I didn't want to meet everyone he went on a few dates with. The admin involved would be exhausting.

I ran a hand through my hair. "Aren't we getting a bit ahead of ourselves? Breanna isn't even pregnant."

And Lucia might not even be around by the time she was. I didn't say that out loud.

An uncomfortable thought struck me. If she did stick around, was there a chance she could have a child with Andy? That would make our children siblings. Something twisted in my chest. It wasn't jealousy. I didn't want to be the one starting a family with Andy – not in the traditional sense anyway. But for a long time, I had. The idea of someone – Lucia or whoever else might be coming down the line - finding it easier than I had was not a comfortable one, even if the response was irrational. I'd only just started coming to terms with the idea that I wouldn't be able to have a baby myself. It would probably be a long time before it didn't hurt to have someone prod that grief.

He tapped the desk twice with his forefinger, righted himself from where he had sort of flopped on the counter, and readied to leave. It felt like an implicit reminder of the favour that we both knew he was doing me by not putting a stop to our IVF process. "Just think about it, okay?" he said. "It doesn't have to be right now, but it would make things a lot easier for me if you did."

I took a step towards the women shopping, as if to get as much space between me and Andy as I could. I just wanted him out of the shop as quickly as possible. "I'll think about it."

One of the women headed towards the changing room, so I pulled a curtain aside for her and gestured for her to go in.

I watched him go. Did he really deserve to have things made easier for him? With everything I was juggling, trying to smooth the path for his love life was not high in my priorities. But that was the habit we'd got into when we were married, and perhaps he just assumed it would continue, whether we were together or not. Another reason to be grateful to be out of there.

As I locked the shop door later that evening, my phone vibrated in my pocket. It was a message from Simone. "Going for a walk, want to join?"

I did. But I was planning to go to the gym before popping around to Breanna's. We would normally see each other a couple of times a week but now that she had signed on to Project Baby I was making an excuse to go and see her virtually every day. It was probably partly to reassure myself that she hadn't changed her mind.

I forwarded any useful information I could find about ways to make pregnancy physically easier, or how to prepare for the transfer itself. It had been nine years since she had been pregnant with Ruby and the advice had presumably changed in that time. If I was being honest, though, it was mostly a way to feel like I was doing something.

The transfer was scheduled for the end of the week, now that Breanna had proved she was mentally okay with it and her screen had come back negative for any illnesses or infections that could have caused trouble. I had been surprised at how quickly it was moving – when it had been me being poked and prodded it had felt like it had taken ages, what with the injections to encourage ovulation and then the awful harvesting. With Breanna being able to skip all that, we could go straight to the transfer, albeit with some medication to get her cycle straight and her body primed for it.

The bell above the door tinkled again. My heart sank. Surely Andy wasn't back again.

I turned around, my muscles tensing as if ready to take him on.

Relief surged through me when it was Simone who stuck her head around the door. "Did you get my message?"

I raised my hand in response. "I did. I was worried about having to get a few things done, but actually, what could be better than a walk on an evening like this?"

I could give the gym a miss. Maybe even let Breanna off the hook for an evening.

Simone grinned. "Errands can wait."

"I'll just swap my shoes. My gym gear's in the car."

Simone had a route she took from the front of her shop along a walking route known by locals as "the loop" - out around the town basin waterfront, across the drawbridge that straddled the river and back around. It finished conveniently right in the middle of a collection of restaurants and cafes. If it had been earlier in the day, I could have suggested we finish off with a coffee but, given the time, we could have ended up having dinner and that would be an unnecessary imposition on my struggling bank account.

I fell into step next to her. "Where's Audrey tonight?"

Simone checked her watch. "She'll be at Mum's. She had a playdate just down the road so I figured it was easier for her to pop over there and that way I can get a walk in before I pick her up."

I nodded. "You're lucky to have your mum's help like that."

She grinned at me. "I know. She'd better not come up with any grand plan to take up cruising or anything like that. I hear it's all the rage with the over-70s these days."

"She wouldn't dare."

Would my own mother want to be much involved with my

baby? She used to express surprise that neither Breanna nor I had moved away from the town we'd grown up in, apart from short stints in our 20s. But she was more of a passing influence in Breanna's kids' lives than the sort of live-in nanny-style role that Simone's had adopted. I saw more of them than she did.

We made our way from the end of the road our shops were on, down to the intersection where we would cross over to the blocks that enclosed the town basin. Simone pressed the button to fire up the red man on the crossing. A woman next to us took a deep breath of her vape and blew blueberry scented air over us. I pulled a face at Simone. The idea of inhaling strangers' breath was a bit disgusting, but it wasn't something that normally crossed my mind. But when it was berry scented it was harder to ignore.

"More importantly - did you talk to Breanna?" Simone shot me a quick look out of the corner of her eye as the light turned green and we headed across the road. I had been wondering when she was going to ask.

"Yes, and she said yes," I bit my lip to stifle a huge grin and did a sort of half-skip.

"That's amazing," Simone turned to me, her eyes bright. "I thought she would but I'm so happy for you."

I nodded. "I've not been telling people yet. Still kind of coming to terms with it."

She touched my arm. "That's sensible, give yourselves time to get used to it all before you get anyone else interfering. I won't pester you for information, but I'd love to hear how it's going, if you want to talk about it."

I let the fizz of happiness wash over me again. "There's not a lot to say, yet. We're booked in for the transfer then we have to cross every finger and toe that it's successful."

"I will do my bit to help with that," Simone said. "Hineteiwaiwa is the atua we say is associated with pregnancy and childbirth, maybe send her a good thought or two."

I smiled. "I will."

She shot me another look. "That's so exciting."

"I know, I can't wait."

We walked mostly in silence for the first 500 metres of the track alongside the water. As we reached the bridge, the sun was already a little lower in the sky. Simone seemed captivated by the way it was sending rays of light like tendrils through the clouds around it and stopped to lean against the railing. "I love summer evenings when it's not dark the minute I finish work."

I found I couldn't move my gaze from her face, which was lit by the softer evening light in a way that gave her an almost ethereal glow. "It's lovely."

Something small and black buzzed in my face, too close for me to make it out. I swiped at it but not in time – my left eye squeezed shut involuntarily as my contact lens shifted. I groaned.

Simone tuned to look at me. "What's wrong?"

I gestured towards my eye, which had started streaming. "A bug's stuck in my contact lens."

"Here," she took a step towards me and reached for me, deftly holding my eye open and peering into it. "Hold still."

My breath caught in my throat and then kept coming at odd intervals. The more I tried to focus on breathing normally, the weirder it sounded.

She inched the little finger of her other hand closer to my eye. Normally I hated anything going near my eye but there was something about her touch that was reassuring. "Look up."

She dabbed her fingertip on to my contact lens and pulled it away. "Got it."

I blinked to readjust my lens. She had let her hand fall so it was cupping my cheek, her face concerned. "Okay now?"

I caught myself as my body seemed to lean into her. What on earth was I doing? "Thanks, much better."

She smiled and moved her hand from my face, leaving the spot where it had been feeling cold. "Excellent."

She turned to follow the path, but my legs were slightly wobbly. Had it really for a minute like she might have been going to kiss me? Or that I was going to kiss her? What was I doing? Was this a midlife crisis? Was I trying to make already complicated life even more difficult?

An image of what it might be like to kiss Simone flashed unbidden into my brain. She always smelt faintly like apples, from what I assumed was her shampoo. I watched her walk ahead of me. If I totally misread the situation, I'd feel like a complete idiot. Anyway, I was getting ahead of myself on something that probably didn't even exist.

Simone was a couple of steps further down the track, and I increased my pace. When I caught up to her, she pointed to a house on the hill in front of us as we rounded the corner. "That's where Hana's parents live. I've always wanted a place like that."

It was big – almost as large as Breanna's - and white, with huge windows on the side that faced the water. Simone and Audrey lived in a house that was a bit like mine.

"Do you ever see them?"

She screwed up her face. "Sometimes. They turn up for Audrey's birthdays occasionally. I don't think they like to be reminded of Hana's relationship with me."

I raised an eyebrow. "What do you mean? You're lovely."

She half-laughed. "When our divorce was finalised, she married a doctor – a male one. Much more respectable for someone in her mum's set."

I hadn't known that. A paddle boarder sailed past us down the river, wobbling ever so slightly.

"I guess people change, don't they?"

Simone snorted. "A lot. She'd never had a boyfriend when I met her."

"Sexuality is very fluid. I'm sure I read something about that recently." I wasn't sure whether I was telling her that for her benefit, or my own.

Simone shrugged. "Especially for women. But you know – not ideal from my perspective. And I never got to stay in that great house again."

We arrived back where we had started 40 minutes after we set out. My watch bleeped approvingly, telling me I had done sufficient exercise for the day. "Thanks for the walk," I pulled my keys out of my bag, ready to head back to my car.

"I'll be thinking of you," Simone kissed me on the cheek. "Let me know how it all goes."

I nodded. "I don't know how long it'll be before I have anything to say, but I will."

She reached for my hand as I turned away. Her tone was serious. "You're going to be an excellent mother."

I had to swallow a lump in my throat and look away to break the intensity of our eye contact. "I really hope so."

She clasped my hands a bit tighter. "However it happens, you will be."

On the morning we were booked for the transfer, I was up by 5.30. That's being generous. I went to bed at 10pm telling myself it was important to be rested. When I wasn't asleep by midnight, I figured I might as well read until my eyes forced themselves shut and I had no choice by to sleep. By 2am, I might have been scanning the words in my book but my mind was not taking any of them in, instead alternating between catastrophising about the potential for things to go wrong and bouncing with excitement about the idea of things going to plan.

I might have drifted off for a couple of hours but as soon as the first birds started to announce the arrival of the sun, I was awake again.

I pulled myself out of bed and wandered to the wardrobe. What does one wear for the day that their sister might be falling pregnant with their baby? If you put it like that it sounded like something that might have ended up on an old episode of Jerry Springer.

I selected a pair of faux leather trousers and a white t-shirt. Low-key and unobtrusive.

In the bathroom, I pulled my hair up into a ponytail and regarded myself in the mirror. I had bags under my eyes so large that they protruded from my face when I turned to look at my side profile. I had a touch of sunburn on my nose from when I'd taken Charlie and Ruby to the park. I always remembered to sunblock the kids but forgot about myself.

Would Breanna have had enough sleep? There was some evidence that if her cortisol levels were too high the transfer might not be as likely to succeed. I'd offered to buy her some calming tea that she could drink before bed, but she hadn't been interested.

I inhaled slowly, counting to four in my head, held my breath for a few seconds then released it.

It was a breathing exercise from a yoga teacher I'd met in my 20s when my mother was in hospital because of a mix-up with the medication she took for her heart problems, and I was an anxious mess. The breathing didn't help so much as interrupt a negative train of thought long enough to force my brain on to something else.

If I couldn't be the one actually pregnant, I wanted to be an invaluable help to the person who was, but I couldn't quite figure out how to do that.

I opened my phone to send a message to Natalie. She knew what she was doing but it wouldn't hurt to spell it out again for her. New stock was arriving about 10am. Frances, a customer who had been coming into the shop for many years, would pop in about midday to try on some of it for photos for social media. I should be back by then anyway. Provided everything went well, we should be out of the clinic within an hour. But things needed to be running absolutely smoothly – there was a chance that the bank's business banking manager was going to stop by to drop off some forms I had to sign. Paper copies, because I also had to get my lawyer to sign them and the bank wouldn't accept electronic signatures from two different places, or something – I'd lost interest half-way through the explanation. Although she claimed that it was an entirely objective process, I was convinced that, if I could just make it seem like we were in control, the bank might be more likely to believe we were, no matter what our account statements said.

It was strange to think that somewhere across town, my last remaining embryo was being thawed. I sent it some good thoughts.

∽

A few hours later, Breanna was lying on a paper-sheeted bed in the middle of one of the clinic's rabbit warren of rooms. Sun was forcing its way through the gaps in the venetian blind-covered window and all the lights in the room beamed down at her. It felt harsh and a little exposed, like the scene in Alien, when the creature is about to burst out of the actress's body. I half-laughed at the mental image – here we were trying to put a creature-to-be into Breanna's body.

I sat on the edge of a chair next to the bed, holding her hand.

She had her eyes closed. Her face was calm and her breathing steady. When I was on this sort of table, it must have looked quite different. I could remember standing up afterwards with my jaw hurting from clenching my teeth so hard.

I rubbed her hand between mine. "Are you okay?"

She moved her shoulders in what might have been a shrug. "The medication's starting to work. Just have to remember not to relax too much."

They had given her something to slightly sedate her, but she had also been told to arrive with a full bladder so that it was easier for the doctor to see what she was doing. I could see why that might not be the most comfortable mix for Breanna. When it was me on the table, I'd been so focused on the outcome that I didn't give much thought to the physical discomfort. It would be quite different for someone who was only here for the process, and only doing it for me. A familiar guilty wave of gratitude rolled through me, and I held her hand even tighter.

The door opened and Amelia entered, being trailed by a nurse. She smiled when she saw us. "It's nice to see you again. This is Farah, who'll be helping me today."

We had only spoken and emailed since the day she had delivered the bad news in her office. She went to the head of the bed and introduced herself to Breanna. "Thank you for doing this."

Breanna turned to look at me. "She deserves every chance she can get."

Amelia straddled a wheeled stool. "Do you have any questions before we begin?"

Breanna shook her head. "I'm okay."

"This is going to feel a bit like having an IUD inserted, have you ever had one of those?"

Breanna nodded and half-grimaced. I looked at the floor. That pinch and cramp was something else.

Amelia patted her shoulder. "It is a bit uncomfortable, but I'll work as quickly as I can."

She gestured to the nurse who passed her a tray of tools as she scooted to the base of the bed.

Breanna cleared her throat. "Just one thing…"

I spun around to look at her.

"Does anyone have any concerns about, you know, my age?"

Amelia looked up, her gaze shifting from Breanna's face to mine. "You're 35, right?"

Breanna nodded. I looked at my feet. There was sweat forming on my palm where it was pressed against Breanna's but I wasn't sure whose it was.

Amelia shrugged. "If I'm being honest with you, it's not ideal. But you're far from the oldest surrogate we've worked with and you're in good health. I have no concerns. I wouldn't have signed you off for this if I had thought it was going to be a problem."

Breanna nodded. I kept my focus on her face as Amelia worked. She flicked her eyes open and briefly locked them with mine before closing them again. She wiggled her fingers a little as if to indicate that I was grasping her hand too tightly.

I was aware of the ultrasound screen pulsing but couldn't look at it. When I'd been in her place, I'd kept my eyes fixed on it and now even the thought of it made me break into a sweat.

"Now I'm using a catheter to push the embryo through into position."

I held my breath. The room had gone completely quiet. I could hear Breanna breathing.

"And there," she sounded satisfied.

I looked at her. "That's done?"

Amelia nodded. "Now all we can do is wait and hope that the embryo implants. We should know within a couple of weeks."

I was familiar with that part of the process – the long wait to find out whether the transfer had worked. In my case it hadn't been the implantation that had been the issue, but the stickability.

She pulled off her latex gloves and looked at us. "Breanna, you'll need to not drive until the sedative has fully worn off. You might feel a bit of cramping and even some light bleeding. If you have any concerns, do feel free to get in touch with my office. Remember, if you have any fever or pain that you can't ease with paracetamol, you need to be seen by a doctor immediately."

Breanna pushed herself up, so she was half-sitting. I put my arm around her shoulders to help her. "I need to put some clothes on, it's a bit breezy up here."

Amelia laughed. "Of course. Sorry, I'll see if we've got the air con set a bit high."

I held Breanna's arm as she climbed off the table. She leant into me a little as she steadied herself on her feet. I tried to pull her in to an awkward embrace, but her body was stiff. A flash of worry hit me. Was she regretting her decision? Blaming me for putting her through that? How much pain was she in?

"Your bag is just here, I'll get your clothes," I rummaged through it to find the dress she had worn in and handed it to her. "Do you need a water? A protein bar? You don't have to get up right away."

Breanna shook her head.

Amelia had one hand on the doorknob. "Take your time, we don't want you leaping up straight away. And remember, no high energy exercise until you take the pregnancy test, and no sex."

Breanna exhaled. "Sadly, that won't be much of a problem."

As we walked back to my car, I handed her a bottle of water. "I know you didn't want any earlier but please try to keep hydrated."

She sighed but took it.

I fished around in my handbag for a small plastic bag I'd tucked into the inner pocket. "And here's a couple of pre-natal vitamins in case you haven't had any recently."

She took them from me wordlessly.

"Are you sure you don't want something to eat?"

She turned to me, her eyes wide. "Amy, stop. I can look after myself."

I took a step back. "Sorry, I'm just trying to help you."

Breanna put her hand to her temple. "I think you're trying to look after the baby. And that's fine, Ames. But you can't micromanage me for the next however long, okay? I will lose my mind. I know the baby is so important to you, but can you remember I'm here, too?"

I took a step back as if she'd slapped me. I had just been trying to help – I didn't realise she had thought it meant I only cared about the baby.

I stuttered. "I know you're here. I'm so grateful. I wish you didn't have to be…"

A lump in my throat removed my ability to talk as I unsuccessfully tried to blink back tears.

She sighed audibly as I put my hands over my face.

"Oh god, I didn't mean to make you cry."

I shook my head. "It's not you. It's … everything."

She pulled me into a hug. "I know."

We were silent on the car trip home. I could see her out of the corner of my eye, gazing out the window.

"Have you got much planned for the school holidays?" My voice was shakier than I expected.

She didn't look at me. "I think we'll just be at home. Don't worry, no extreme sport planned."

I shook my head quickly. "That's not what I meant."

She half-smiled. "I know."

"I could come and take the kids out. That new playground opened."

"Yeah, that could be cool. Charlie loves a flying fox. Just don't let him get too ambitious."

I cursed under my breath as my fuel light flicked on. Breanna gestured to the gas station a few metres ahead. "We can stop?"

I shook my head. "I'll be fine for a while yet."

She half-laughed. "I forgot you run it down to fumes."

I pulled the car to a stop at a pedestrian crossing as an elderly couple meandered across the road. "When's Brad home next?"

She leant back against the headrest. "Not for ages."

I reached out and touched her arm. "Do you still miss him? Or are you used to it now?"

She shrugged. "I honestly don't know if I'll ever get used to it, because I'm constantly hoping that it's going to end soon. It's hard on the kids, though I guess they don't really know what they're missing."

When we pulled up outside her house, she moved to gather her things. There was no one around but, in the distance, I could hear what might have been a ride-on lawnmower navigating one of the impossibly large gardens of her neighbours.

I passed Breanna her bag from the backseat. "Did you tell him we were doing this today?"

She shook her head. "No, I figured I'd catch him up when we know that it's definitely happening."

I ducked my head. She was right, no point getting ahead of ourselves. It was only me who had the next 18 years planned out in my head.

CHAPTER SIX
BREANNA

We were told not to do a pregnancy test until at least two weeks after the procedure – and even then, we were really meant to wait until the hospital could do it for us to get an official result. But Amy could not wait and 14 days after the transfer, I had an event in my phone calendar, scheduled by Amy, to set aside at least an hour in the morning.

First, I had to get the kids off to school. It was still early in the school term, so there was still some novelty to propel them on their way. Charlie was ready to go just after 8, heading off down the road on his bike with Carter from next door. Ruby was still in her room. I peered around the doorframe. "Almost ready to go?"

She had two t-shirts out on the bed and was assessing them. "Which one should I wear?"

I took a step closer and put my hand on her back. "I think you'll look lovely in either of those."

"Maia's going to be wearing pink today so I should wear purple," she gestured to the shirt on the right. "But I like the cat one." She looked up at me. There were only a couple of years left before her school would enforce a uniform.

"I think you should wear whatever makes you happy, it's okay if you and Maia are wearing the same colour."

She shook her head. "She'll be upset with me. Pink is her favourite colour."

I put my arm around her and kissed the top of her head. "You don't have to do what Maia wants all the time, you know."

She rolled her eyes. "I don't. I'll wear the purple one today and the cat one tomorrow."

"That sounds like a good compromise. Come out to the kitchen when you're ready and I'll pop some sunscreen on you before we leave."

As we headed down the road ten minutes later, I could see Charlie and Carter stopped on the footpath. I pulled over and rolled down the windows. "What are you two doing?"

Charlie looked up quickly. "Just waiting for Jayden. He won't be long."

"You'd better be at school by the time I'm coming back down this road, alright?" I tried to keep my voice stern, but it was a beautiful morning, still cool but with that rich summer sunshine that makes every colour brighter. I could understand why they might be trying to linger in it. "And you left your lunchbox. Can you pick it up from Ruby's class?"

Charlie half-nodded as I pulled the car back into the road.

Ruby barely looked back as she clambered out of the car in the carpark and headed into school. Watching her go, I conducted a mental scan of my body. Did I feel any different? With both Ruby and Charlie, I had not found out I was pregnant for four weeks and the only signs had been a bit of breast tenderness and nausea. But since I turned 30, my breasts had become tender every period, so it was hard to tell whether that was a sign or not.

As I pulled out of the carpark and nosed back into the road, Charlie and Carter were riding in through the gate. I waved to them, but he ignored me.

When I returned home, Amy was sitting on the front doorstep, her car parked on the street in front of my house. She looked up as my car pulled into the driveway. She had her hair pulled off her face in a severe ponytail. She was wearing huge black sunglasses and a blue-and-green maxi dress.

I pulled my car into the garage and went through the house to open the front door for her. As she almost pushed past me into the hallway, I took in the swirling colours of her dress. "You look fabulous, got big plans today?"

Amy blushed. "Thanks, but no. Just trying to dress up a little more." She was talking too fast, fidgeting as she hesitated, waiting for me to follow her into the house. "I've been hanging out in my loungewear a bit too much lately and it's probably not the best ad for the business, even when I'm not actually in the shop."

I didn't answer but brushed at what might have been a toast crumb on the right leg of my yoga pants. Was she judging me?

She put her hand on my arm. "I didn't mean for you. You always look great. And you work from home, you can do what you like." A weed eater cranked into action outside. I checked the calendar. It was the gardeners, perfectly on time as always. I hadn't seen them arrive, but they must have been just behind me.

"Comfort prevails. These are an expensive brand, though, so you can't judge me too much. I can't remember which one though." Even without meaning to, I was speaking more slowly than normal in an effort to encourage her to calm. It wasn't working. She was excited and worried, but it was just a tiny bit grating. The more uptight and stressed she got, the more worried I became about letting her down.

She flicked a look up and down my body. "Lulu, I think. I was actually thinking about getting into a bit more activewear in the shop. There might be a market for it – we don't have a lot of options in town, do we? "

She dropped her bag on to the sofa in the main lounge and took a deep breath. "I'm sorry, I'm nervous talking."

"I know. It's okay. Have you got the stuff?"

"We sound like a movie, doing a drug deal or something."

The dishwasher was clanking in the kitchen like something was hitting the side of the machine. That would be Charlie's haphazard stacking. Trying to get the kids to take on more of the chores in preparation for me potentially needing to slow down was not going particularly well. Was I allowed to have a coffee before we did this test? But then Amy would probably be horrified if it wasn't decaf.

She handed me a package wrapped in brown paper. "Here you go."

It had been nine years since I had done a pregnancy test but there appeared to be little change. Would I even be able to pee? It was meant to be done first thing in the morning but there was no way I would have been able to hold on until after the kids were gone. I accepted it from her and turned to head towards the bathroom. After a couple of steps, I realised she was trailing me. "Were you planning to come in?"

She stopped, as if surprised and unsure what to do next. "Sorry. I don't know what I'm up to. I'll wait here. I'll make us a cup of tea, shall I?"

I smiled and put a hand on her arm. "Sure. Sit in the kitchen, I'll be right back, and we can set the timer together. I promise I won't look until you're with me."

It was an unusual situation, to be standing in your kitchen with your sister, both trying not to look at a piece of plastic that had been doused in your urine minutes earlier. I placed the test on a piece of paper towel and set the timer on my phone. Amy flicked a glance at it, but I waved her away. "No point looking for a minute."

I placed a tea towel over the top to make the point. That would have to go in the wash with a lot of disinfectant. I pushed her cup of tea towards her. "Drink this, it might make you feel better."

She took a sip. "It's good, what is that?"

I checked the label on the box that was still sitting on the counter. "T2 French early grey, it's got a bit of vanilla or something in it. My favourite."

Amy sniffed it. "Sounds a bit spendy for me. I tend to stick with the more budget-conscious brands."

I took a sip of tea but said nothing. Amy's money troubles were still a bit of a mystery to me. She had got the raw end of the deal in the split with Andy, but she still came out with enough to buy a nice enough house without a huge mortgage – nowhere near as big as ours, anyway – but she was constantly broke. She was worried about the business, but last time we'd talked about it properly it was still covering its bills.

She looked towards the test again. "What's the chance of a false negative?"

She pulled the instructions out of the packet, which was lying on the bench next to her. "Apparently more common than a false positive."

I let my gaze wander out the window, trying not to think about the seconds ticking down. "It's okay, we've got the blood test coming up in a few days' anyway, that'll confirm it either way."

"This is just for my peace of mind."

I watched her, trying not to laugh. When was the last time she had had peace of mind about anything to do with this process? "If you could call it that."

The timer went off, a shrill beeping that bounced off the kitchen walls.

I lifted the tea towel and we both leant over the test.

"Is that..." Amy's voice was quiet.

"I think it is..." my heart had started hammering in my throat so hard that it felt as though other people should be able to see it. A wave of nausea worked its way up my chest.

"It's two lines," she looked into my face, her eyes shining.

"It's two lines," I confirmed. "I think I'm going to be sick."

I half-ran to the bathroom nearest the kitchen and shut the door behind me, leaning against it. The room was spinning around me. There was no going back now. Somewhere inside me there was the start of a small human. My niece or nephew. And all of Amy's hopes were tied up in it.

I splashed water in my face, making eye contact with myself in the mirror, feeling suddenly lonely, despite Amy's obsessive attention. The nausea bubbled in me again and I rested my head on the cool porcelain of the bathroom vanity.

Amy knocked on the door. "Are you okay in there?"

I swiped at my face again and stood. "I guess it's just a taster of morning sickness."

I leant against the door for a second before I opened it. As I stepped through, she grabbed my hand and twirled me around in a circle. "It's two lines! I can't believe it."

I let her wrap me in a bear hug, then release me as if she was worried about squeezing me too tight and rupturing something precious. "Nor can I."

She leant against me. "Thank you so much."

I pressed my lips together in a thin line. "I know you'll be here to support me."

I'd agonised about how, when and where to tell the children.

Amy would have prepared some sort of Pinterest-inspired reveal for them, probably involving a small pair of shoes or a onesie hanging on the line. But what I knew – and she probably hadn't thought about with her castles-in the-air approach to life planning – was that my kids might have a different emotional reaction to the Instagram-ready videos she had seen online. We weren't offering them a new baby sibling. We were offering them a cute little cousin who they would no doubt be very fond of. But that cousin would be almost a decade younger, and we were also letting them know that their mother, who was very much the default parent in their lives, could be a bit distracted for the next little while.

I picked my moment when they were home from school that afternoon and had eaten. There was nothing quite so scary as my children operating on an empty stomach.

I gestured for them to sit with me on the couch. It was better to tell them before they twigged that something was happening, rather than leaving them to try to piece it together if I was acting strangely. "I need to talk to you guys."

Charlie raised an eyebrow and stretched out on the floor in front of me. "What's going on?"

Ruby snuggled into my side. "What?"

I could almost feel Amy trying to listen in from the shop. She would have asked me to record the conversation if she didn't know better.

"You know how Auntie Amy hasn't got any children..."

They both nodded.

"And you know she's tried a few different things to make it happen..."

Ruby frowned. "She's not married to Andy anymore. So she can't have a baby, right?"

I looked down at her. "That's not really quite how that works. We can talk about that later. But right now, no, she hasn't been able to have a baby. But she's asked me to help her."

Ruby leant back and looked at me. "How?"

I blew a breath out. This was harder to put into words than I expected. "Amy's problem is she can't grow the baby inside her. So she's asked me to do it for her."

Charlie pushed himself on to his forearms. "Are you sending us to live with her?"

I could see him trying to imagine fitting all his video game consoles into her small living room.

I laughed despite myself. "No, of course not. You're stuck with me. She is giving me the egg that her baby will grow from, and I'm going to do that in my tummy."

"Oh," Charlie rolled on to his back and stared at the ceiling. "Okay. Is that it?"

I reached for his foot and rubbed it. "It means I'll be pregnant for quite a few months. Do you have any questions about that?"

He shook his head. "Do I have to do anything?"

"No."

"Then no," he stood and wandered through to the second lounge, where I heard him turn on the TV for his PlayStation.

Ruby was still watching my face. "Does it hurt?"

I pulled her into me. I was still trying not to dwell too much on the birth. "Some parts might hurt a bit, but it's worth it to give you a cousin and Amy a son or daughter. I'm so lucky to have you two, I want that for her too."

"She'll still want to see us, won't she?"

I kissed the top of her head. "Of course."

She played with a bit of my hair that was hanging loose. "Will you love the baby too?"

I nuzzled her hair, where the smell of shampoo mingled with sweat. I had wondered about that. When the kids were born, I would have died before I let anyone take them from me. Now I was assuming that I'd be able to just hand the baby over, simply because he or she didn't come from my egg? I had to trust that I'd be able to keep some level of distance. I sniffed Ruby's head again. "I'm sure I will, the baby will be my niece or nephew. But you'll always be my number one girl."

She seemed to turn the thought over in her mind. "Okay. I'm hungry."

She had just eaten but there was no harm in a bit of emotional support food. "Me too. Let's go find a snack."

When the kids were asleep, I called Brad from my bed. As soon as the call connected and he saw my face, he sighed. "It's happening, then."

I shifted in my position propped up against the pillows. "How did you know?"

He leant back on what looked like his bed. "You look different."

"Don't be silly." I frowned. "Unless you mean I look puffy? I guess I could be retaining water already."

He held my gaze for a bit too long. "You just looked nervous, so I figured you had something to tell me that I wouldn't want to hear... You're a good sister. I hope she appreciates you."

I lay back on the pillows. "She does. But you're better at rubbing feet. When are you coming home to do your duty?"

He lifted one eyebrow. "I think there are other duties I'd rather do first." He frowned at where the thought went next. "Or is that going to be weird now? Maybe Amy doesn't want us getting up to anything..."

I cut him off. "What Amy doesn't know won't hurt her."

Somehow, I had to keep reminding him that whatever I was doing for Amy, I was still his wife. It was hard enough sometimes, given the distance. This couldn't be another thing that broadened that distance between us.

He smiled. He had one of those smiles that totally transformed a face. The first time he had turned it on me I had been almost speechless. "I'm trying to move things around so that I can be home soon. It's been too long."

I pulled the duvet around my shoulders. "It feels like a really long time this time. The kids will be moved out by the time you come back if you're not careful."

He screwed up his face. "I know. Maybe it's time to think about finding a job at home."

I shifted my gaze from his face to the ceiling, my limbs suddenly heavy. He had said the same thing every six months or so for the past five years. I was well past the point of getting my hopes up – now these promises just dragged me down. There was always a reason why it didn't work. The economy was bad. Or the economy was good and there were too many people jumping at opportunities that wouldn't last. The money was too good offshore. Projects had come up that needed to be finished. My desire to be the fun wife on the other end of the video call evaporated. "I'll believe it when I see it."

He didn't bother to argue with me. "I love you, all of you."

I met his eyes. I so wanted to see something there that showed he understood how hard it was for me, and what he was missing out on. "I know. I'd like to hear it in person a bit more often, though."

"I know."

Before I even had my glasses on the next morning, I could see a flurry of notifications of emails had popped up on my phone. Was it Amy, digging out new links about pregnancy to send me? I fumbled for my reading glasses and swiped open the app. My heart sank as I pulled my phone closer to my face, not quite believing what I was looking at. Mary Jones had again filled my inbox.

I could just delete the messages. What benefit would come from reading them? Each one I scrolled past made my heart beat a little faster. I'd had a terrible night's sleep, coming up with lists of things that could go wrong with the pregnancy, and wondering when we'd next see Brad. Now this.

Getting rid of them had been my editor's advice – just delete and block and don't think any more of it. But I'd blocked the original email address, and this person had set up a new one with the same name to be able to send me another message. Part of me also wanted to know what she was saying. If I deleted them without looking, they would play on my mind all day and anything I imagined would probably be worse than the reality.

I tapped one open. "You and your kids act like you're the best parent in the world. I know you're not. I know your secrets. Pretty soon everyone else will, too. What will your lovely neighbours think of that?"

My heart was hammering. There were only two real parenting

secrets that I held on to – the unclipped car seat and a second, also from when Ruby was a baby. When Brad was at work and I was trying to answer a call and breast feed her at the same time, I'd dropped her. I could still remember the thud of her hitting the floor. I'd cried for hours and checked her constantly for bruises for about a week. But I'd hardly told anyone about that.

This person had to be grasping for anything to upset me.

Could they really know where I lived? The thought prompted an uneasy shiver up my spine. I had taken my address out of every directory and asked to be anonymous on the electoral roll after a letter from a reader early on arrived at my home. It was a very sweet note, referencing a piece I'd written where I talked about having small children, but the fact that someone I didn't know had been able to find out where I lived had rattled me. The messages all seemed to be the same, sent over and over.

I created a new folder in my inbox, selected all the emails and shifted them across. At least that way they wouldn't be sitting, blinking at me through the rest of the day.

I was hit with an urge to wash away the sick feeling the emails had given me. The morning sickness hadn't started properly yet – it wasn't fair that this anonymous person was making me queasy already. I hauled myself out of bed and headed for the shower. It was day one of 300 or so of doing my best to bring a niece or nephew into the world in the best shape possible. A shower before the school run might be a good start.

The emails were still running circles in my head when I sat down to work a couple of hours later. I assumed it was a woman based on the "Mary Jones" in the sender field of the email, though I had no proof. Statistically it was more likely to be a man harassing other people on the internet.

As I opened my word document to start writing a new column, my hands shook. Every time I started a sentence, I deleted the words before I could finish it, imagining her reading them. Maybe I should write to myself for advice – either to see what I could come up with in response, or just for the catharsis of putting words on the page. For almost five minutes, I was frozen and completely unable to function normally. Was this how my career would end? Forced into statis by someone sending anonymous abusive messages?

I shook my hands as if it would shake away the nerves. Maybe a walk around the block would help clear my head. But as I got to the door, a shape appeared on the other side, outlined in the frosted glass. Gasping as though I had been punched in the chest, I took a step back. The cup of tea and toast I'd had for breakfast rose in the back of my throat. The door creaked open. I raised a hand to stop it, my palm slapping against the wood.

There was a yelp of surprise on the other side. Amy's face peered around the corner. As her eyes met mine, her smile vanished. "Breanna, what's wrong?"

My hand was to my throat. "It's you."

"Of course it's me, who did you think it would be?"

I closed my eyes and concentrated on filling my lungs, then slowly exhaled. "The emailer..."

I pulled her inside, reached for the door and locked it.

She frowned. "They're back? Let's go and sit down. You look like terrified."

My hands were clammy as she guided me to the couch and bustled around, placing a cushion behind my head, and passing me a glass of water.

"What are we going to do about this?" She placed a hand on my forehead in a worried way that reminded me of my mum, even though I couldn't produce a memory of her ever having done so. It was surprisingly comforting, and I leant into it for a couple of seconds.

I opened my mouth to reply but she was still talking. "This much stress is really not good for the baby, you know."

CHAPTER SEVEN
AMY

You know how sometimes everything just seems to be going wrong for so long that you kind of convince yourself that things will never get any better?

I didn't even realise I'd got myself stuck in that type of mindset until it ended.

I'd obviously been desperately hopeful that the transfer would work, and Breanna would become pregnant. But a significant part of me had expected the worst and it was hard to accept the good news, even when it stared me in the face, the test lying there on her kitchen counter. Was it really happening? Had we really managed to make it work?

A few days later, as I slipped into a long black dress with a wide tulle-supported skirt, cinched waist, and the most flattering neckline I'd ever seen on myself, I realised that I'd also kind of expected Simone to change her mind about taking me to the awards, too. Even now, I was expecting a text at any moment to tell me that she couldn't go, or she had realised there was someone she should be taking instead.

But the only text she sent me had been telling me that she was looking forward to seeing me. Now I had only about 45 minutes until she was due to pick me up. I still had to find the right jewellery to accessorise, fix my hair into some sort of up-do – that had never been my strength – and attempt some makeup. I'd even bought some of the equipment that had only become popular this century, like highlighter, a contour stick, and some primer. We had never bothered with any of that when I was in my makeup prime at university and slapping it on every night – back then we just put foundation everywhere – sometimes even over the lips, and hoped for the best.

Armed with a YouTube tutorial, I carefully drew lines on my face and buffed them out with a big makeup brush. When I'd finished, the effect was surprisingly effective. My green eyes looked bigger and my skin was glowing. That was quite a feat considering my face was relatively dry at the best of times and I spent a lot of my day under bad air-conditioning. I imagined myself through Simone's eyes. Would she be surprised at the transformation?

I caught myself. There would be a room full of far more attractive women than me there. I tapped my fingertips together to bring me back to Earth. It would be a fun night out with my friend, and we were going to enjoy it. We'd been texting all day about the pregnancy test being positive, and we had a chance to celebrate.

I was waiting on the street outside my house, idly stroking Crumpet, when Simone pulled up in her car. It was a silver station wagon and impeccably clean. After shunting Crumpet back to the house, as I opened the passenger door I was hit with a wave of air-conditioned air freshener.

Simone was dressed in a pair of sequined shorts and a cream blouse. Shorts were an unusual choice for an event like this but the way she wore them made me wish I'd thought of it myself.

She grinned at me as I slid into the seat. "It's the māmā-to-be. Congratulations again."

"Thanks. You look fantastic." I craned to see what she had on her feet. A pair of plain black platform sandals. "That is the perfect outfit for you. But what happened to the dress?"

She shrugged guiltily. "Sorry. My sister borrowed it for a wedding she had to go to, and I still haven't got it back. So, I'm improvising."

I shook my head. "Don't be sorry, this is phenomenal. This suits you much better, it has your personality all over it. You just had this in lying around in your wardrobe?"

She laughed as she pulled the car out into the road and headed towards the centre of town. "Don't sound so surprised, I'm not a completely lost cause. And I have to level up to be seen with you, anyway."

I turned to the window to hide my smile, waving quickly to a neighbour a couple of doors down who was walking through his front gate with his dog. "Hardly…What do you think they'll feed us?"

My stomach was starting to grumble. In the busy-ness of getting ready, I'd forgotten to eat.

She frowned. "It's hard to say. I don't know who's catering this year. I'm sure it'll be a good night."

She had something playing quietly on her stereo that sounded like TLC – not the sort of thing that most of her clientele would produce. Was it for my benefit?

I hadn't been to a business awards event for three years. When I first started the shop, I'd put a lot of effort into entering and putting myself forward for the customer's choice awards. But as time went on the need to keep the business operating took precedence over spending the time to put together a nice awards entry. The idea of opening the books to the judges became less appealing too, particularly because one year a judge had been the owner of another clothes shop in town. We weren't really competition – she was selling menswear – but I got the sense in the way that she grilled me the year I entered that her business bank account was probably a bit healthier than mine had become.

Simone's perfume was a soft musk that mingled with the artificial pineapple of her air freshener. I looked around the car, taking in what looked like freshly vacuumed floors and spotless seats. There was even a small rubbish bin attached to each door. Had she cleaned it for tonight? There was a photo of Audrey attached to the dash.

"This is like going on a date except everything's so clean and you smell amazing."

I regretted the words as soon as they were out of my mouth, but she laughed. "You must have had some shockers."

An image of Andy popped into my mind. He liked the apartment spotless, but the car was another thing altogether. It had always had piles of files in the back seat and bits of his lunch tucked in the drink-holders in the doors. When he started doing a keto diet a few years back, that meant I was often finding bits of chicken bone stashed away. I counted it as a win when it was one from that day and not from the week earlier.

"And anyway," she winked at me. "What do you mean 'like' a date, I've gone to a lot of effort here."

My face flushed with heat and I opened my mouth and closed it again, unable to speak. Was she joking? It was hard to tell.

I shot a glance at her out of the corner of my eye. She was undeniably attractive with her high cheekbones, highlighted by her hair swept up into a messy updo. With her olive skin, she could pull off a red lip of any shade in a way I could never hope to. There was something more than that, though, although I couldn't put my finger on it.

I checked myself. Was I really crushing on her? I'd never dated a woman before, or even come close to it. But what good had sticking to dating men ever done me? No one had ever really made me very excited. Even when Andy and I were about to get married, I probably too much time planning an imaginary future with a perfect husband, and not enough on considering what the real-life man I was about to get was really like.

But with Simone it was like one side of an electrical circuit connecting with another. When we were together, everything was just... better. I'd thought that was just the sign of a good friend but maybe it was time to stop kidding myself.

I pulled myself up. How arrogant was I to assume she would even feel the same way? Wasn't that the cliché for people who weren't straight? Just because she was attracted to the same gender didn't mean she was attracted to everyone in it. I could be flattering myself to imagine it could even be a thing.

I looked out the window at the stream of houses going by, behind a uniform wooden fence. The council had widened the road a year or two previously and given everyone the same replacement.

But even if this wasn't going to turn into something with Simone, was I now into women more generally? Would I have to come out? How did one even do that at my age, and with a baby on the way? It wasn't the kind of thing they did at playgroups, as far as I knew.

I looked at her, mentally pulling the handbrake on my runaway internal monologue. It might not be women I was into, but it was definitely her. Was there a word for that? Straight except...

She was focused on the road but turned to catch my eye briefly. "You must be so happy about the pregnancy."

I grinned. It was the best thing I could imagine to take my mind off my sexuality crisis. "I almost can't believe it."

She stopped the car at a red light and leaned over to hug me, the gear stick pushing into my hip. "I'm ecstatic for you. You must be over the moon." She stretched to reach for something in the back seat. "I've got something in the back here for you."

She handed me a small bag.

A car's horn beeped behind us, snapping Simone's attention back to the traffic lights. The car in front of us was moving off. "Oh, piss off," she muttered. "So impatient. Important life stuff here."

I laughed, retrieving a small velvet box from the bag. I opened it. "This is beautiful."

It was a small pounamu taonga, a smaller version of the chunky greenstone she wore around her neck.

She shrugged. "We give them for momentous events in my family. I thought it would suit you. For becoming a māmā."

I fixed the woven cord around my neck and looked at myself in the car's passenger mirror. My eyes were shining, and my cheeks were flushed.

"Thank you."

She reached out and squeezed my hand. "You're welcome."

She pulled the car into a side street, taking us past a KFC, its drive-thru humming with dinner customers. "Does it feel real yet?"

I shook my head. "Not really. But people do it every day, right? I have to keep reminding myself that. It's just me who's found it so hard for the past few years. I shouldn't expect the town to throw a parade just because my luck might be changing."

Simone shrugged. "I think every time anyone has a baby it feels momentous, like you can't believe that other people do it all the time, too. I remember when I was pregnant with Audrey, I couldn't understand how the rest of the world was just carrying on. Like people were just going to the supermarket and doing their thing while I was preparing for my whole life to change."

"That's how I feel too."

"There's probably an extra element when you're not doing it the 'traditional' way," Simone pulled the car into the side street where the city's main events centre was situated next to the huge, glass library. "There's more of a focus, right? Because it's not something that could take hold any time, you have the build up to that one time then you see if it happened."

I nodded. "That's true. I guess your experience is quite a bit like mine."

She put her left hand over my right one, resting on my knee. I looked at it, as if I could keep it there with the power of my eyes. "I had one shot with the turkey baster approach, I didn't have to go through everything you have. You're amazing. Do you care whether you have a boy or a girl?"

I shook my head, making my earrings jingle. "Not at all. I just feel that there's a child-shaped hole in my life that I need to fill."

She looked at me. "I get that. We thought she would complete our family. Didn't work out quite like that, but I couldn't imagine life without her."

There was traffic backed up from the entrance to the events centre carpark. Some people were already getting out of their cars and wandering in. Simone crept the car forward until we were in the carpark and slid into the first free spot. All around us, women were teetering in overly high heels and men tugging at suit jackets that they probably hadn't worn since the last awards.

"Shall we do this?" She caught my eye as she opened the car door. A streetlight above caught on some of her sequins, sending colourful patterns on to the roof of the car.

I took a deep breath as Simone reached over and adjusted my dress to conceal my bra strap. "Yes, let's."

Whatever "this" was, if she was doing it, I was, too.

We were seated at a table with an older couple and two of their employees.

As the awards presenters took to the stage, Simone passed me a glass of champagne from a tray a circling waiter was holding. "You might need this. These things can go on."

I had a vague memory of sitting so awkwardly through the ceremony that my legs had gone numb and I collapsed when I stood to try to leave. It had looked like I'd had too much to drink and given the state of some of the other attendees, no one had believed my protests.

I took the glass and raised it to my lips, the bubbles popping against my skin. I'd have to do my best to drink slowly – my tolerance had gone out the window in the time I'd been abstaining.

The older woman nudged her husband. "How about grabbing one of those for me?" She hissed.

People at the next table turned to look at her.

Her husband looked around the room. The waiter who had been at his shoulder had moved on. "I can't see them."

She pursed her lips. "I'll get up and get one myself, then."

She squeezed out of her chair, holding her taffeta skirt in place as she sidestepped through a gap between the tables. As she passed me, she tapped my arm and indicated my drink. "You've got a keeper there."

Simone laughed. "It doesn't take much to impress her obviously."

I sighed. "Well, you know, women who date men – our standards aren't always particularly high."

She turned and fixed me with an unblinking gaze that made my midsection erupt with warmth. "Well, you know, you could change that."

"The expectations? Or the dating men?"

She grinned. "Either."

As she turned back to the stage, my heart was pounding in my throat. Were we really doing this? I pulled up my phone to send a discreet text to Breanna but then put it down again. What would she think, if I was out like this when she was at home getting ready for months of pregnancy just for my benefit? I regarded the glass in my hand. Maybe I should be giving up the wine again, too. And the cheese. And probably those canapes that were made out of barely cooked meat. A waiter passed carrying a plate of sushi as the last of the hors d'oeurves circulated before the main entrees were brought out. She wouldn't be able to have that, either.

I put my phone back in my bag. If I opened the emails, I'd just find bills – new ones, old ones, bills for the bits of fertility treatment I still had to fund and reminders – that needed to be paid.

The MC took to the stage. He was one of the local radio presenters who'd been on air in our town for almost longer than I had been alive. The bright lights beaming on to the stage reflected off the top of his bald head.

He cleared his throat. "It's wonderful to be here tonight, celebrating some of the best of Northland business. You've flourished through tough economic times and continued to inspire us with your creativity and innovation."

I half-laughed under my breath. "It's good to know that some of us are flourishing," I whispered to Simone.

She took my hand and squeezed it. "It'll come right for you, too."

Would it? I looked around the room. How many other people here were barely covering the rent?

Simone looked at me. "Chin up, it's okay. You know this is mostly pretend anyway. No one tells the truth when it comes to these things."

Three-and-a-half hours later, Simone and I pushed open the conference centre doors and walked out into hazy rain. It was welcome refreshment on my skin, which had acquired a sheen of perspiration from the close muggy air of the function. Simone's hand was on the small of my back and it was as if all the blood in my body had rushed to that spot.

She turned to face me. "That wasn't too bad, was it?"

I shrugged. "Would have been better if the award had gone to the rightful recipient. You were robbed."

She laughed. "There's always next year. I think these things are a bit of a lottery, honestly."

She waved to a group of men who were standing on the curb, probably waiting for a taxi, before turning to me. "Do you want to head out somewhere, or do you need to get home?"

A passing group of women shouted something in greeting and she smiled over my shoulder at them. One of their group picked her way across to us in her stilettos. "What are you girls doing next? We're headed to Raven if you want to join us."

Simone looked at me. "We could?"

Raven was a bar on the waterfront that usually made me feel old when I got within a 20-metre radius. It was the kind of place Breanna and I would have gone when we were younger but around the time she had started staying home because of the kids, some sort of generational shift had taken place around me, and I was suddenly part of the group who was whispered about with a condescending "good for them" sort of tone any time we went out after dark. As if we'd broken out of a rest home for a sneaky gin instead of simply having committed the sin of being the wrong side of 30. But maybe there would be safety in numbers – we weren't the oldest of the group heading out.

Simone was waiting for me to respond.

I turned the idea over in my mind. I'd been half-thinking I could invite her back to my house for a drink instead. "Oh... I don't really mind. We could go out for one? But you're driving...."

She grinned. "I'm more than happy to be on the diet cokes with you. Let's go."

The bar was one block over, on the now-almost-deserted main street of town. Another change since we were teenagers was that most people now seemed to go home by 9pm.

In the time I'd lived in Whangarei I'd seen Raven change from a dodgy student bar, complete with cage for dancing in, to a Mexican-themed nightclub, to a family restaurant. It was now a cocktails-and-tiny-Asian plates sort of place. We could cut through a small arcade, past a shop selling crystals, what used to be a nail salon and a raw vegan food café to get there in under five minutes. Simone and I didn't talk as we picked our way across the puddles of the carpark and down the tunnel to the arcade. Some of the paint on the mural on each wall before the shops had started to peel. She hummed something under her breath that I half-recognised.

As we rounded the corner at the end of the arcade, we collided with a group standing outside. "Is this the line to get in," Simone asked the man closest to us.

I recognised him. He and Breanna had dated in high school before she went university. He had been at Christmas once, a year that Mum was quite well and Dad was still around. He gestured with his chin towards the bouncer. "He's checking IDs for some of the young ones at the front. We just all arrived at the same time."

He caught my eye. "Hey."

I smiled. "How are you doing? Still living up here, obviously."

He nodded. I couldn't remember his name. "I just got back from a few years in Sydney. Mum's not well."

I cringed slightly. "I'm sorry to hear that."

He waved it away. "She'll be okay."

He looked from me to Simone, and I was suddenly self-conscious. What did he make of us? Did we look like a couple? I shifted my weight from high heel to another. The woman ahead of him grabbed his hand to pull him towards the door and Simone and I fell into step behind them.

There was something about walking into the bar with Simone that felt different. It was still largely the same crowd as ever, with a rowdy group of awards attendees thrown into the middle. Many of them looked as if they rarely, if ever, got out of the house for a night out and they were determined to make the most of it. The bouncer gestured us through wordlessly. Obviously, there was no need to check our IDs.

Simone pointed to a couple of stools at a table near the door, where we could sit at the bar leaner and get a view out of the window on to the street. A couple of cars with overly noisy exhausts were idling next to each other at the lights. She gestured to the bar. "I'll go and get us some drinks."

The sequins on her shorts sparkled as she made her way across the room. A man turned to watch as she walked past. I glowered at him but he didn't notice.

She returned with a coke and a glass of champagne with a frothy head. "That looks a bit excited," I took it from her.

She grinned. "Must have been taking tips from me."

I took a deep sip. It was a nicer one than they had been serving at the awards. "This has been fun, thanks for inviting me."

She settled on the stool next to me. "There's no one else I'd rather have."

I took another sip, watching the bubbles collect on the glass. "Sorry you didn't get the award."

She shrugged. "Like I said, I think it's all down to the luck of the draw sometimes."

The woman who won was the wife of one of the judges in the main category. Simone was too classy to complain, though her business must have turned over three times as much as the specialty eco party planner, and the customer reviews were much better.

We looked at each other for a couple of seconds. Before I was fully aware what I was doing, I was leaning towards her and had her hand in mine. She put her fingertips against the side of my face and pulled me towards her until our lips met. A rush of energy pulsed through me and the room seemed to wobble beneath the stool I perched on.

I'd never really understood kissing in the past. There was something vaguely off-putting about the idea of putting your mouth on another person's and mingling saliva. But this felt like she was pouring energy into me. Was this what I had been missing?

We broke apart and I stared at her. "That was amazing."

She laughed. "You just never knew what you were missing out on."

I certainly hadn't experienced anything like that with Andy. He seemed to share my indifference to kissing because it took up time on his quest to other things – which had also been approached with something of a "get it done" attitude.

I cleared my throat and studied my glass. "You know, I kissed a girl once before, in university. We were at a bar and had been drinking that horrible green stuff. What's it called? Absinthe, we had a few of those and then all of a sudden, she was right there in my face and kissing me. It was nice, soft. I don't know what happened to her, I don't think I ever saw her again…"

I trailed off. Simone was leaning away from me slightly.

"Sorry, I was babbling."

She waved it away. "It's okay."

A thought pulled me up. Whatever this was – was it really bad timing? I was about to be knee-deep in nappies. That couldn't be conducive to anything romantic. Simone caught my eye and half-smiled, and the muscles in my neck untensed a little. It wasn't like I was setting out to meet a stranger on the apps. It was Simone.

We finished our drinks in near silence. The bar was loud and although I kept looking at her at her and sometimes found she was meeting my eye, I couldn't think of anything that didn't sound silly to say. Someone should study that phenomenon – it wasn't that long ago I could have told her about the contents of my rubbish bin or my need to clean out the attic and not have worried about what she thought. But everything had changed.

When Simone pulled her car up outside my house an hour later, my heart was hammering in my throat. I avoided looking at her. "Do you want to come inside?"

I could feel her smile. "Is that what normally happens on your man dates?"

I turned to her, my brow furrowed. "Can you stop calling them that?"

She laughed. "It's funny to get a rise out of you."

I pulled my bag over my shoulder. "I don't invite everyone in, no. But you are welcome if you'd like to."

The words came out a little colder than I had intended. She wasn't judging me, just gentling needling, and I had replied as if she had given me an insult. I tried to smile but nerves were making every gesture feel forced and awkward.

She shook her head. "I have to go and play tennis in the morning, so I'd best be going to bed. I've had a lovely night, though."

I met her eyes, trying to hide my disappointment. "Me too."

We looked at each other in silence. Was she going to try to kiss me again? Should I lean towards her?

She cleared her throat. "I'd better be going."

My stomach dropped. "Sorry, yes. Okay."

She reached for my hand. "Don't look like that. I'm just tired and I know my game will be off tomorrow if I don't get straight home to sleep. I'll call you tomorrow and maybe we could have lunch on Sunday, if you're not busy?"

I shook my head. "That would be great. I'll see you then."

"And Amy?" She leant across again. "Keep me updated with what's happening with Breanna, okay? I'm so excited for you."

"I will." I pushed the car door shut and watched her drive away, my hand clasping the taonga that still hung around my neck. It had been an amazing night, and she wanted to see me again. So why did I feel so disappointed?

CHAPTER EIGHT
BREANNA

I leant against the bathroom sink, inhaling the last of the scent from my shower steamers, which promised to rejuvenate and energise. My toothbrush was propped on the double vanity against the mirror, with Ruby and Charlie's positioned alongside it. They had their own bathroom closer to their bedrooms but for reasons I couldn't determine had shifted into using mine. It was like when Brad was away, we became a tighter little unit, occupying a smaller and smaller part of the house.

I wasn't feeling queasy – yet - but I was so tired that it sometimes felt as if I could not move my feet. Walking from room to room in my house was like wading through jelly. Ruby had looked at me with big, worried eyes when, lying on the couch, I almost burst into tears at the idea of getting up to attend to the beeping washing machine for the third time in one day after Poppy, coming home from a walk by the river, ran across all of our three beds with her muddy paws.

It was probably the effects of the medication, which I had to stay on for a full 12 weeks of pregnancy. I mentally ticked them off. Six-ish to go.

I was closely monitoring any changes in my body. There was a bit of bloating, and I could feel the start of that firm lump appearing above my pubic bone that would eventually turn into a full-blown baby bump. So far, nothing that other people would notice as a pregnancy.

The doorbell rang at the other end of the house. Outside, a tui that spent many of its days leaping around in the branches of the pohutukawa by my bathroom window imitated it.

When I reached the door, I could see the outline of my mother standing on the front porch. I checked my watch. She was a bit early - I hadn't expected her until closer to lunchtime. She brushed past me with a kiss on the cheek. "How are you, darling?"

I followed her to the kitchen, where she put her handbag on a stool at the breakfast bar.

I shrugged. "I'm fine. Just tired. But what's new?"

There wasn't any point getting into the emails with her. If I was shaken, she'd be beside herself with worry. Experience told me that, even though I couldn't yet figure out how, the discussion would evolve so that I ended up being the one who comforted her about it. I was too exhausted for that.

She half-rolled her eyes, shuffling on to another stool and crossing her arms on the marble benchtop. "I hope Amy appreciates what you're doing for her. Your father would have told her not to put you through it, not with the children and everything you do."

She indicated at the house around her. It could probably do with a bit of a tidy – there was some homework on the kitchen table and a few Nerf bullets on the tiled floor - but it wasn't too bad. I'd even put on a proper set of leaving-the-house clothes in preparation for her visit.

Our mother approached Amy's quest for motherhood with quiet bemusement. She'd assumed that it finished with the demise of her marriage to Andy and had been astonished when she discovered it had not.

"I just don't know why she'd want to do it, being a single mother," she fluffed her copper, shoulder-length hair back into voluminous position, waiting for me to make her a cup of coffee. "It will be so hard for her."

I tried to think of something diplomatic to say. "It's important to her. I have the kids on my own a lot, don't I, and I cope?" She was never there for my middle-of-the-night meltdowns, anyway.

Mum sort of faintly scoffed. "You have Brad earning a good income, it's not really the same."

To be fair to our mother, we all had concerns about how sustainable Amy's income was, given how the retail sector in general was struggling and Amy's shop in particular. But she was an adult woman with a good brain and a solid work ethic when she applied it, so it was not like she wouldn't be able to get work if she needed to.

Mum hadn't been able to be much of a hands-on parent when we were small, because she had been so unwell so frequently. Even when she was mostly recovered, she was often short on energy. She'd usually been a sort of benevolent presence who cared about us but couldn't summon the enthusiasm to do much more than smile and ask us how our day was. It was Dad who took us to our sports matches and birthday parties most of the time, when he wasn't at work.

Did Amy's desire to be a mother make our Mum wonder what she'd missed out on? She'd been in better health since a year or two after Dad died and so had been able to take an interest in my children but it still never felt as if the interactions came naturally to her. I pulled a box of chocolate biscuits out of the pantry and waved them in her direction to offer her one. "I love her. I can do this for her."

My mother took another sip of drink. "I won't interfere. But there's more to life than motherhood, you know."

I looked at her. Was that a dig at me? "I am aware of that. But it matters to her."

She was nibbling the edge of a Krispie. "She'll find it hard to find another husband with a child."

I groaned inwardly. It was going to be one of those conversations. Since my mum went back on the dating scene, she was full of opinions about what it would take to meet a partner and who might be suitable for whom. "I don't think that's a high priority for her right now."

Mum pursed her lips. "I'd be much happier if I knew she had someone special. It's not healthy to be alone, you know. Do you think you could introduce her to someone?"

I stopped myself from shaking my head too quickly. That was not something that I wanted to get involved with. "Do you have someone special?" I tried to nudge the conversation in another direction and took a biscuit that might have been called a Chit Chat from the box. It was a poor substitute for a Tim Tam but at least some sugar would keep me going through this conversation.

Mum was 70 but could have passed for ten years younger, with her carefully coloured hair, which she styled into waves every morning, and perfect makeup. She was always well-dressed, mostly thanks to Amy. Since she retired, she'd joined a book club and a bowls club and had even taken up pickleball.

Her cheeks had reddened. "I've been out a couple of times with a nice man. It's nothing serious, though."

I gestured for her to go on, grateful for the new direction for the conversation. "Tell me more."

She gazed off into the middle distance. "He used to be in insurance, he and his wife separated a few years ago. No children."

"And what do you like about him?"

She frowned as if that was an impertinent question. "He's good fun. We went for lunch yesterday and he introduced me to something called a mojito."

"Cocktails on a Tuesday, how luxurious."

She smiled but said nothing.

"And how are you feeling?"

She waved it away as if her health hadn't been a major concern through my younger years. "I'm fine. The new medication the doctor has me on has been very helpful. I'm able to walk around the block without getting puffed. I really just wanted to pop in today and make sure you're okay."

I took a bite of a chocolate chip biscuit. "I'm fine. I'm glad you're feeling well."

"And how are the children?" It always came as a bit of an afterthought.

I smiled. "They're fine. Charlie's got the start of the proper soccer season coming up and Ruby's still throwing herself into everything. Her allergies haven't been bothering her, touch wood." I tapped on the fruit bowl, which might have been kauri.

Mum nodded. "We never really heard about allergies when you were children."

I pulled my lips into a thin line. I did not want to get into a conversation about why allergies were now so prevalent. Eight years of Ruby's life had exposed me to quite enough conspiracy theorists, I didn't need Mum suggesting it was something I'd done that had created it, too.

When Mum had gone, I returned to my desk. I'd been asked to contribute to a new feature that website was running, where we asked celebrities for the best bit of advice they had ever received. It mostly involved asking PR people to send the questions to their clients and then collating the obviously made-up answers.

But each time I went to check my emails, my body wanted to fight me. My hands would shake, and my vision went a little blurry. I was always bracing myself for another abusive email. There was something about the messages that really rattled me. As if this person knew me on a more personal level.

As my office clock ticked up to the hour, I readied myself to check my inbox again. At first glance, there appeared to be nothing untoward. An email reminder from a celebrity's rep who seemed to have forgotten that I had already given her a date for when the piece about her client would run. An advertisement for an activewear shop that continued to send me hopeful messages even four years after my sole purchase. Now they were recruiting for "brand ambassadors" to post pictures of themselves on Instagram. Geriatric pregnancy chic probably wasn't quite what they had in mind.

But as I pressed the "refresh" icon, my heart sank. Another email. Mary Jones again, with the same frenetic punctuation and random capital letters scattered throughout.

"I know where you live. I'm going to Make you Sorry. And Ruby. And Charlie."

I slammed my laptop shut but the words might as well have been burned into my retinas. My editor's number was in my recently missed calls. I stabbed at her name. She answered on the second ring.

Before she could speak, I cut her off. "I need you to get me some security. Or something."

"Whoa..." it sounded as if she was walking out of a busy room into a quieter space. "What's going on?"

There was a ringing in my ears. "Whoever this psycho is says she knows where I live and knows my children's names."

Krista exhaled through her teeth. "Okay, hold on. Is it likely she's worked their names out from somewhere else?"

In the shock of reading the email, I hadn't thought of that. I had locked down my social media accounts and I didn't mention the children by name in my columns, but it was always possible that if someone stalked me hard enough, they could find out details like that. This wasn't a very big town, after all. Was it just the next step in her – or his – ruse to freak me out?

I took a deep breath. "I'm still going to think about reporting it to the police."

Krista spoke quickly. "Yes, do. I've recorded the ones you've already told me about with our people team and I'll add this one to the file. But it would be sensible to have a record with the police. Is your home secure?"

I flicked a glance at the front door, then the French doors to the back garden and the huge picture window that ran along the side of the lounge. "If someone really wanted to get in, they could, but isn't that the case with any house?"

I could hear her moving something on her desk. "If you're really scared, I could find somewhere for you and the kids to stay for a while."

I could just imagine telling Ruby and Charlie that they had to go and stay in a dodgy motel somewhere. Knowing my employer, it wouldn't be a flash place, like the hotels Brad booked us into on the rare occasion we had a trip away while he wasn't working. We'd probably all be staying in one room, and for how long? But the idea of keeping them in the house when there was potentially a threat made me feel ill, too. I'd be up all night listening for every sound.

I sighed. "Let me think about it."

I could imagine her in her office in Auckland, looking out the window at the harbour bridge. "Okay, I'm going to give you the number of someone who can make it happen quickly if you need to, right?"

I hung up only slightly less frazzled. There was no reason to believe this person really had any real information on me. But that didn't do much to calm my nerves.

I picked up the phone to call Megan. She was the only person from work who understood what it was like to live in Whangarei. Auckland was that much bigger, so that a faceless threat did not have quite the same impact as one in a town of 80,000 people where anyone you passed on the street could be the person wishing you ill.

She answered on the first ring. "What's up?"

I tapped my pen on my desk. "Sorry to bother you, I know you're busy."

Her voice was warm. "Not at all, I'm happy for the distraction. what can I do for you?"

"Remember I told you about the emails I've been getting?

They've sent me another one and named my kids, it's freaked me out a bit."

She made a sound that might have been a gulp from a water bottle. "Oh yuck, that's disturbing."

"Krista's asking if we want to go somewhere else for a few days while they look into it, but I'm not sure it's quite at that level."

"Is there someone in town who might have a reason to want to hurt you?"

I turned the question over in my mind. "I honestly can't think of anyone."

I kept to myself most of the time. When I did see people, it was generally because I was helping out – at the school board, or the odd charity fundraiser or the very occasional night out with the school mums I was closest to.

Megan was still talking. "If it were me, I wouldn't leave. Stick it out. It's probably just someone who's found out the names through google or something and is trying to upset you. Don't let them win."

She was probably right.

"I need to head to court but just keep your wits about you, okay? I'll check in on you later on."

I stared at the phone screen after the call ended. How exactly was I meant to do that?

I turned back to my computer. The words were still reluctant to flow. Every time I wrote something, I read it back in the imaginary voice of Mary Jones. Would the person who was tormenting me read this? Would it encourage them to do something more?

Maybe I needed to take a few weeks off to collect my thoughts. But then I would probably need all the leave I could get when the baby came. A calendar reminder popped up on my phone. A health check-up to ensure that my body was responding appropriately and hadn't decided to reject my sister's baby. With our shared DNA, it was less likely but there was still a chance.

I had 30 minutes to get there. Grateful for the chance to stop working, I gathered my things ready to head for the door. Arranging my keys between my fingers just in case as I opened the front door, I peered out into the street. It was empty apart from a man further up mowing the strip of grass in front of his villa, the original one in a street that had slowly become filled with homes. I locked the door, then tested it was locked, and locked the dead bolt above. None of the windows were open. I turned to my car, which I had left parked on the street. It felt safer, somehow, out in the open. There was nothing on the backseat. Sliding in behind the steering wheel, I locked the doors behind me. I put a protective hand on my stomach as I edged my car out of its parallel park and into the road. I could hear Amy's voice in my head: Stress won't be good for the baby.

The check-up was at my normal GP's office. She shared a practice with four others, in a pink building on the intersection of two roads that were too busy for the amount of foot traffic the medical centre generated. The waiting room always smelt as if someone had recently cleaned something awful with bleach.

I settled on a plastic-coated seat in the corner and looked around at the faces of the other patients. There were mothers who looked as if they hadn't slept in a week, holding the hands of children with runny noses. Old couples who appeared to have matching injuries to their shins. What was it about being old that meant it took forever to heal? They were probably there for another reason altogether. I watched as one man handed his wife a magazine and took one for himself. Would Brad be doing that for me when we were 90? I laughed to myself without humour at the idea that he might still be clinging to an oil rig out in the middle of the Indian Ocean somewhere, still promising me that he'd be back in a few months' time.

The waiting room door opened with a thunk and Amy arrived in the room.

She spotted me in the corner and scurried over. "How are you feeling?"

I patted her on the leg as she sat next to me. "This is just a routine check-up, remember? You don't even have to be here." I kind of wished she wasn't, if I was honest.

She smiled. "I'll be at every appointment. I told you."

"What about the shop?"

"Nat's off sick so I've closed for an hour. It's okay, it's not a busy time of day, anyway."

"Won't you be heading into the lunch rush?"

She shrugged. "Don't think I've had one of those for a while."

My doctor, Angela, appeared in the corner of the room. She had her hair pulled up into a ponytail and was wearing a blue sundress. She waved me over and I followed her into her consultation room which was off a long hall with faded blue carpet. From the window I could see the hills up towards my house. This part of town was much rougher than where I lived, with overgrown grass in many of the front gardens and the odd rusted car propped on lawns. The house closest to Angela's window had a plastic tricycle in the back garden, the red and blue sort that every New Zealand child had a turn on at one point in their young lives.

I settled on a hard plastic blue chair, and Amy lowered herself on to one next to me. Angela smiled, taking us both in. "How are you feeling?"

I shrugged. "Fine, I think."

"No concerns?"

Where to start? None related to the pregnancy, particularly. I shook my head, avoiding her eyes. She reached for her blood pressure cuff, looking across me at Amy. "This must be your sister?"

Amy waved. "I'm the grateful recipient of the baby."

Angela laughed. "I don't doubt it. She's doing an amazing thing for you."

I sighed. It was so awkward, being praised constantly. "I'm just helping my sister." It sounded terser than I had intended.

Amy leant forward as if she was going to take my blood pressure, too. "Does everything look okay?"

Angela studied the reading on the blood pressure monitor. "Breanna looks to be in perfect health."

"Her weight hasn't changed much, as far as I can tell, is that what you'd expect?"

I glared at her, trying to project a silent "back off". "I'm not a prize cow. I don't think you need to be worrying about my weight."

Angela half-smiled. "Breanna's right. Nothing to be concerned about, there."

She turned to me. "Are you sure you're okay? You seem a little on edge. Not your usual self."

I nodded. "I'm just dealing with a bit of drama at work. Sorry."

She cocked her head. "Don't apologise – you're important in all this too, you know. Take care of yourself."

To my embarrassment, my eyes were burning with tears. I swiped at them. Amy was watching me. "What's wrong? Is it the email?"

I nodded. "Let's not talk about it now." I rubbed at my face with the back of my hand.

Angela waited a few seconds. "You sure you're okay?"

I sniffed. "Yep. Sorry."

She seemed to be weighing up whether to say something else but decided against it. "I was just going to ask whether you have a lead maternity carer yet."

The midwife who had dealt with my first two pregnancies had been a reassuring, no-nonsense woman who wore sensible shoes. I would have gone back to her, but she had retired soon after Ruby was born.

I reached for one of the tissues in a box on her desk and wiped my nose. "I'll need to find someone. I'll see if I can get any recommendations. It's been a while since any of my friends have had a baby."

Angela made a note. "That's okay. We have a little time before the specialist and I will be happy to hand you over to regular maternity care, anyway. We need to get you booked in for your first scan, though."

Amy twitched. She would be ecstatic at the prospect of seeing her baby pop up on a screen, even if it was at the stage where it looked more like a tadpole than a real human. "What's that one for?"

Angela had turned to her computer and was filling out a form but looked over at Amy. "Just to check everything's progressing as it should in there. We can't do it until about the 10th week of pregnancy, so that's in about four weeks' time, by my calculations."

Amy looked at me. "That will be so exciting." She appeared to check herself and took my hand. "Can I do anything?"

I collected my bag and thanked Angela. "No. Let's get going."

When I got home from the appointment, the entry way from the garage to the house was spotless. The cleaner, Grace, had arrived while I was out and started at this end, mopping the tiles and vacuuming and dusting the kids' rooms. I thought I did a decent job, rushing around with the vacuum cleaner and swiping at spills as the kids made them, but then once a week she would come in and show me that the benches I thought were clean had really been covered in a fine layer of filth.

I wandered through to the back of the house, where she was working in the kitchen. She smiled and waved, headphones covering her ears and saving me from having to think of something cheery to say. I stared out over the garden, resting my hands on the wood between the windowpanes of the French doors. The grass was freshly mowed and the cherry trees at the far end were lush.

At that moment, it would have been good to have a best

friend to turn to. Poppy nosed my hand. "I know you're here," I stooped to kiss her furry head. "But it's not quite the same."

I had the mums from school and the kids' sports, but they weren't close enough that I could turn to them with a problem that didn't relate to the kids or the house – the two things we had in common. Grace was lovely but any time we chatted, she made it extremely clear she wanted to be able to finish her work and get going as quickly as possible.

There was my school bestie, Lucy, but we'd lost most of our connection since she moved to Melbourne, even though we assured everyone we hadn't when we did catch up. Sometimes talking to Brad when he was away made me just feel more alone.

Maybe that's what it's like when you're an adult, though. It's hard to make friends, particularly when you're not going into an office every day and forced to be alongside other people. Megan had said she was around if I needed a chat. I pulled up the messages app on my phone and opened one to her. "Fancy a coffee? I could do with some adult company."

She replied almost instantly. "Sure, this afternoon? Where suits?"

I glanced at the clock. "Pop round here before I pick up the kids if you like?"

I rearranged a stack of magazines on a coffee table, which Grace had already tidied. Might as well make the most of the house while it was pristine. I had work to do but it could wait.

CHAPTER NINE
AMY

What does it mean when someone says they'll call and then they don't? Does it mean they don't care? That they have forgotten? That they're regretting having suggested they might in the first place?

I dragged a piece of paper towel across the blue tiles of my kitchen bench in angry swipes, as if it was responsible for leaving me hanging.

After my almost perfect night with Simone, I had expected things would go smoothly. It was meant to be men who were the painful ones not texting when they said they would, right? That was certainly my memory of my pre-Andy days.

Although back then I'd never cared hugely much. This time I cared – a lot. And I had assumed that because it was Simone and because she was my friend, it would all be a bit easier. She normally messaged me pretty regularly, anyway. I had scrolled back through our messages several times over the past few days, and there we were, sending funny reels to each other or pointing out when the woman who busked on the street outside our shops expanded her repertoire. Someone must have complained about her having only three Bob Marley songs on high rotate.

All of that should have meant that when Simone said she

would get in touch, she would, and it would all be so easy – no need whatsoever for me to turn into a neurotic ball of worry staring at my phone for hours on end. Turns out, it was a lot harder.

I oscillated between trying not to text Breanna to check how she was (still pregnant, nothing to report, and messages growing curter) and trying not to text something inane to Simone.

I had waited until the afternoon of the day after the awards to send her a message thanking her for a fun night. I was still on a high – dancing while I did the dusting and singing along to Whitney Houston without worrying about the neighbours.

She didn't reply until hours later, when she obviously double-tapped it to send me a heart reaction and replied "me too". I had had to sit down with disappointment. What happened to the idea of lunch? I would have been happy to just hang out and get a coffee to drink at the park with Audrey.

It would have been driving me completely up the wall if not for my twin distractions. The first was the pregnancy, which was the best diversion possible. The second was my attempt to arrange a loan from the bank to get me through until the end of the long summer slowdown, when everyone in town was either away on holiday or at the beach.

I had been holding on for the new year, convinced things would somehow pick up once we put a long, depressing 12 months of tough economic times behind us. Our town is quite heavily reliant on two things for work and income – farmers and the now-mostly-closed oil refinery. Various town planner types would like there to be more of a tourism industry but with the more attractive Bay of Islands further up and Auckland not very far south, there's a tendency to skip right over us. Cruise ships were allegedly coming but I wasn't convinced they were my target market, either.

With the farmers getting less for their milk and fewer jobs to go around, it meant less money sloshing around in town and fewer people willing to spend proper money on clothes – particularly when you could pop online and get them from China for a tenth of the price. You couldn't tell from the photos that the cheap imports were made out of material that would stick to your skin and make you sweat, and would fall apart on the second wash.

A woman in town had set up a "no fast fashion" group where they swapped clothes and recycled things to try to save the environment. I grew up with enough Captain Planet to agree wholeheartedly with the sentiment, but it felt like a personal attack. My clothes weren't intended to be fast fashion, but we all got lumped in together.

The loan I had applied for was only small, but it would be enough to be sure that I could pay the mortgage and pay Natalie. And it would give me a little buffer in the bank for the baby when it arrived. It was scary enough to be responsible for a whole new human life, but to do it without always having enough to cover the groceries was a bit too tight, even for me. I would have to take some time off, although I hadn't quite worked out how long. The baby could come with me to work on occasion, but probably only if it were one of those magical ones who did a lot of sleeping – people might be less inclined to spend if a small human was shrieking at them. Breanna rolled her eyes when I even suggested this was a possibility but not all babies had to be like Ruby and Charlie, the never-sleepers, did they?

I started to wonder whether Rose, the bank manager, and Simone had been sharing notes because I was still waiting to hear back from her, too. It didn't help that we'd gone to school together and hadn't been on great terms there. But that was at least 20 years ago. We were all adults, right? She couldn't let me forgetting to invite her to a party when I was 16 get in the way of a loan application now.

I polished the tap on the kitchen sink. When was the last time my house had been properly cleaned? Probably before I moved in. Breanna sometimes talked about stress cleaning, but I had never understood that. Cleaning usually just made me feel more stressed because once you began, you just noticed more and more that needed to be done.

A message buzzed on me phone, prompting my heart to leap into my throat. It was from my mother. Wanting me to ... I read it again... have coffee with her and her new boyfriend? I cringed. The last thing I felt like doing was going and making small talk with my mum's new boyfriend when I couldn't even manage to get my own personal life in order. She had barely even mentioned him to me. I didn't pay a lot of attention to her dating life because something about it made me deeply uncomfortable, even though we all were – as she continued to remind me – adults.

I couldn't say no, though, could I? I'd have to have a great reason. But I wasn't going to spend any money on it. They could come round for a pot of tea from my kettle. I told her so in a brief message. She replied immediately. "Let's go for lunch at that restaurant by the water. Our shout."

Our? Just how serious was this new man? But a free lunch was a free lunch.

I returned to wiping down my fridge. How did that even get dirty? As I attacked the vegetable drawer with a vengeance, I pulled myself up. This was ridiculous. I was ruminating like a teenager over what should be a perfectly adult conversation with Simone.

The bird in the tree outside my kitchen window was chirping noisily. She seemed to have been successful in hatching some babies in the nest she'd carefully built. I saw her and another bird flying to and fro.

What would Breanna tell me to do? In normal circumstances I'd have asked her for her advice from the beginning, but I still felt guilty about the fact I was even bothering with anything as frivolous as my love life when she was handling something so much more important for me.

Once she got over the shock of it being a woman, she would no doubt suggest I just take the initiative and find out what's going on. After all, it was what I did in most other aspects of my life. Why was it so hard this time?

I bashed out a message to Simone before I could think too much more about it. "Coffee after work tomorrow?"

The time seemed to drag as I waited for a message in reply. "Sure."

My heart sank. That was it? She didn't sound very excited. Could she have asked me how I am, or about the pregnancy even? I dragged myself to my feet and reached for my raincoat. A change of scene would be good for me. The sky outside had that purply grey tinge that indicated a thunderstorm brewing but I should be able to walk around the block a couple of times to clear my head before it came pelting down. And maybe being washed by the rain might even be therapeutic.

Simone and I only had one place we would meet for coffee after work, and she was already there when I arrived. Somehow, our town had collectively decided that no one wanted a coffee after 3pom so all the cafes closed and the only place we could go was an ice-cream parlour near Sage.

The day had been slow, but I had sold a pair of expensive jeans just I had been about to close the doors, so it wasn't a total write-off.

Simone had ordered two drinks in matching takeaway cups, and they were positioned on the glass table she was perched at outside. If I drank anything but decaf now, I'd probably be up all night researching pregnancy supplements or stewing about birth plans, but I wasn't about to tell her that.

The table was one of a scattering in the pedestrian mall near our shops, just beyond the pub. You just had to watch when you sat down that you weren't lowering yourself into a sticky icecream puddle on the seat.

I shot a glance at the sky. The clouds were still threatening but had lost some of the heavy feeling they had had. If we were going to get another bout of rain, it might still be a few hours away. I kind of hoped it would pour again, the hydrangeas in my tiny garden were still looking parched. I checked myself. That was a very middle-aged thought to have had.

Simone raised her hand to me and I slid on to the seat on the other side of the table. The wood was hard under my legs. I took a deep breath, forcing energy into my voice. "How was your day? A few people in town today."

She looked up from her coffee cup, which she cradled between her hands. "It was okay, how was yours?"

I sighed and reached for my coffee, taking a large sip. "It was fine."

A boy who might have been about 13 or 14 shot past us on his skateboard, wobbling just enough to make me worry as he hit a bump in the paving stones.

I looked back at Simone. "You know that's not what I want to talk to you about. I'll just come straight out with it, okay? Is something wrong?"

She coloured slightly and looked away, tossing her hair over back over her left shoulder. She was wearing a form-fitting blue singlet and light jeans with holes in the knees. "No. Why?"

I spread my hands out on the table. "Please don't act dumb. You haven't properly talked to me since the awards night. What is going on? Did I do something wrong? Am I a really terrible kisser?"

She laughed at that and I smiled.

"No, you're not. At all."

"Then what?"

She stared at me. I could almost imagine I could see her brain working, weighing something up. "Amy," she started, then stopped.

I pulled myself up to my full posture. "What?"

She exhaled hard. "I just don't want to give you the wrong impression."

My stomach turned over. This was far more humiliating than any time I'd been turned down by a man. It wasn't just embarrassing, though. It was aggravating. She had been the one driving what had happened. I hadn't asked for it. Now she was acting like I was some weirdo she had to let down gently.

"I get it. You're not into me like that. You don't have to sugarcoat it."

She shook her head. "That's not what I meant."

I turned away. A seagull was tiptoeing across the road, as if even it was trying to get away from this mortifying exchange. Someone threw it a chip.

"I am into you... like that, if that's how you want to put it," she was talking quickly. "It's just..."

"Just what?"

She put her hand over mine. "I've been hurt once before by a straight woman who was curious about testing the waters and I don't know if I can handle going through that again. Especially not with you. You mean so much to me."

I watched her face. "You think I just want to see what it's like and I'll rush back to men again?"

She shrugged. "Maybe. I was a little bit concerned that your uni girl and I might be one and the same."

I turned my hand over so I could grasp hers. "That's not what this is. You're right that this is new to me but you're not an experiment."

She said nothing for what felt like far too long. Teenagers in the distance were shouting at each other across the road. I studied her face.

"You've got a lot going on, too," she murmured.

"I know. I'm not expecting anything from you with any of that."

She shook her head. "I'm happy to help you, I just mean should I be adding anything to your plate right now? You've got enough to worry about."

I closed my eyes. "I want you to add to it. I'm as surprised as anyone by how I feel, but I really do."

"Okay," she said at last.

"Okay?"

She met my eyes and smiled. "Okay, I trust you. I agree you're not just anyone. And I'm sorry for going all quiet. But you know…You've got your relationship with Audrey that I don't want to mess with, either…"

I moved my hand so our palms squeezed together, a surge of relief tingling down my arms to my fingertips. "I know. You're one of my best friends so we can't muck this up. And of course, nothing would ever change for me and Audrey."

She laughed, breaking the tension. "It's lesbianism not base jumping, I'm sure we can manage it."

I let my eyes linger on her face, taking in the curve of her cheek, where the sun reflected off what might have been a swipe of highlighter. She'd put makeup on to come and see me. I took a deep breath. She was gorgeous, funny, smart… and willing to have a go at being my girlfriend? The me of a couple of months ago would never have believed that everything could fall into place so perfectly.

I became aware of a woman standing next to my left shoulder. I tensed, half wondering whether if I pretended I wasn't aware of her, she would go away.

She cleared her throat, demanding I look up. It was Rose, the bank manager. That was one way to quickly kill the buzz. She was wearing a uniform suit with sensible black heels and had her dark hair styled into a severe bob that looked as if it would not move in a cyclone.

"Amy," she nodded. "How are you?"

My heart was hammering fast enough to prompt my Apple watch to ask me if I was working out, but whether it was due to Simone's hand in mine or Rose peering down at me, I wasn't sure.

Rose was still talking. "I have been meaning to call you all day, so I'm glad to have run into you. Do you think you could pop into my office tomorrow? I just have a few questions for you."

I nodded. "I'll come by first thing."

She seemed to be about to say something but then moved to turn away.

"Hi, Rose," Simone met her eyes. "It's nice to see you."

Rose smiled in a way that I'd never seen her do with me. "Simone, how are you?"

Simone shrugged. "I'm well – must be time for another one of those networking nights, is it?"

Rose nodded. "Good point, I'll put something together. Catch you tomorrow, Amy."

She waved over her shoulder as she headed towards a car parked on the side of the road. It was a cute vintage Aston Martin. She had definitely developed a bit of style since we were teenagers, when she had an awkward bowl cut with a frizzy, curly fringe.

Simone watched her go. "She's an odd ball. She did put on a decent 'women in business' night, though. Good canapes."

I turned back to her. "She's a bit scary. Think she's still punishing me for being a bitch to her in high school."

Simone laughed in surprise. "I can't imagine it."

"It wasn't intentional – just a few unfortunate oversights. You know how everything is so serious when you're that age."

Simone nodded. "Things to look forward to with Audrey." She paused. "And with your little one."

I hesitated. The idea of raising a teenager was so far in the future that I'd not given it a lot of consideration. "I have no idea how I'd handle that. Is hiding in my room for five years an option?"

Simone smiled. "I think it's like any stage – you never really know what you're doing, you just bumble your way through and hope for the best."

We drank our coffees in silence for a minute or two. I kept flicking glances at her, as if she might disappear if I didn't keep checking she was there.

"Is your meeting with Rose something exciting?"

I half-laughed. Simone must have a rather different experience of dealing with bank managers than I did. I had never had a bank manager meeting that could be described as exciting. I traced a line in the wood of the table, where bits of dirt and snags of paper napkin had caught. Would she be put off if she knew how truly messy my financial situation was?

When Andy and I split, I had prided myself on having come out of it with my own home, my business and even a little bit of money in the bank. But making a baby was expensive.

It was hard to keep up the relentless enthusiasm required for marketing of the business when I was careering from one disappointment to the next. Do you know how much energy it takes to put together a Facebook live showing off the shop's new stock when you have just heard the latest attempt has failed? And everyone kept telling me that success in retail these days was all about making people connect with me, to build a brand of me rather than the shop. Yuck.

I decided to keep my voice as neutral as possible. "Money's a bit tough at the moment. You know there haven't been as many people shopping and all that. And there have been a few medical bills lately. I just wanted to take a little loan to tide me over."

Simone nodded. "I understand. We could look at some ideas to get people coming in, if that would help? You could have one of those cheese-and-wine tastings where you give people just enough champagne to spend a bit of money. Or..." her eyes seemed to light up. "You could do some sort of charity fashion show. We could probably get some news coverage of that."

It was easy to catch her excitement. "I'm not sure I'd know where to start with that. Wouldn't I need a lot of contacts to make it work?"

She shook her head. "I can help. I'll put a few calls in tomorrow. When would you want to do it? The sooner the better?"

I hesitated. This was surely the kind of thing that took a while to pull together. "It won't be long before we start to get more of the new season in. But doesn't it take a bit of organising? What would we do, a percentage of sales to charity?"

She shook her head quickly. "No, it should actually be really easy and all upside for you. We just sell tickets and that money goes to a charity, then we get sponsors to put on food, convince your mates to walk the catwalk. It'll be great."

She leant across the table, the pounamu at her neck swinging and dropped a quick kiss on my lips, sending warmth down my spine. "You'll be back on track before you know it."

I had always thought that "walking on air" was one of those expressions that people used that didn't really mean anything.

But as I left to walk to the shop the next morning, it really did feel as if there were little air cushions under my feet. Simone had sent me a "good morning" message, Breanna's pregnancy seemed to be progressing as it should, and the sun was shining.

Even the prospect of going into the bank first thing and sitting down with Rose wasn't enough to pop the bubble of my happiness. Crumpet was sitting on the handrail of the porch as I locked the door. The clouds were hanging low over the hills in the distance, but the sun would burn them off before long. "You'll get your sunshine back, don't worry," I stroked his ginger fur, which seemed to be coated in a fine layer of dust. "What have you been rolling in now? I bet it's going to make me sneeze."

He closed his eyes slightly and arched his back up into my hand. I kissed the top of his dirty head. "I'll see you soon."

As I headed out on to the street, a message popped up on my phone from Ruby. Breanna had recently signed her up to a kids messenger service and she had worked out how to pepper me with emojis when she was getting dressed for school or last thing at night. There was also "guess what I've drawn" which was often an unusually stressful test. Breanna usually forbade them from having their devices in the mornings to ensure that she could get them out the door to school but I suspected she had stashed her iPad somewhere in her room and Breanna was turning a blind eye to it.

"Don't forget," the message read, followed by a string of hearts and smiley faces, as well as what looked like an explosion and a cat face emoji.

"Forget what?" I replied. It wouldn't hurt to tease her a little bit.

"My birthday," came the indignant reply. "Capybara party. Capybara cake."

"Are capybaras coming?"

The icon burbled indicating that Ruby was typing. Finally, a reply. "Can you bring one?"

I smiled at the thought of a large rodent turning up on Breana's doorstep. Ruby told me a few times that they liked spa pools. The spa pool next to the swimming pool in their perfect back garden would be just the spot for a capybara party.

"I'll see what I can do," I replied. Breanna was still waiting to hear when Brad would be back for Ruby's birthday. He had missed Charlie's last and Charlie had not yet quite forgiven him.

"How's Mum doing?" I pressed send a little guiltily.

The message came back straight away. "Sick." It was followed by four green-faced emojis.

"Give her a kiss from me."

I followed it with another message. "But don't tell her I asked you to."

The main area of the bank was full of people when I arrived. It was only opening four days a week now and every morning there seemed to be a queue of people that stretched from the one teller working to the door. They were all on shifting and jiggling in frustration as they waited for the elderly woman at the front of the queue, peering over the counter at a man with glasses and a frown. He didn't seem to understand what she was asking and she was not able to hear more than every third word from him. Everyone in the queue was either stabbing at their phones or checking watches – real or imaginary.

Rose appeared from a room off to the side of the main area and gestured me in. Her office was small and almost completely devoid of any sign of her life outside the bank. There was a computer on a desk, two chairs and a filing cabinet. I wondered briefly what anyone put in a filing cabinet these days. She gestured for me to take a seat on the opposite side of the desk from the door, so I had to walk right around her.

The only windows in the office had been covered by venetian blinds. There wasn't even a picture on the walls. If I hadn't seen her clamber into her cute little car and remembered what she was like as a rather studious teenager, I might have suspected she was a figment of the bank's imagination.

She pulled her chair in to the side of the desk opposite me, her bright red oval fingernails tapping on the keyboard to locate a document on her computer screen.

"How are you, Amy?"

I smiled. "I'm really well, thanks. How've you been? How's work?"

She looked at me without smiling. "It's fine, very busy as always. Not as exciting as your business, I suppose."

I shook my head. "I'm sure it's very satisfying, helping people and all that."

I tried to think of something else small talk-ish to say but my brain had stopped cooperating. She said nothing but returned to the screen. She put one finger to her perfectly lined and lipsticked red lips and at me across the desk. "I'm sorry to call you in but I thought it would be better to chat through this in person."

I shrugged. "Sure, do you need any more information from me?"

She shook her head. "I'm afraid your loan application isn't going to work as it currently sits." She leant forward and lowered her voice. "I understand your personal circumstances could be about to change, too."

I shifted my weight back against the chair. The back rest moved awkwardly as if the whole thing might be about to give way. "I'm sorry?"

"I've heard that you are pursuing another option to have a baby – more power to you – but we need to factor that in to the personal expenses part of your lending, so I thought we could talk through that…"

I cursed under my breath. This town. We hadn't even announced the pregnancy yet and people were gossiping. Would it be one of Breanna's friends? Or someone who spotted us at an appointment? Maybe it didn't really matter. "I don't think I'm in a position to do that yet, there are still a few moving parts."

She turned back to her screen as if looking at it a second time might give me a different result. "Alright. Well, as it stands, the affordability just doesn't seem to be there, I'm sorry."

What sort of bank speak was that? "You mean I'm not earning enough to pay the loan? I can promise you that I'll make the payments. I can get a boarder into my house if need be."

For a few months, anyway, until the baby arrives, I finished in my head. "There will be no other interruptions."

She shook her head slowly. "You could but we still might struggle to get there. Your income has been very low the past few months. In fact, there are some notes on your file wondering whether you can repay some of the overdrafts you already have."

I swallowed. "Is that really necessary?"

She drummed her fingernails on the table. "I can put in an application for that to be deferred, if you like."

I cleared my throat. "I'd appreciate it." I pushed myself to stand. "So, you're saying there's nothing you can do?"

She shook her head again. "I'm sorry."

I pulled my bag over my shoulder. "This meeting could have been an email or a phone call, couldn't it? I'm late to work."

She opened her mouth to respond but I let the door swing shut behind me. Sixteen-year-old me had clearly been right not to invite her to my party.

CHAPTER TEN

BREANNA

The ultrasound room was dark in the way that an expensive spa might be. But instead of an inviting massage table with soft towels and aromatherapy candles burning, there was a medical set-up in the middle, covered in a paper sheet.

I clambered on to it. Amy took her spot next to the head of the bed, exactly where Brad had been for the scans that he had been in the country for when I was pregnant with our kids. Back then, I'd spent the weeks before the scan reading up on what we might see and what various measurements could mean so that my head was spinning with numbers and facts when I lay on the bed. This time, I let my body relax. It was rare to get the chance to lie down in the middle of the day, I might as well make the most of it.

Amy took my hand in hers as the ultrasound technician entered the room. I could feel the beginnings of sweat on her palms. The woman, wearing dark blue scrubs, pulled up a seat on my other side and gestured for me to lift my button-down striped shirt.

"I'm Tanya. Shall we get started?" She smiled from me to Breanna. "Is this your first baby? I'll just pop some gel on, it might feel a bit cool."

Amy laughed. "Don't get the wrong idea, this is my sister. And no, not her first baby."

I turned to look at her. Her face was lit with excitement and her eyes sparkled even in the dim light.

Tanya returned her grin. "That's lovely that you're here."

I squeezed her hand. "It's her baby, she has to be."

Tanya eyes widened in surprise. "Oh, a surrogacy?"

I nodded and she looked at me. "That's a very selfless thing for you to do."

I shrugged, embarrassed again. I shifted my gaze to the ceiling as she tucked a paper towel into the front of the waistband of my denim shorts.

Soon, an image filled the screen. At just over 12 weeks, you could make out the shape of a human – not like the eight-week scan I'd had with Charlie where he just looked like a bouncing blob, or some sort of weird computer game where an alien had to get out of a maze.

Amy was clearly captivated as Tanya moved her wand around my abdomen, stopping every few seconds to snap an image and tapping her keys to note something. Amy gestured to the screen when she was moving across the side of my stomach. Her eyes were filling with tears. "Look at that little hand."

Amy's gaze was fixed on the image but out of the corner of my eye I could see the smile had faded from Tanya's face. The scan had been over in 10 minutes with my kids but this was already out to 15 and she was still focused on something.

I willed Amy not to look at her and focused on breathing smoothly. My heart rate was displayed on the top of the monitor screen, and Amy would notice if it picked up.

The room felt very quiet. But was that just because I was picking up a weird vibe? Maybe it was always like this. I focused on my breath again. Calm down, calm down.

Finally, Tanya cleared her throat. I turned to look at her, as if I could convince her to give us positive news with the power of my stare. "All okay?"

She sucked her lips into her mouth in a way that made them almost disappear. "I'm sure it's nothing to worry about, but there's something there that I'd like to have your doctor look at. I'll send the images over to her and ask her to give you a call."

Amy was at alert. "What is it?"

Tanya turned her body away from us a little bit, as if shielding herself from Amy. "I can see something a little unusual around your baby's heart. I'm afraid I can't say for sure – it may very well be absolutely nothing. But better to be safe than sorry. I'll get that to your specialist right away. It's always better to get on to these things early."

Amy and I watched her scurry out of the room as if trying to get away from us as quickly as she could. Amy's face had gone slack and grey. I rolled over to pull her in towards me. Her breathing was out of its normal rhythm, as if she was fighting with her lungs.

"Don't think about it too much until we know more. There's always weird stuff happening with babies in there and usually it turns out to be absolutely nothing."

She flinched away from me. "Did anything like this happen with the kids?"

I pulled my shirt down. "Well, no. But I do know of people who were told there could be problems and their kids are totally fine."

Amy stood as if she was on autopilot. Her voice was expressionless and her eyes almost seemed unseeing. "I'll call the doctor."

I stood from the table and took her hand to lead her towards the door. "Wait til we're in the car at least, okay?"

She nodded but it was for my benefit. "Do you think this is related to Mum?"

Our mother's heart problems were congenital, and it had crossed my mind with my own children that they could be inherited. But what was the point of delving into that now? "I honestly don't know. If there is something, it probably doesn't matter so much where it came from, just that we get it sorted. Right?"

Her attention was fixed on her phone. I smiled dutifully at the receptionist as I followed Amy, storming through the waiting room to the carpark outside.

"I don't think Google is going to help you," I nudged her as I pushed the front door shut behind us.

She looked at me, her eyes big. She was balling her hands into fists, then releasing them, over and over. "I have to do something."

We didn't speak as we walked to the car. Amy was immersed in Google, trying to find anything she could about what might possibly show up on an early scan in relation to a baby's heart. What could the outlook be? What treatments might we need? What might I as the pregnant person do to help the prognosis?

After three attempts to pull her away and remind her that no good ever comes from self-diagnosing via search engine, I left her to it, took the keys to her car from her shaking hand and drove us back home. I'd work out how to come back for it later.

I took her to my house, where she perched on the couch and stared into space in between calls to her specialist.

I pulled my laptop out and set up on the kitchen bench so that I was at least in the same room as her. I had to get some progress made on a feature that was due by the weekend, otherwise there was going to be a major problem. I had written two paragraphs when I became aware of the sound of Amy sobbing, her face buried in the intricately embroidered cushions on my couch, which Brad had brought back to me on one trip when he'd come home via Thailand. I stood and crossed the room in three steps, squeezing on to the couch beside her and putting my arms around her. I rested my face against her hair.

"I'm so angry," her voice was muffled.

I frowned. "Why angry?"

She groaned. "I got my hopes up. I thought we were going to be fine. Now we're here and it's so much worse. I thought all the difficult stuff was over. I'm so angry at myself."

She turned to look at me. "I don't know how to keep going. It's so much."

I inhaled. "We'll get through it. There's every chance it all still will be fine. I'm here with you. You haven't done anything wrong."

She nodded and swiped at her face with her hand. "I guess you don't have much choice but to be here."

I kissed her forehead. "We are in it together. Your specialist will know what the right thing to do is, and we'll do it."

She reached down and ruffled Poppy's ears, who was snuffling her feet. "I hadn't thought about what it would be like to have a baby with a major health issue."

I watched her, taking one of Poppy's big brown paws in her hand. She hadn't? What with the sister having a geriatric pregnancy? Even beyond the pregnancy...she had seen what it had been like juggling Ruby's allergy. Had it never crossed her mind that her baby might not be precisely as she imagined? It was so typical of her. I pushed the thought away, guiltily.

I chose my words carefully. "I'm sure you'll be a great mum and you'll be able to deal with whatever this little person needs. I think a lot of being a parent is about readjusting expectations. And Mum and I can help as well. You're not alone."

Amy's phone rang and she pounced on it. The name on the screen was Amelia Scott.

I watched her as she listened to the woman at the other end. "Tomorrow? Yes, we can be there tomorrow."

She looked up at me quickly for confirmation, as if realising too late that she should have checked. I nodded. I'd be working late tonight to make up for it but what alternative was there?

Sometimes, the waiting is the worst thing when you're dealing with a medical issue. Waiting for an appointment, waiting for test results, waiting to hear about a follow-up consultation. When Ruby had allergic reactions as a toddler, we'd spent what felt like months waiting for the results of tests to come back to tell us what we were dealing with.

But I've discovered being rushed through, with no waiting at all, was actually much, much worse. When there's a problem that the doctors have decided needs so urgently to be addressed that you needed to be seen immediately, the fact you're not waiting around is no bonus whatsoever.

Amelia Scott's offices were in an office building, shared with an accounting firm and a surveyor. While the ultrasound had been in a building that could have been a beauty spa, the specialist's offices could have been any professional setting. We might just as easily be signing the forms to buy a house as turning up to find out what was happening with a pregnancy.

The scan began the same way as it had the day before, with me lying in the middle of yet another room. Amy was on the edge of her chair, her knees jiggling as she stared at the screen before it had even sprung to life.

Amelia looked first at Amy and then at me as she walked into the room with us. She touched my hand lightly as she took a seat on a stool opposite Amy. "You know the drill by now, I'm sure."

I nodded. A sonographer entered the room and straddled the stool on the other side of the bed. "This is Linda," Amelia gestured. "She'll run the scan today and I'll be working closely with her to see what we can determine is going on in there."

Linda started to move the wand over my midsection, studying the screen. Amelia pushed her stool around so she was closer to the screen and the pair studied it, moving to capture different angles and making notes. After about 10 minutes, Linda stilled the wand and Amelia turned to us. "I know you indicated there is a family history of congenital heart problems."

Amy nodded mutely.

Amelia gestured to the screen. "It's early in the pregnancy but there are some indications that your baby may have something that we need to treat. I'm going to refer you to a foetal cardiologist for an echocardiogram, but we won't be able to do that until the pregnancy is at 18 weeks. In the meantime, we'll conduct regular scans so that we can keep an eye on baby's development."

"Will my baby be okay?" Amy's voice was small, and I turned to her instinctively.

"Congenital heart defects are rare, and because of your family history the risk was always a bit higher. But some issues resolve themselves without the need for us to do anything. Let's just see what we're working with and take it from there, okay?"

"Is there anything I need to do?" I couldn't think what it might be but if she had told me that standing on my head once a day would help, I would have done it.

Amelia shook her head. "At the moment, it's business as usual for you. Just don't push yourself to any unusual levels of exertion or put yourself in any situations where you might experience rapid movements or force."

"No rollercoasters, basically," Linda offered, with a smile.

"No exercise, right?" Amy asked.

Amelia cocked her head to the side. "If you're used to exercising, Breanna, you should carry on. But don't take up Cross Fit."

As we stood to leave, I put a hand on Amy's wrist. "This might be absolutely nothing."

She moved away from me when we were out of the room and away from the view of Amelia and Linda. Her voice was strained. "Maybe. But what if it isn't?"

I pulled my hand in. She didn't look at me, fixing her eyes on the corridor ahead and stalking along. I had to walk a little faster to keep up with her. We stood side by side as the lift doors closed, staring straight ahead as we waited for it to inch towards the ground floor.

"Stupid defective genes," Amy burst out just as the doors opened again.

I pulled her out of the lift and towards a pair of chairs in the building's foyer. A woman in a suit shot us an inquisitive look as she walked past.

"It's not your fault, it's no one's fault," I held her hands and tried to make eye contact with her in the same way I would if one of the kids was having a meltdown. "These things happen, and the doctors know what they're doing."

She wiped at her eyes with the back of her hand, looking away from the row of mirrors on the wall behind me. "I know but that doesn't make a difference."

She turned away from me and stood up. "I need to get to work. I don't know how much all this is going to cost."

I followed behind her. I knew enough from Ruby's experience that private treatment could add up. "How much of this are you having to pay for yourself?"

She slowed to open the swinging glass entry door. "Well scans aren't fully funded these days, so that's at least $100 a time and how many of those have we got ahead of us? Then the specialist – she's $250 every time she breathes on us. I exhausted my Government-funded fertility treatment a long time ago."

She stormed across the carpark and yanked her car door open. "I'll drop you off on my way to the shop."

I followed her. "I'll drive. You're in no state."

Brad was due to call at 10pm, when the kids were meant to be safely in bed and we would have time to talk. It must have been weird for him, being so far away and getting little glimpses of what was happening through the day in text messages, like peeks through the curtain of a neighbour's house.

Usually, the kids would be in bed by 9, read a bit and then lights out by half past. But I am convinced there is some kind of telepathic communication that goes on between parents and children so that on the nights you really need them to be asleep by a certain time, they refuse. At 9pm, they were in bed. At 9.10pm, Charlie felt ill and needed a bowl next to his bed. At 9.15pm, Ruby heard a weird noise outside her window. At 9.25, Charlie remembered he needed to find his handball to take it to school the next day. At 9.30, Ruby wanted to know whether Poppy had a favourite colour.

"Just go to sleep please," my voice reverberated off the walls of the hallway walls between their rooms.

Ruby looked at me with wide eyes.

"You can't be mucking around like this at bedtime, it's late."

In his bed in the room opposite Ruby's, Charlie screwed up his face. "You don't need to be so grumpy."

"Honey, you are old enough to be able to do better bedtimes than this, go to sleep."

I stomped back to the couch and instantly felt guilty.

The burbling ringtone sounded just after 10. I positioned myself, lying back against the cushions with my phone propped against my knees so that I could see his face. Poppy sniffed my head.

He grinned when the call connected. "Hi beautiful. How are the kids? And how's Amy?"

I scratched Poppy behind the ears. "Hello to you, too."

He smiled. "It's nice to see you. Bedtime go okay?"

I avoided his eyes. "Not great but we got there, I think."

"Miss you guys."

I sighed. "We miss you, too."

He leant back, crossing his arms. "What's been going on? How's the pregnant life? It took a while for the guys here to realise that when I said my wife's pregnant it didn't mean you'd been sneaking around."

I cringed. "I can't handle jokes about this right now."

I tried to explain the scan, Amy's distress. It was hard to put into words that sinking feeling that had started when the first sonographer had hesitated.

Brad listened mostly in silence. "I'm sorry I'm not there with you."

I bit my lip and stared at his eyes on the screen. His brow was furrowed, and he had cupped his face in his hands. I couldn't make out much of the room behind him. There was a table of some sort and a whiteboard.

"Have you had any more of those emails?"

I sighed hard. Another rubbish point of conversation. "No. I'm trying not to think about them."

He nodded. "Must be a bit scary, though. Is your work doing anything about it?"

I turned slightly away from him to look out the window. Sometimes meeting someone's eyes on a video call seemed even more intense than an in-person conversation. "They will if I want them to. I'm okay at the moment."

"It must be hard alone, I'm sorry I'm not there to make you feel safe."

I frowned at him. "Let's change the subject. When are you home? The kids are looking forward to seeing you. Ruby's dying to show you the plans for her capybara birthday."

He leant back on his chair again and steepled his fingers. "I've been wondering how to tell you. They've asked me to go straight into another contract so I was thinking I might have to skip my next home visit."

I blew a strand of hair out of my face. "Really? You won't be here for Ruby's birthday?"

He leant forward on his hands and looked up at me through his eyebrows. "I'm sorry, Bre."

I ran my hands over my head. Most of my hair had fallen out of its ponytail. "You can't be serious."

He was quiet.

Resolve hit me. "We can't go on like this."

He stared at me. "What do you mean?"

"When does that mean you come home? Another three months?"

He checked a calendar on the wall next to him. "That's right."

"You'll miss our anniversary too. And the start of Charlie's soccer season. This is ridiculous, Brad. How can you be a father when you're never here? What do you think it's doing to the kids, growing up with you just some weird guy on the screen? They might as well have been raised by Blippi at this point. Or Mr Beast."

He lowered his gaze. "I'm sorry."

I shrugged. "Are you, though? You could do something about it. I'm over this. Seriously, over it."

I slammed my laptop shut. It was so easy for him to do this absent father thing from the other side of the world, thinking he was doing his part by sending home the money every fortnight and then expecting us to fall over him with praise and gratitude when he found the time to turn up.

Meanwhile here I was doing all the real work of it all, looking after the nightmares, tending the illnesses, mediating the conflicts, and resolving the dramas with friends – as well as just the dull mundanity of everyday life. The millions of minute pieces of parenting that built our kids' existence.

I could just imagine the kids growing up to be adults who wrote letters to advice columnists like me asking if they were justified in going no contact with a father who had done nothing much to care for them growing up.

I leant back in my chair. This was not what I signed up for. The kids and I deserved better, and I had to assume that at some point he was making an active choice not to give it to us. Sure, he probably couldn't earn what he was getting over there back at home but we'd been sensible with his earnings so far. We could make it work – if only he wanted to. He hadn't even asked what I thought.

I tiptoed down the hall towards Ruby's room. The kids' lights were both still off but there was a definite rustling from hers. I peered around the corner. She was under the duvet, with it pulled over her head. I could see the lump where the top of her head was moving against the covers. A light shone out from the edges, where they almost-but-not-quite met the mattress. I cleared my throat, and she hastily pushed the cover over to one side, presumably collecting whatever was giving off the light with it, and flipped over, pretending to be asleep. But the light still shone through the pastel purple duvet.

"What's going on in here? I told you, you need to go to sleep."

I pulled up the duvet to reveal her iPad.

She cracked open one eye. "I was just having a look to see what I want for my birthday. I couldn't sleep."

I sighed and slid into her bed beside her, tucking my feet under the duvet and moulding my back on to hers. Her hair smelt like the milk and honey shampoo that she'd used to wash it an hour earlier. It still wasn't completely dry.

"I'll lie with you for a bit. I'm sorry I get grumpy, I'm just so tired."

"Do you think I could have some new crocs?"

I nuzzled her head. "Let's talk tomorrow. Time to sleep now."

"Or what about one of those Rainbocorns with the 50 surprises."

I held her closer. "Time to sleep."

She wriggled around and looked at me. "Can I invite Annabelle to my party?"

I let my head flop against her pillow. "I don't know Ruby. You and Charlie are always asking for stuff. It's exhausting."

Her face fell and guilt washed through me again. It was Brad I was angry with, and Amy I was worried about. But she and Charlie were here and so they always ended up taking the brunt of it. She turned away from me, subtly moving her body away.

"Sorry, Ruby. I've got a lot on."

She wriggled further away.

I reached for her but she slithered out of my grasp.

"Sorry, darling."

She said nothing. I counted her breaths until she fell asleep a few minutes later, running my finger in circles on her back. At least that much she would allow. Guilt pushed me down into the mattress. Why could I never get this right? No matter what I did, someone was always upset with me. I put a protective hand on my stomach. Must moderate my stress. It was proving easier said than done.

CHAPTER ELEVEN

AMY

Simone's eyes were bright as she pushed through the door of the shop, carrying two big boxes, one under each arm.

"Where do you want me to set up?"

In a matter of weeks, Simone had developed the charity show from the start of an idea into a full-blown event, with 100 tickets sold, women from around town booked in to model clothes, and a sponsor that I had a strong suspicion was her shop offering a glass of champagne and canape to everyone who attended. At $20 a ticket, it meant we could give a decent donation to women's refuge, hopefully get a mention in the local paper and potentially get some sales from the latest collection.

It was so easy for Simone, and such a battle for me. What I was good at was styling and clothes, and helping people find their confidence in a great outfit. I wasn't at all skilled at all the other stuff that came with running a shop.

I had propped a trestle table for food and drinks in one corner, covered in a white tablecloth. We had cleared a space in the middle of the room to be a make-shift catwalk and dotted a few chairs around. "Most people will stand, won't they?" I surveyed the room. It looked good. Bright, fresh and light.

Simone nodded. "Definitely. And it's not a long event. How many pieces are you sending down the catwalk?"

I scanned the shelves. "Maybe 12 outfits – tops and bottoms – and three or four full dresses. It's still party season, isn't it?"

She shrugged. "You know me, I just wear the same thing most of the time, whatever I'm doing."

I laughed. "Except for your sequinned shorts."

She locked eyes with me and smiled, making me blush.

She was in her uniform of ripped jeans, but the tank top was one I hadn't seen for a while, a band that might have been from the 1980s. "You'll maybe switch to your going out jeans for tonight?"

She winked as she placed the boxes on to the table and started pulling champagne flutes from them. "If you're lucky."

I reached out to rest my hand on her hip. "Thank you for everything you're doing."

She shrugged. "It's nothing."

I rolled my eyes. It wasn't nothing. Somehow, Simone and I had skipped most of the fun things you might imagine when you first start seeing someone and gone straight to the heavy stuff – saving my shop, managing the pregnancy worries. Andy would have never put up with it.

We spread the glasses out across the surface of the table. "What time are the canapes arriving?"

Simone checked her watch. "Should be here any minute."

Natalie emerged from the back of the shop, holding up two dresses. "Which of these do you think would be better for the show?"

One was a long casual blue dress with a white stripe up the side and the other a bright pink midi dress with red flowers. "They're both great – maybe the pink has more impact? Just make sure you put it on someone blonde, it would be a sight on me."

She nodded. "I think you're right."

Simone caught my eye. "You enjoy this."

I took a deep breath. It was a welcome distraction from the worry about the baby. "Yeah, the fashion bit I do."

I turned at the sound of someone else coming into the shop. It was Breanna, carrying two large white boxes, which she brought over to us. They were full of tiny pieces of toast, topped with what looked like pate and a tiny cherry tomato. "I didn't know you were bringing food?"

I looked from her to Simone. She shrugged. "Simone filled me in on what was happening, I wanted to help."

"You didn't make these? Where did you find the time?" I looked at the more closely. She was meant to be conserving her energy. "I don't think you can even eat these."

She smiled and ducked her head. "I did not. I bought them. And you're right, I can't."

I dropped a kiss on her cheek. "Thank you."

Simone took the box from me, letting her other hand trail down my back. I reached for her hand and squeezed it as she stepped away from me to put the food in the right spot.

Breanna did a double-take, her eyes wide. "Can I talk to you outside for a second?"

As the shop door closed behind us and the evening air hit my face, she took a step closer to me so we were almost touching. Her eyes were bright. "Are you going to tell me what was going on in there? Why are you and Simone all touchy feely all of a sudden?"

My cheeks where hot. "I was waiting for the right time to tell you…"

She shifted so that she was still looking directly into my eyes, even as I tried to duck away. "Tell me what?"

I watched her face as I tried to find the right words. "Simone and I are… seeing each other."

She shrieked but I tapped her arm to silence her. She shook herself. "Sorry. But Simone? Really? Since when? And since when have you been into women?"

"Since her, I guess. It started at the business awards."

She cocked her head and stared at me, hard. "You sure you're not just having a moment?"

"You mean like it's just a phase and I'll grow out of it? No."

She nodded slowly. "Sorry, I didn't mean it like that. I'm just so surprised. I didn't pick it."

"Neither did I."

"Mum will be astonished."

I snorted. "Let's get to that when we have to."

She put her hand on my arm. "I'm happy you're happy."

"You're not angry that it happened while you're dealing with all the… you know," I gestured at her stomach.

She screwed up her face. "What? No."

An hour later, the shop was as full as I could remember it being, as women from around town sipped their glasses of wine and watched the models traipse through the middle of the room in the outfits I'd picked out. We were down to our last bottle of sponsored wine. I nudged Simone. "Do you think I should go and grab some more?"

She looked around the room and shook her head. "No, we've almost finished the show. People will mingle for a bit then head home, you watch. You've got the balance just right."

There was a round of applause as Natalie rounded up the models to walk out and bow together. She gestured to me. I was supposed to say something. Feeling the combined gaze of all the women in the room land on me, I took a step forward. My mini dress was a little shorter than I would have liked. "Thank you all so much for coming. It's been great to see some familiar faces and meet some new ones, too. Thank you very much for supporting such a worthy cause – Natalie and I will be very happy to answer any questions you might have about the stock."

There was a murmuring of approval and the crowd started to disperse a little, moving around the shop to look at the racks.

Breanna appeared at my elbow. "I'm going to have to get back to the kids. Well done, you guys, it's been a great night."

Simone gave her a side hug. "Thanks for your help, you've been amazing."

She watched her leave. "Your sister is a star."

I turned away from her, an uncomfortably familiar jealousy rising in my chest. "Everyone says that."

She gently touched my lower back. "Go, get behind the counter, I think that woman wants to buy something."

She was right. An older woman was waiting at the counter with a pair of trousers over one arm and a blouse in the other. I had to give Simone credit, it looked like we were going to make more sales in one night than we had in a week.

Two weeks after the scan where the sonographer raised the potential for alarm, we were booked in again, for the first of what I was told would be fortnightly visits until we knew exactly what was happening or had a new plan of action for it. I had taken out another credit card.

The date was marked in my diary with a big red circle around it, but it didn't need to be – every cell in my body seemed to be counting down the days. I dreamt that I missed the date and woke up in a cold sweat.

I'd always imagined I'd be looking forward to all the scans during a pregnancy with excitement, fizzing about finding out the gender, checking out the number of toes or the cute little nose. But that had been taken from me through this process too. As the scan grew closer, I just got more and more anxious. I just wanted to get it over and done with so that I knew things were on track and we were a step closer to the echocardiogram.

Simone had been doing her best to take my mind off things. But when we went out for dinner and all I saw were mothers with their kids eating chicken nuggets and smearing the sauce all over their faces. I wanted to shout at them when I saw them snap at kids dropping sugar sachet son the ground. Did they not know how lucky they were? How impatient I was to have my dinners interrupted by demands for more fries or something. Audrey gave me a bunch of flowers she had picked from the neighbour's garden. "I'm not totally sure the neighbour knows," Simone hissed as she passed them over.

We went to a movie but I'd burst into tears when the main character had a positive pregnancy test. It was like being back at the beginning with Andy. Then, he'd inched away from me little by little as each disappointment piled on the one before, and as one hormonal meltdown gave way to another. I couldn't let that happen with Simone.

After the movie, I'd pulled her aside outside. "You don't have to do this."

She gestured for me to walk around the side of the building to where there was a bench on the side of the street. The road was well lit but mostly deserted, the evening air heavily humid and still buzzing with cicadas.

She settled next to me and reached for my hand. "Do you remember the first day we met?"

I bit my lip. It would have been soon after the shop opened. She had come across to introduce herself.

"You were in the middle of your shop with boxes all around you, and you were excited – seriously, so excited – by a delivery of bright red ball gowns. Do you remember?"

I smiled. They were great dresses.

"And I was, you know, me about it, but you showed me the material they were made from, the designer and where they were made – and you held one up on Natalie. I couldn't believe how it transformed her, with her incredible skin. I'd never thought about clothes as something that transformative before."

I nodded slowly. "Okay. But I hardly ever show you dresses now."

She laughed. "I know. But when you're you, you show me a

new way to look at the world, and it's amazing. Your ability to imagine things that hadn't even occurred to me, it's crazy. I know you're going through a tough time at the moment but I know you'll get through it. I'm just here to help until then."

I swallowed hard. My parents and Breanna had always made it seem as if my grand plans and big ideas were a problem rather than a benefit. I squeezed her hand but couldn't get any words to come out.

On the morning of the scan, Breanna drove herself to the sonographer's office. She said it was because she had errands to run afterwards but I suspected it was because she was finding spending time with me difficult. Every movement she made or twinge she reported put me on high alert. Sometimes it was as if she was scared of speaking to me at all.

I settled in the corner of the waiting room and watched the door for her arrival, staring at a magazine that I could not read. I could see a glimpse of my reflection in the glass of the painting opposite me. I had pulled my hair back off my face in a claw clip and swiped some concealer on the dark circles under my eyes. Stress had dented my appetite and my cheekbones jutted through the skin. My heart had already picked up the pace, as if it remembered what had happened last time. Our appointment was at 9.15. Where was she?

Just as the clock ticked over to the appointment time, the door opened and Breanna arrived with a gust of wind. Her face was flushed and she was clutching her phone and keys in her hand. She was dressed as if she was going to a work meeting, in a blue blazer and tailored blue trousers with a grey stripe down the side. It was a good look for her. In normal times, I'd have asked her where she got it.

I half-waved to her and she hurried over to take her seat next to me.

I couldn't help myself. "How are you feeling?"

She brushed herself off, arranging her trousers so they were smooth across her legs. "I'm fine. Just busy with work. I have to go and catch up with Megan after this. How are you holding up?"

I shrugged. "I'm getting there."

She looked at me but didn't say anything for a few seconds. "How's the shop?"

I cringed. "Hanging out for that moment when people decide they like shopping again."

She put her hand on my leg. "I'm sorry it's tough. The charity show must have helped a bit? What about that marketing woman?"

The marketing expert had been recommended by a friend of Breanna's who ran a surf shop in Sydney. She worked online and apparently could turn around any business with her catchy ideas for videos and funny memes. The only problem was that she wanted more than $1000 to get started. You could get three scans and a decent number of onesies for that. "I don't think that's going to work out right now. We did quite get a few sales at the charity evening, hopefully that's helped with the brand as well."

Breanna smiled. "That was a good idea from Simone. She's lovely."

The sonographer peered out from one of the side rooms and gestured us through.

We knew the drill by now. Breanna clambered on to the bed and presented her midsection for inspection. I took my seat on the chair next to her. I reached for her hand but she didn't offer it this time, instead positioning both hands in the small of her back to take the pressure off. I rested my palm against her thigh, as if maintaining physical contact would make us closer or send some good vibes to the baby.

"I'm Claire, I don't think I've met you ladies before," the sonographer was getting her equipment ready on the other side of the bed.

Breanna nodded. "You'll probably see us again. I think we've got approximately 46 scans booked over the next few months."

Claire looked at a folder that must have contained our notes. "Are you serious?"

I coughed. "A slight exaggeration but not much. We've got to keep an eye on things to make sure everything's progressing as it should be for our little person."

She cleared her throat. "Well then, let's get on with it and see what baby's up to in there. Are we finding out what we're having?"

I locked eyes with Breanna. We hadn't discussed it. "Not this time. Maybe the next one."

Breanna nodded and gestured to me. "Save it for when she isn't so worried."

Claire consulted her notes. "Okay, I'm just asking because you never know which bits they're going to want to show to us."

She scanned down the page. "So we're looking at baby's heart particularly but just a general growth check-up, too."

I willed her to get on with it. Just one piece of good news was all I needed. Surely it wasn't too much to ask?

She arranged Breanna's clothing so that she had a clear work area. Maybe I should have been a sonographer. It wasn't one of those jobs that they pushed at you at school, was it? Back then, it was always "be a teacher", "be an engineer", "go to law school". How many other potentially interesting jobs had passed me by? There were so many things I could have done with my life instead of getting into a major retail debt hole spending my days convincing people to buy dresses they didn't need.

I gave myself a mental slap. Focus.

Claire swiped the wand across Breanna's stomach and looked at the screen. A blurry image appeared, and I tried to make out which part of the baby I was looking at. I was almost positive I could see the outline of a leg, and there was the profile of a gorgeous little face. "Look at that cute little nose."

Claire half smiled but didn't say anything. Her brow

furrowed as she returned the wand a second time, and then a third. She flicked a glance out of the side of her eye to check whether we were watching and then swooped it over again. My stomach seemed to migrate down through my body towards my toes. What was happening now? The soft background music and gentle humming of the air conditioning made me want to scream. She was going back over and over the same patch of skin.

"I'm just going to get a second opinion," she pushed herself back off her stool and walked out of the room.

Breanna and I exchanged a glance.

"This can't be good," my blood seemed to be pumping ice and my heart was pounding as if I had run a marathon. The room was wobbling under me, and I had to rest my head on the side of the bed.

Breanna patted my back. "I'm sure it's okay. She'll be back in a minute."

I breathed in the soft linen scent of the sheet Breanna was lying on. The paper did not reach right to the edge and the bit of white cotton that stuck out around the sides had the texture and smell of a hotel bed.

The door creaked open, and Clare returned, joined by an older woman with her hair pulled back into a severe bun, high on the back of her head. She took the spot where Clare had been sitting and shot us a look without speaking. She guided the wand back over the same area. Again, she went back and forth, looking at different angles. The two women looked at each other. I clenched my fists. What was going on?

"I'm very sorry," Clare's voice was quiet when she finally spoke. "We've not been able to find a heartbeat."

A moaning sound filled the room, and it took me half a second to realise it was coming from me. It was as though all the blood had left my body and I was just an empty shell. The screen had been shut down so I couldn't even see the little face any more

"Are you sure? Could you test again?" Breanna's voice trembled.

Claire shook her head. "We've both looked thoroughly, and we can't find anything. You'll need to go back to your specialist to confirm but I'm very sorry to say it looks as though your pregnancy is no longer progressing."

Her eyes glistened as if they had tears in them. A surge of fury rushed through me. What did she have to be upset about? She didn't even know who we were an hour ago.

The older woman put her hand on Claire's arm and guided her out of the room. "We'll give you two a minute."

My arms felt like lead on the bed. My feet might as well have been welded to the floor. How was I ever going to move again? This was my last chance to have a baby and it was finished. My baby was gone.

"What did we do wrong?" I forced the words out.

Breanna had rolled on to her side and was awkwardly cradling my head. "We didn't do anything wrong."

I sat back and stared at her. She had tears dripping down her face. "But we must have. We must have. It must be my fault somehow. Is it because I'm such a mess? Why would anyone want to have me as their mother?"

Breanna shook her head, wordlessly. "These things happen and it's no one's fault. It's just so, so sad. I'm so sorry."

I put my head back down on the bed. "I don't know what to do now."

She stroked my hair. "Let me come and stay with you tonight. Mum can look after the kids. I'll message her now."

I let her rub my shoulders and upper back. "What's the point?"

"You shouldn't be alone. Let me take care of you."

My stomach twisted. "I mean what's the point of any of it? What do I do with myself now?"

Breanna shhhed me like I was one of her children. "Don't think like that. You've so much going for you."

A cold shiver ran through me. "What happens to the baby now? Do they have to get it out of you, or does it just happen?"

Breanna swallowed hard. "I have no idea. But I guess Amelia will tell us what to do."

Claire opened the door and looked in at us. "Can I get you anything? I've sent the files over to your specialist, she should be in touch with you this afternoon about booking an appointment."

Breanna shuffled around so that she was sitting on the bed. "No. I think we should go outside."

Claire cocked her head. "Take as long as you like. I'm so sorry for your loss."

We staggered to our feet. It took all my energy to put one foot in front of the other to make it to the door, and then out on to the street. At the carpark, I turned to face Breanna, helpless. The world was still happening, but it felt as though I was viewing it through a screen.

She gestured for me to get into her car. "One step at a time."

As Breanna nosed into the traffic, a woman with a pram stopped at the traffic lights on the corner and pressed the button. Breanna clocked her and put her hand on my knee. I leant back against the headrest and closed my eyes. "It doesn't make me angry, anymore. Being the only one who can't do it. It just makes me so sad."

Breanna put her foot on the accelerator and turned on to the road towards my home. "Me too."

We lay on my couch side by side, our feet extended towards the coffee table. There was a reality show on the TV but neither of us were watching it. Every so often Breanna would look at me and pat my head or my shoulder.

I shrugged her off. "Don't you have work you should be doing?"

She shook her head. "I've called in sick. Is the shop okay?"

I drew my knees into my stomach. I didn't really care. "Natalie's got it."

She picked up the remote and flicked through the streaming services. There was a dog barking in the distance. The cloying humidity of late summer stuck stick to my skin and pushed me down further into the sofa.

The phone rang. Amelia. I showed Breanna the caller ID.

"Do you want me to answer it for you?"

I shook my head and pressed the button. Amelia's voice was quiet.

"I've seen the recording of the scan," she said.

All the muscles in my face were slack. "Yes."

"You'll need to come into the office so we can confirm it, but I'm sorry to tell you that the scan technology is very reliable. It seems likely that we've been unsuccessful."

I swallowed hard and made a sort of strangled sound.

"I'm really sorry, Amy. I know how much you've wanted it."

I screwed up my face, tears spilling over my cheeks. "What happens now?"

She sighed. "It's likely that it will resolve itself naturally, Breanna will pass the tissue as if it were a heavy period."

The tissue. My baby.

She was still speaking. "If that doesn't happen within the next few days, or if it doesn't seem to have happened fully, we may need to intervene."

She tapped something on her keyboard. "I'll make an appointment for you to come in, I'll text you the details."

I couldn't say anything, and she waited for a few seconds before hanging up the phone.

The door to the spare room seemed to flash in the corner of my eye. It would have been the nursery. Now it was destined to remain white and minimalist, just as Andy would have liked, with a throw across the bed that always remained perfectly in place, unless Crumpet decided to make a nest in it.

I knew Breanna envied how I could put things in a spot in my house and they would still be there when I got home. There were never bits of laundry lying in the hallway to fall over or empty dishes stacked on the bench. It wasn't even worth trying to describe to her how quickly I'd have traded places.

"We could do a little ceremony in the garden," Breanna said quietly. "If we can see the baby, we could get a little box."

"It'll be tiny."

She nodded.

"You might not even notice it. It might get flushed away."

Breanna was pale. "I'll do my best. I'll make sure you know exactly what's going on."

I leant back against the sofa and looked at the ceiling. "Do you need pain killers?"

She shook her head quickly. "I'm fine at the moment."

"Will I tell Andy?"

Breanna turned to look at me. "How much did he know? You might not need to."

Light rain was hitting the window. It was like being holed up in a bunker together, with the world storming along without us outside.

I rested my head on my arm and stared at the TV. "What would you tell me if I wrote to you?"

Breanna interlaced her fingers while she thought about it. "I would tell you I'm so sorry. And I'd probably tell you to try to find other things to focus on to get you through. Like your hobbies and your business, Simone ... the things that give your life meaning that aren't having a baby. I might point out all the people who don't have kids but who have amazing lives. I know that advice would be annoying and not very helpful though."

I nodded. "I don't really have any hobbies. The infertility ruined my marriage."

She coughed. "I don't know that Andy was the right one for you. And look, it seems like Simone's pretty serious about you."

Simone had texted me three times, obviously increasingly

worried by my lack of response. "The business…" I let my voice tail off.

She cocked her head. "What's really going on with the business?"

"It's not going to last much longer. I can't keep putting on events like that. And what else is there to do? The competition is too strong and this town, you know people here don't have a lot of money. When was the last time you went and spent hundreds of dollars on a dress?"

She tapped her mouth with her index finger. "Well, I don't need to because you won't let me. You keep giving me lovely things for barely anything."

"But you know what I mean. When would you be shopping like that if you didn't have me? You'd be going online to the one-day sales sites or having things couriered in from Australia or Auckland or whatever, you wouldn't be heading into town to a shop that only opens during the week when you're meant to be working and for a couple of hours on a Saturday morning when you're meant to be watching the kids' sports, would you?"

She half-smiled. "When you put it like that… but what if you opened at different hours? You're right that it's not that easy to get into town – what if you opened in the evenings or Sundays or something?"

I shook my head. "I can't staff that. I can barely get enough staff for the hours we do open. I can't pay anyone enough to make it worth giving up all their family time. Most people have those, remember."

She squeezed my hand. "You have a family. I'm right here. The kids love you. Mum…"

I closed my eyes as she stroked my hair.

"I'll go and get us something to eat, okay? You stay here. Do you want some trashy mags?"

I frowned. "I haven't read one of those in years. Haven't they all gone out of business, too? Seems like it's the fashionable thing to do."

"Maybe the ones we read as teenagers, but I reckon I can go and find you something to take your mind off things a little bit. I'll be back in ten minutes. Maybe less."

She let the front door slam behind her, leaving the house still and quiet, apart from the ticking of the clock on the wall in the kitchen.

The late afternoon sun was stretching across the hall, lighting the glass pane in the front door. The outline of the hills just showed through. So, this was what it was going to be like. Just me and Crumpet when he could be bothered coming to find me. No little feet tapping down the hall. No muddy little gumboots at the front door after a trip to the park. No trampoline in the back garden.

Breanna was back just under 15 minutes later but as soon as she opened the door, I knew something was wrong. Her hair was a mess as if she had been raking her hands through it, and her eyes were glazed with worry.

She put a bag down on the couch next to me, which contained a small plastic container of summer rolls from our favourite Vietnamese takeaway.

"I have to go."

I coughed. "What? I thought you were staying the night."

She reached for her bag, which she had left beside the couch. "Ruby's had a reaction, she's been taken to the hospital. I have to go and be with her."

"Can't Mum do it?"

She turned to look at me. "I'm so sorry to leave you, Ames. Mum has picked her up from school. But I have to go and be with her, she needs me. I've got Charlie to think about, too. Can I call someone to come and be with you?"

A surge of hot anger flowed through me. Why was it always me who had to be left behind, to cope on my own? Yes, I was jealous of an eight-year-old. But it wasn't just that. I was always going to be second best, to everyone. As I watched her, getting her things together, rage rose within me.

"Fine, go. I know the baby never meant that much to you, anyway." The words were hot with anger.

Her face fell. "What on Earth are you talking about?"

I gritted my teeth and spat the words at her. "I've been trying to get you to take supplements that everyone said would help, and cut down on your exercise to take the pressure off your body, and you wouldn't do it. Just kept taking on more work, more stuff for the school, having to be the mum-of-the-year. Now look what's happened."

She was staring at me. "You're blaming me for this? You are unbelievable."

She spun on her heel and headed for the door. As she turned to open it, she fixed me with a hard stare. "I know you're grieving but that is out of line."

I said nothing. It wasn't fair to be angry with her, but the anger was forcing its way out of me, almost out of my control.

She flicked her hair over her shoulder and wrenched the door open, then let it slam behind her.

I turned away and stared straight ahead at the wall. My pulse was pounding in my temples and my jaw hurt from being clenched so hard. A message from Natalie popped up on my phone's screen, pushing my heartbeat up another gear.

"Sorry to ask – will you be in tomorrow?"

I threw my phone against the couch cushion, leant back and stared at the ceiling. The blood pulsing in my eyeballs almost made the ceiling wobble.

I reached for my phone. "I'm closing the business."

I sent the message then turned off my phone. I would have a large glass of whiskey, or four, then try to go to sleep. Whatever happened next would have to be something I dealt with in the morning.

CHAPTER TWELVE
BREANNA

When I got to the hospital, Ruby had already been taken through to a ward. She was lying on a bed in a room with three others in it, a window at the end overlooking the car park and road beyond. My mother was sitting beside the bed, holding Breanna's hand. There was one other chair free on the other side of the bed, next to the small metal cabinet that held a bell to call the nurse and a plastic cup of water.

They both looked up as I entered.

"Mum," Ruby's voice was shaky.

I hurried to her and put my arms around her. "What happened?"

Mum dropped her hand and stood up. "The school said she must have eaten something at their shared lunch today that had some nuts in it. You'd think people would be more careful."

I shook my head. "It's okay. They do their best. I knew a shared lunch would be risky. But did your epipen not work?"

Breanna looked out the window. "I'm not sure where it is."

I swallowed the urge to snap at her and focused on moderating my voice. "Didn't you give it to the office to look after? Remember we carefully printed those labels to go on your pens, one for the school office, one for dancing, one for home?"

She shrugged. "I'm not sure."

I could feel the tension rising in my voice. "We need to find it Ruby, or get you another one. That's very important."

At least they weren't as expensive as they used to be. When she was a toddler, it was almost a week's mortgage payment to cover each pen.

Mum caught my eye. "Let her relax."

I sank into the empty chair next to the bed and studied the weave of the white sheets, not trusting myself to say anything.

"Did you let Brad know?"

Mum and Brad had a funny sort of relationship – sometimes I thought he had her spying for him to make sure things were happening as they should be at home. Other times I wondered whether she secretly hoped he would stay away permanently.

She shook her head. "I was waiting until we knew what was going on but when Ruby got here the doctor stabilised her quickly."

I pulled out my phone and sent him a message. We had exchanged a couple of curt messages since our disastrous phone call, mainly about the kids.

"Did you meet her here? Did someone from the school come with her in the ambulance"

She nodded.

"Mrs Parton came with me," Ruby said. Mrs Parton was the school principal. I'd thought she was a bit intimidating when I first met her but as we got to know each other through my work on the board, I'd realised she was muddling through just as much as any of us were. She would have been beside herself with worry about Ruby.

"Thank you. I'll get in touch with her. I was with Amy."

Mum caught my eye and raised an eyebrow.

"I'll tell you about it later." I indicated Ruby with a tilt of my head. She would have to know at some stage but there was a limit to how much an eight-year-old could cope with in one day. Even I was struggling. There was a lump in the back of my throat that had formed when we heard the baby hadn't made it, which I could not get to go away.

"How long do they want to keep her in for?"

Mum shrugged. "No one's said. Hopefully a doctor will be around soon. The nurse said it shouldn't be too long."

I leant back against the chair and stroked Ruby's hair. We had been in this exact position many times over the years, particularly when she was young and everyone was still trying to work out exactly what it was that set her allergies off. I'd sort of told myself that she was old enough that I could worry a little less and expect her to manage more of it herself. Perhaps I'd been proved wrong.

"How was your day apart from this?"

Ruby half-laughed. "It was okay. Mrs de Boer was away so we had a reliever."

"Was she nice?"

She shrugged. "She just let us watch movies."

I ducked my head. I could expect an email later from the parents who liked to let me know every time a day did not live up to their educational expectations, then. Screen time was either completely evil and must be avoided at all costs, or we were luddites if we didn't do all our work on screens, depending on who you listened to. If only they would write a letter to my column, and I could tell them they should all calm down and reduce their anxiety for a happier life. For all of us.

My hand drifted to my phone. Amy would still be at home by herself. But I was still too annoyed with her to initiate any contact. If I held my body very still, I could feel something that was a little bit like a twinge in my abdomen. Maybe racing across town might have triggered something. But maybe I was imagining it.

I flicked my calendar app open. Charlie would be finishing school and going straight to cricket practice, so we had some time. I could ask his best friend's mother to pick him up from there and take him to her house. How long would we be in the hospital?

Mum caught my eye. "Do you have work you need to be doing?"

I shook my head. "It's okay. I had taken the afternoon off anyway. I'm just trying to sort Charlie."

She looked surprised but I ignored her. It was rare for me to take any time off work unless we were going on holiday – my annual leave days were preciously guarded so that I could use them to be at school trips and camps. When only one parent was ever able to be there, it doubled the load. I bit my lip. "Can I show you something outside for a minute? I'll be right back, Rubes."

Mum followed me to the ward door. I pulled her around the corner into the corridor. She looked at me expectantly.

I lowered my voice. "I need to let you know that things aren't going well with the pregnancy. I might be about to have a miscarriage. I'm not sharing that with the kids yet. But just cover for me, if you have to, okay?"

Mum's eyes widened. "Oh no. What's happened?"

I sighed and looked at the floor, tears making my vision swim. "There was a problem with the baby's heart and today they didn't find a heartbeat."

She put her hand to her mouth. "What kind of problem?"

An orderly pushed past us with a trolley of supplies. I waited until she was a little further down the hall. "We didn't get far enough to find out."

Mum put her face in her hands. "Was it genetic? Our family has history…"

I shrugged. "I don't know."

"What a disaster. I knew she shouldn't push on with this mad plan of hers. Not with our predisposition to these things."

I kept my voice level. "It was worth a shot."

"If she'd ever actually talked to me about it, I could have helped her…"

I sighed and turned my gaze out the window. Across the road, houses lined the bush-clad valley. A new subdivision had been carved out near the top of the other side. Was it Janet Frame who described New Zealand wooden houses as boiled sweets, all painted different colours? Around town, those boiled sweets were being bulldozed, or intermingled to the point of disguise with townhouses doused in a uniform coating of beige.

"I think Amy tries not to distress you."

Mum looked at me. "What do you mean? I always want to help you both."

I put my hand on her arm. "I know, but we both want to protect you, too. Give her a call tomorrow, maybe. I need to get back to Ruby."

I didn't let her say anything further and headed back to Ruby's bedside. She was scribbling something on a piece of paper, drawing a line of what looked like capybaras wearing sunglasses. A doctor tapped on the ward door and peered into the room. Ruby half-smiled when she saw her.

The woman waved and strode across the room, her shoes squeaking on the lino. She positioned herself to the bottom right of the bed and looked in turn at Ruby, Mum and me. "This probably isn't where you wanted to end up today."

I rubbed Ruby's leg through the thin sheet. "We've had a pretty good run of avoiding the place."

The doctor nodded. "I see from your notes that you're doing an excellent job of managing Ruby's allergies."

I didn't say anything. It wasn't like we had a lot of choice. When she was small, I'd stay up at night googling what I might have done during pregnancy to cause the allergies. Now the best I could do was to make sure we planned out all our meals to stay well clear of anything that might set her off. The teacher had a full list of everything she was allergic to and the shared lunch had been meant to come with a full list of ingredients on every container contributed. But you could never trust other parents to take it as seriously.

"I'm happy to let you go home," the doctor was speaking directly to Ruby but flicking glances at me. "In rare cases the anaphylaxis can return in the next couple of days, so I need you to call emergency services immediately if there is any sign of that, okay? And keep your epipen handy. Do you need another prescription?'

I nodded. "Yes please."

She gave me a sympathetic look. "It's a hard thing, helping kids with allergies. You want to give them some autonomy but it's also important to help them keep things under control. You're doing well. Has Ruby had any further tests lately?"

I turned to look at Ruby, who was already wriggling up the bed, ready to get up. "We haven't. We did skin prick tests a couple of years ago and there weren't any signs that things were improving so I thought we'd just wait."

The doctor tilted her head to the side. "It could be worth it. While she's obviously had a reaction to something today, I wouldn't be surprised if some of her other allergies are becoming less of a concern. We do find kids grow out of some, even if they don't completely get rid of all of them."

She smiled at us over her shoulder as she headed for the door. "I'll get your discharge papers together, won't be long."

After she left, Ruby slithered off the side of the bed and dived into her schoolbag, which was next to the feet. "I want to show you something I did at school today."

Mum reached out for her. "Take it easy, please."

Ruby thrust a pile of paper at me. She pointed at a picture of a dog. "I want a pug like that."

It was a cute cartoonish drawing, with big eyes and a flopping tongue. "You're a great artist. Did you copy this from the YouTube guy?"

She shook her head. "No, I did it myself. Can we get another dog?"

I groaned involuntarily. Imagine the mess and the chaos another dog would add to our household. "What would Poppy think of that?"

Ruby frowned. "She wouldn't mind. She'd like a friend."

"And who would look after two dogs? It wouldn't be easy to take two of them for a walk."

She raised her chin defiantly. "I would."

I rolled my eyes. "You would for the first couple of days and then it would be all on me. And what if you turned out to be allergic? I'm pretty sure it helps that Poppy has been around since before you were born."

She looked indignant. "I'm not allergic to any dogs, it's not just Poppy. I hang out with Sophie's dog all the time."

"You do?"

She scowled. "She brings her to dancing sometimes."

I hoisted myself on to the side of the bed and wriggled so that I was tucked in next to her.

She looked up at me. "Can we go?"

I glanced at the door, waiting for the doctor's return. "It can't be long."

An unmistakeable twinge in my lower abdomen made my breath catch in my throat.

Ruby went to sleep almost the minute she got home and slept through until late next morning. It was unlike her – usually she was up as soon as the sunlight touched her curtains.

Twice in the night, I crept into her room to reassure myself she was still breathing. The first time I checked on her, she was spread across the whole mattress, head tilted back as if presenting herself in complete submission to sleep. The next time, she was curled in a foetal position near the base of the bed. When did adults lose that ability to sleep so freely? Sometimes it felt as though I'd hardly moved in the night from start to finish.

She'd been determined to go back to school and, while I would have preferred to keep her home where I could monitor her properly, it seemed unwise to encourage her against it. And her teacher had such a fright that it was unlikely anything would come within three metres of her that shouldn't.

She woke with about half an hour to spare to get there, quickly bolted a bowl of cereal and threw on the first clean pair of bike shorts she could find in the washed laundry, and a hot pink t-shirt. Charlie was already out the door, on his bike with a resentful glance over his shoulder, concerned his sister might be getting a day in front of the TV.

My cramps continued overnight. As I stood from bed, there was an unmistakeable heaviness. When I stripped off my pyjamas to get into the shower, I saw it. The bleeding had started. So far it seemed just like a normal period. How much was worse it going to get?

Amy still hadn't told me when we were meant to be going back to the specialist to confirm the awful diagnosis of the sonographer. But the fact that it had already clearly begun sounded a note of finality. There was no more wondering whether the sonographer had been right. No needing to test for falling hcg or anything like that. It was definitely happening.

When I got back home after dropping Ruby at school, I walked around to the back of the house, where there was a small garden shed. On the top shelf was a packet of perennial wildflower seeds that I had bought a year earlier and never got around to planting.

I reached up and retrieved it, a puff of dust exploding into the air. Cradling it in my hand, I walked slowly to the cherry trees at the far edge of the garden. Amy could come up with her own memorial for her baby, but I needed to do something for my niece or nephew, too.

I settled on the ground in front of the trees and used my finger to make a track in the dirt, pouring the seeds in. "Sorry I never got to meet you," I whispered, one hand on my stomach. "We'll think of you when these flowers bloom. And every other day, too, probably."

I lay on the grass and stared up at the sky.

Before I went inside to try to work, I headed around the front of the house to check the letterbox.

I was clutching my phone, but couldn't bring myself to use it to send Amy a message. She hadn't contacted me at all since the horrible way we had parted the day before. I was used to her moods, but it was incomprehensible that she could accuse me of not caring. I had laid my body on the line for her and her dreams, without so much as a mention of what it would cost me. She hadn't even asked after Ruby.

The letterbox was full of junk mail. Cards from real estate agents telling me they had sold my neighbour's house. A handwritten letter from someone wanting to convert me to the Latter-Day Saints. When had they stopped door knocking and started writing letters instead? To be honest, I was happy about it. I never knew quite what to do when strangers knocked on my door.

At the bottom was an envelope with my first name written on it in blue ink. The handwriting wasn't familiar.

I slid my fingernail under the join in the envelope as I walked back up to the house. There was one sheet of paper inside it with just a few words on it – "believe me now?"

I let the paper drop from my hand at the same time as another cramp rolled through me. I stumbled back towards the house, pushed the door shut and leant against it, my heart hammering in my chest.

I pulled out my phone to call Krista. "I need to go ahead with going to the police," I spluttered as soon as she answered. "I put it off last time but it's not a bluff. They know where I live."

"Slow down," she sounded frustrated. "What do you mean?"

I slammed the front door behind me and locked it. "The person who's been emailing me - they wrote a note and dropped it in my letterbox."

She sighed. "Okay. Okay."

I could hear her tapping on her keyboard.

"We need to get you out of there. I'll get some accommodation sorted for you for tonight and we'll go from there. Does the people team have the emails?"

"Yes."

"Okay. I'll find out where they got to in terms of tracing them. You're right that we need to escalate this to the cops. Can you make it to the station to make a report? I can get someone to meet you there."

She was at least two hours' drive away. The only person from work anywhere near was Megan. I had been meant to have lunch with her the day of the terrible scan but had cancelled with no explanation. She had seemed miffed and at the time I hadn't cared. I hadn't had a chance to get in touch with her to clear things up.

"I'm fine, I can handle it by myself."

She hesitated but seemed to decide that was true. "I'll be in touch soon. Take care of yourself. Are you feeling better?"

I hadn't told her why I was on a day off. All she knew was that I had been unwell and out of action, which was extremely unlike me. I was the person who worked until the day before I gave birth and would take my laptop to bed with me rather than call in sick.

"I'm fine," I lied as another cramp squeezed my abdomen. There was no point trying to explain to anyone what was really going on.

I pressed the button to end the call and switched over to my messages. "Brad, I need to speak to you. Can you give me a call when you get a minute?"

The phone marked that the message was delivered but ten minutes later, as I climbed into my car to head down to the police station, there was still no reply.

As I pulled my car away from the curb and headed down the street – holding my breath as I squeezed between two four-wheel-drives parked on either side of the too-small road at one point – I swallowed hard. For all Amy's protestations that I had everything that anyone could ever want, now that I needed someone to help me, they were proving difficult to find.

The police station is the most modern building in town. When it opened a few years back, there was a letter to the editor of our local paper bemoaning that the two most attractive buildings were the court and the police station. That sort of indicated what most of the residents spent their time doing, the writer said.

There was an unfortunate grain of truth to that, but I figured, as I slid my car into a carpark in the road outside, surely it was better to have an attractive one than whatever the alternative was. Maybe it was up to everyone else to get the rest of town looking a bit better.

The automatic doors pulled apart to allow me into a quiet waiting room. There were rows of plastic chairs along either side and a coffee table in the middle with an array of magazines that might have been last updated in 2003. The floor was cream laminate, and the room was dominated by a large wooden bench with a Perspex screen. There was no one sitting at the desk but a woman in the back of the room raised her eyebrows in greeting.

"Can I help you?" She had an accent, but I couldn't place it.

"I need to make a police report. I'm being stalked. Or harassed. Or something. I need to tell the police about it."

She rustled around under the table and produced a sheet of paper on a clipboard. "Take a seat and fill this out."

I scanned the document. The emails were sitting in a folder in my email app so I could easily work out the times and dates of the harassment. I jotted down as much as I could and pushed myself to my feet, feeling a gush of blood at the same time. I probably had another hour-and-a-half before I would be trying my super-with-wings pad's patience.

I stepped lightly as I crossed to the desk, trying to avoid my shoes rapping on the floor. The woman frowned as she took the clipboard from me. "Thanks, an officer will be in touch."

"That's it?'

She shrugged. "We'll assign it and take it from there. You should hear from someone in the next week or two."

"Week? What should I do in the meantime?"

She looked startled. "Um, well… you should note down any further interactions you have with this person. Call the emergency number immediately if you feel that you're in danger."

"I feel a bit in danger, given this person knows where I live and is trying to scare me."

She nodded. "I understand. Someone will be in touch as soon as possible."

I sighed. "Right."

I retrieved my phone from the bottom of my bag as I turned to head for the door. I pulled up an email to Krista. "I've filed a report – not that I have much faith anything will happen. Is IT trying to trace those emails?"

It was a sorry situation when I had to put more faith in the guy who told me to turn my computer off and on again every time something went wrong than the police department.

She replied quickly. "Yes, we're on it. Would you want to stay with Megan while we sort this out?"

I screwed up my face. We didn't know each other that well. "I don't think she'd love having her house overrun with my kids."

She replied again: "You're right, sorry."

Outside the police station, I turned towards my car and then hesitated. Simone's shop as only about 50 metres away, across the intersection and along the road in front of me, almost directly opposite Amy's. I could go and talk to her, see if she could look after my sister or maybe even relay some messages. I turned and headed for the crossing. It was worth a shot.

Less than five minutes later, I was pushing open the door of the music shop and blinking in the darker interior. Simone had the lights set up to make the sparkles on the drum sets glimmer. There was a row of electric guitars along the wall, like beacons shining for those who dreamt of a rockstar life.

It had never appealed to me. All the travelling around, not going to bed until the middle of the night, not being sure where your next pay cheque was coming from – although in that regard my foray into journalism had not been a spectacularly better option.

Simone was in the back corner of the shop. I squinted. There was someone with her, leaning against her chest, Simone's arms wrapped around her back.

"Amy," my voice sounded too loud, even with the shop's radio blaring.

Simone looked up, and tapped Amy on the shoulder, indicating she should turn around. I took a step towards her, but she moved away, her face pale. "I can't see you right now."

I stumbled over my words. "I just came to tell you..."

She glared at me. "You left, I needed you."

Simone placed her hand on her arm, as if trying to calm her. She whispered something in her ear that I couldn't hear.

I stared at her. "I had to go and be with Ruby."

She turned so she was looking over my head, refusing eye contact. "But you didn't seem upset at all."

I hesitated. This again? "That's incredibly unfair. I have to hold it together for everyone else, that doesn't mean that I don't feel anything."

She was wild with grief. Her face was covered in tears and her eyes and nose were red. There was no reasoning with her when she was like this. She had not been able to get the world to do what she needed, and there was nothing she could do about it.

I carried on. "I do care, Amy. I care so much for you, and I care so much about the baby. It just can't be the only thing I care about... I had to help Ruby."

She flicked her hand in my direction, dismissing me. "That's right, I'm not a mother. I don't know what it's like to be someone's number one. Guess I never will."

Simone patted her again, but the action had no impact. We locked eyes over Amy's head.

"I think you're being too hard on your sister," Simone said quietly.

Amy frowned but said nothing.

I took a step backwards, the dragging weight in the lower of my abdomen threatening to pull me down. "I'll leave you to it – I just wanted you to know that the miscarriage... well, it's happening. I'll go to the appointment with Amelia if you tell me when it is. You don't have to be there."

Neither of them said anything but Simone kept her eyes on me, as if trying to communicate something. Her fingertips were tracing Amy's spine.

"I'm sorry, Amy. I'm sorry it didn't work out."

Amy flicked a glance at Simone. "Okay. Thanks for trying, I guess." She still didn't make eye contact with me.

CHAPTER THIRTEEN
AMY

I stayed with Simone in the shop for an hour or two before it became apparent that my snotty, sniffling presence was making her customers uncomfortable. She touched me gently on the shoulder to get me to move when I put my head on the counter as she tried to sell a man an expensive harp. It was the kind of thing I'd have to take a mortgage out for. He frowned as she tried to arrange the paperwork around my head.

I pushed myself up and looked him square in the eye. "I'll go."

She touched my waist lightly. "Why don't you go and get a bowl of chips or something at the pub, I'll meet you there soon."

And see other people? The thought made my stomach clench. But what else was I to do? I didn't want to go home by myself. The pub was too bright, too busy, and far too cheery. But it was one of the few options I had.

The woman behind the bar grinned at me as I approached, but I couldn't summon a smile in response. "What can I get you?"

I hesitated. I'd told Simone I was coming for something to eat. But maybe a glass of wine would be a better salve for my mood.

The glasses hanging by their stems above the bar twinkled in the sunlight.

"Just a house sav please."

She nodded. "Take a seat and I'll bring it over to you." She doubled back and raised an eyebrow. "Are you okay? You're not looking yourself."

I sighed. No doubt what little make up I had remaining from yesterday had smeared across my face. Had I had a shower? I couldn't remember.

"I'm fine, I'll just quickly tidy myself up."

I headed for the bathrooms in the corner. The door had a frosted window in it, and I could see someone coming in the other direction as I reached for the knob. I stepped aside to let her past me before I entered. How much was a drink going to cost me? I ran a mental tally. The mortgage payment would have gone – just – but there might not be a lot left in my bank account. The credit cards were completely maxed out. I just made the minimum repayment to keep the bank away.

I stared at myself in the mirror. How had it got to this? How many years had gone into trying to have a kid? And all for nothing? I'd been so focused on having someone to leave "everything" to, to make all my work worthwhile and in the process, it had all fallen apart and there was basically nothing left to worry about leaving, anyway.

I plunged my hand into my tote back to retrieve a lip gloss and a powder. The powder went on in patches, clinging to where my tears had left my skin dewy. Maybe I could ask the bartender to turn down the lights a bit so no one would notice.

I settled at my favourite table in the corner of the pub, where I could see the room but I wasn't in anyone else's line of sight. There was a group of men in the corner, some of whom I knew had businesses on the next road over. What were they doing at the pub at – I checked my watch – 3pm? Maybe their trade was going better than mine. Not that that would be hard. I guess plumbing supplies are one of those things that people keep buying at a greater rate than shift dresses. A couple of them were real estate agents – or as a boss I'd once had referred to them as "middle-class unemployed".

There was something about them that annoyed me. Maybe that they took up so much more space in the room than their number suggested they should. Maybe it was that they were so loud, as if no one had ever told them that not everyone wanted to hear their opinion. Maybe it was their confidence that everyone else would fall in line for them and it wouldn't matter if they ignored all their phone calls for the afternoon – from clients, wives, kids – because everyone would just accept they were busy important men with other things to do. Unlike me, who had to be on call for everyone and never got anything in return.

I was glowering at them when a woman sitting in the booth next to me caught my eye. It was the same one who had been coming the other direction when I went into the bathroom. "They're a type, aren't they?"

I smiled despite myself. "I guess everywhere has them."

"Imagine what it would be like, if there was a group of women in here making that much noise, there'd be complaints on the local Facebook page, the bartender would probably chuck us out for being drunk. The burn would be so savage you'd see the marks on the stools when we left."

I half-laughed. "I know."

She eyed me for a minute as I tried to keep my face neutral.

"That's not the only thing bothering you, though, is it?" she said at last.

I leant back into my seat and slithered my weight down a bit. I had to stop being so obvious.

She gestured to the space next to me. "Could I join you?"

I shrugged. Simone was probably an hour away, at least, and the company might take my mind off things. "Sure."

She stepped out of her booth and slid into the other side of mine. "It's nice to meet you. I'm Mia."

I nodded in acknowledgement. I had seen her around. She had that glossy look of someone who was relatively new to town, before she realised that she didn't need to perfectly blow-dry her hair every day or wear high heels to work. They seemed superficial considerations, but I had found those who didn't make that adjustment ended up bristling against the small-town environment so much that they had to go back to the city. Maybe it was signalling something deeper. I was lucky if I blew my hair out once a week. Right now, it hadn't seen a brush in days. I ran my hand through it.

She looked at me straight-on, making eye contact in a way that almost made me nervous. "So what's going on in your world?"

It was a weird question to ask a total stranger but there was something about the open way she looked at me that made me want to talk to her. I rolled the stem of my wine glass between my fingers and watched the liquid start to move in a whirlpool.

"I'm at a low point, I guess you could say."

She nodded. "Not to be rude, but I can kind of see that."

"My last chance at having a baby just failed. My business is in pieces, and I don't really know what I'm going to do next."

She didn't push me, but I kept talking.

"I've been trying so hard to find my place in the world, to feel like I fit in. But now it's all gone."

Mia cocked her head to the side. "A baby was going to help you fit in?"

I shrugged. "I know it sounds weird. But growing up ... I always thought when I had my own kids, I'd have the connection my sister had with her dad. He was her biological dad, not mine.

"In this town, pretty much everyone is a parent, too. But it's a club you can't really tap into properly unless you're part of it. I'm stuck on the outside."

Mia put her drink down. "This sounds like a really tough spot to be in – it's hard to find your place as an adult, sometimes."

We both went silent as one of the men laughed far too loudly at something.

"Even if all your people are in kid-land at the moment," Mia said slowly. "As their kids get older, some of them will come back out again."

I took in her dainty watch with a smattering of diamonds, and her just-pressed dress. What would it be like to trade places with someone like Mia? To be so polished and confident? "Yeah, maybe."

"What did your sister and your father bond over, that you didn't have?"

I tried to remember. "They used to go fishing together."

Mia tapped her oval, French-tipped nails on the table. "They didn't take you?"

I looked up at her. "Can you imagine? Definitely not. You spend all day on the water, end up smelling like fish..."

She shrugged. "Maybe it wasn't the biological thing, then? Maybe it was just a shared interest? Did he freeze you out?"

Someone had turned the music up slightly and it seemed to crowd out my thoughts. A memory of Brian popped into my head. He was lying on the floor next to my bed, holding my hand when I couldn't sleep. How many nights had he done that? I'd struggled to sleep for years. "No."

She leant back on the booth. "I'm from a bog-standard nuclear family and my mum and sister were much closer than I was with her. They used to do triathlons together. I was the weird one staying at home reading my book."

I traced my finger through a drop of water left by condensation on the table. "Yeah, I get it."

"I'll get you another drink," Mia gestured to my wine glass. "Look, I'm not saying that your feelings aren't valid. I just wouldn't get too hung up on it. Families are weird. Humans are weird."

A message popped up on my phone. Andy. "Have you thought any more about a coffee with me and Lucia?"

I threw my phone on to the soft cushion of the bench seat. No, I hadn't. And why would I now? I clenched my teeth and inhaled through them, reaching for my phone again. "I haven't," I replied, slowly picking out the letters on the screen. "But there's no need now because there won't be a baby."

I pressed send. Another line ruled under another part of my dreams.

Mia arrived back with a drink which she put in front of me. I looked up. Her hair was shimmering a little with the lights from the bar behind her.

"What is it you do for a job?" We hadn't talked about her at all.

"I'm a lawyer. Just in town for an environmental hearing. I live in Wellington."

I nodded. "I saw something in the paper about that. You want to dredge the harbour to make the port bigger."

She half-laughed. "My client does. I'm just here to make the argument that they should be allowed to."

"Do you think they should?"

My parents had lived out by the harbour for most of our lives. I didn't normally pay much attention to what was going on with the businesses out there, but it would be different if the port was allowed to dredge. The argument seemed to be going back and forth about how much beach we were prepared to lose to allow for bigger ships, which should bring more people and money into the region. I was a bit sceptical – there had been lots of promises of development that was meant to bring more people in, but it had so far seemed only to generate larger council rates bills.

Mia didn't look at me. "It's not my job to have an opinion. I think that lots of smaller parts of New Zealand risk being overlooked though, and it's good for them to have opportunities for development that come from within rather than waiting for the government to pour in more money."

I shrugged. "I don't think it serves us that well to think that we'll solve our problem just by letting our businesses get bigger, though. Sometimes it feels like all we have are those scenic spots."

She looked at me. "Would it have helped yours if people up here had more money to spend?"

I closed my eyes briefly, trying to picture it. "When you put it like that, yes. But I don't think it's that simple."

She smiled. "I didn't come in here to argue about it, there's quite enough of that in my future as it is."

She leant back and took a sip of her drink. "What's your business, anyway?"

I exhaled hard. "A clothes shop. But I think maybe I'm just actually not that good at the business side of the business. I should have just been a stylist. It's a pity there's not a huge need for those up here."

She tapped her lips with her finger. "Maybe not in person, but perhaps you could do some sort of online thing?"

I shrugged. "I've messed it all up, anyway. Everything's turned to rubbish. My big dreams have fallen to pieces."

Mia took a sip of her drink. "Might it be time to think about what dreams you could pursue instead?"

I turned away from her.

"Things don't have to be perfect to be great," she said.

The pub door swung open and Simone spilled into the room, looking around for me. It was brightly sunny outside, and her eyes were struggling to adjust to the dimmer interior.

When she spotted me, her face relaxed a little and she half-smiled, but frowned when she saw Mia sitting across from me. As she drew nearer, I stood up to pull her in next to me and introduce her. My legs were slightly stuck to the leather of the booth seat, where a layer of sweat had started to congeal.

"Mia, this is Simone my..."

I hesitated. What was I meant to describe Simone as?

Mia scrambled to her feet. "Look, I've got to get going. I'm really sorry to hear about what you're going through."

Simone was looking from one to the other of us as if trying to work out what was going on. Mia half-waved, put her cross-body bag over her shoulder and turned away from us.

Simone looked at me. "Who was that? And what was she talking about?"

Mia was already halfway to the door.

"I dunno," I shrugged. "She said she's a lawyer in town for work. We bonded over mutual dislike of those guys."

I gestured to the men who were on to another round of drinks and had somehow picked up another decibel. Simone nodded. "And how are you holding up? How many of those have you had?"

She gestured to my drink, which I had almost finished.

I shifted my weight away from her slightly. "This is only my second. You don't need to check up on me." It might have been my third, but I wasn't going to admit to that.

She nodded. "I know. But you know, drinking isn't that helpful sometimes if you're feeling sad. And when was the last time you ate something? Did you ever get any chips?"

I grimaced. "You know what's not helpful? Pouring all your time and money into one goal and one dream and having it all fall to pieces."

She bit her lip. "I'm sorry that it feels that way. But please don't snap at me. I'm trying to help."

I sighed. "I'm sorry. It's just all so much. Mia said some things that have got my mind spinning. And now I want to talk to Dad and I can't because he's not even here."

Simone put her arm around my shoulders and leant her head against mine. "You haven't told me much about your dad."

I sniffed. "Brian. I've told you about him. I'm sure."

She inhaled quickly. "Oh Brian, yes. I remember."

I folded my arms and rested my head on them. "And I've mucked it up with Breanna, too, after everything she's done for me."

Simone sighed. "You were really hard on her. But she loves you."

I looked at her. "I know."

CHAPTER FOURTEEN
BREANNA

I was still torturing myself with unanswerable questions when I got home. How could Amy be angry at me, after everything I had put myself through for her? It was unbelievable.

I had tried to tell Amy for years that she was getting too caught up in this. She wasn't paying attention to her business or her marriage with her single-minded focus on having a baby. Now she was left in the position where she had emerged empty-handed and there was not a lot else for her to fall back on. There would be even less if she pushed me away.

I should have encouraged her to do more therapy when they suggested it through the surrogacy progress. What happened to the pilates classes she used to do on her lunch breaks? She had talked about training to be a teacher.

She used to paint, didn't she? Why had she let things like that go? Adulthood is one long process of trying to hold on to bits of yourself while the world around you demands its slice. She seemed to just throw all the pieces away.

I wandered into the kitchen, checking the windows as I circled the room. Everything was double-locked and all the doors were bolted. The kids' breakfast dishes were still on the counter, so I swiped at them with a dish brush and thrust them into the dishwasher. I had to get the house partly clean so that when we decided it was safe to come back from wherever my work was putting us up, we wouldn't be coming home to rancid dishes in the sink and laundry half-done.

Krista had said the directions for the accommodation would be sent through by late afternoon. I estimated I had about an hour to get the things we needed packed and ready in the car and the dog to the kennel. The kids were in a rare trip to after-school care while I got sorted. Charlie had put on such a performance about not wanting to go when he was younger that I did everything I could to avoid it. But they had accepted it this time and it made me wonder if it was something I ought to have added into our routine. It was probably another case of mum guilt making life harder than it needed to be.

Packing up and leaving the house was probably a bit of an over-reaction. But every time a tree branch tapped against the window or roof in the night I was on edge, and jumping at shadows.

I pulled some shorts out of the clean washing pile for Charlie. No matter what time of the year it was, he would wear shorts and usually bare feet. I'd given up wincing watching him walk across hot pavement or the sharp edges of the tarseal on the road.

A dress or two would do for Ruby, and her dancing gear. It couldn't take too long to work out what was going on, could it? Krista said she had everyone she could think of working on it at our end, even if the police were likely to take their time about it.

Ruby would be the most rattled about what we were doing and why we weren't at home. Was it better to give her the truth and risk her not sleeping for a week - and possibly having nightmares for months - or come up with some sort of cover story that one or other of them would most probably end up being able to see through? Being busted in a lie could cause more stress.

I exhaled hard and sat down on Ruby's bed, where I was

folding her clothes for the suitcase. When would it be my turn to have someone else look after me? Brad left me to manage our home alone. Amy expected me to give her a baby. Even Mum expected me to stick to the script and paper over our family's emotional cracks.

∽

Two hours later, I had the kids in the car and was following directions on the GPS to the house where we were meant to be staying for some unknown amount of time.

I studied the map's overview. It was somewhere out the back of town, past where our house was, beyond where the suburbs gave way to homes with bigger plots of land, then lifestyle blocks pretending to be rural. It was further out again, right into pure farmland.

Was it safe for us to be isolated? I took a breath. I must stop getting ahead of myself. The expressionless computer voice of my phone's map app ordered me to continue driving straight ahead, so I obeyed.

The road was mostly clear of traffic, apart from a dairy tanker that crested the hill in front of us, coming the other direction, and a station wagon being driven at a creeping pace in the middle of the lane in front of us.

"Can we get ice-creams?" Ruby leant forward from the back seat to tap me on the shoulder. A sign on the side of the road promised real fruit ice-creams, alongside avocados and strawberries. A couple of goats were leaning against a fence next to it, craning their necks to get at a tattered shrub on the other side. I shot a glance at the directions on my phone screen. We still had a fair way to go.

"Maybe we could get one later, I just need to find the place we're going to stay, okay? Then we can explore from there."

It would have been better if I could have convinced someone

to come and stay with us, but I didn't have anyone I could easily call. There I was, back to the old dilemma of no real friends. I had made myself the person who could cope with anything on my own and now I had to do it. Megan was going to come up for a coffee but I didn't want to ask her to stick around.

"Where are we actually going, Mum?" Charlie was staring out the window. "I'm meant to be playing football with Harry before school tomorrow."

I checked the directions. "It's not too much further. We're just going to spend a little while staying in the country. A change of scenery will be nice. You'll see Harry at school tomorrow, it's just a bit more of a drive in."

He was staring at me in the rear-view mirror. "But why?"

"We need to have a few things done to the house. And my boss is keen for a review of this place."

It wasn't an outright lie – I just wasn't telling him that the things I needed to have done were making sure it was secure and that no one was going to try to break in and hurt us. And a review wasn't a novel idea for them, either. There had been enough occasions over the years where I had had to review anything from a Wiggles concert to a high-end restaurant with them in tow that a review of a strangely rural Airbnb didn't seem too unusual.

Ruby was also watching me and making some sort of silent judgement. "Are you okay, Mum?"

I turned quickly to catch her eye and tried to smile. "Just a lot on my mind, honey."

She didn't look satisfied with the answer but didn't push it.

Eventually, my phone told me to turn right into what looked to be an unmade road, snaking up a hill that had a Buddhist monastery at the very top, with views out across the town towards the sea in the distance. A huge house on the right was known by locals as "the castle", complete with a human-sized chess set in the garden. Unfortunately, the GPS instructed us to keep going past the top of its driveway.

"Where are we?" Charlie sounded mystified.

I turned to look around. "I'm honestly not sure, but I think the place is just up here."

As the car approached the top of the next hill on the winding road, a small white weatherboard house came into view. It was surrounded by a post and wire fence and had a couple of large trees out the front. It was the sort of place that might once have been a farmhouse but had been cut off from the farm by someone who had ambitions of turning the land into something more profitable.

There was a small gravel parking area out the front. Somewhere in the distance a peacock was screeching, sounding alarmingly like a human baby.

Charlie's face was creased into a scowl as he pushed open the door of the car and stepped out. "What is this place?"

Ruby clambered out after him, looking at the hills around her. "Look, sheep," she pointed to a paddock on the other side of the road. "Do we have to look after the animals? Can I feed them?"

I hadn't thought of that. "Ah, no I don't think so. We're just staying in the house for a little while, for a little break away. Sheep kind of feed themselves anyway, don't they? You can probably go and say hi to them, though."

It was a property that was listed on Airbnb but clearly wasn't overcome with bookings. Krista had no doubt settled on it because it was cheap. I entered the code into the lockbox on the outside wall, retrieved the key and scrabbled in the lock to open the door.

Charlie went in ahead of me. "There had better be internet."

The eternal refrain of my children. "I'm sure there will be. I have to work, remember."

"I'm hungry," Ruby was eyeing the small kitchen off to the right of the large living room we had walked into. The far side of the room was entirely glass and offered a view across the green hills of the valley. You could get a glimpse of the town beyond.

"I packed a few snacks in the car," I gestured towards the

front door. "Let's go get the rest of the things and we can think about what we want to eat."

I couldn't imagine wanting to eat, my stomach still churning. At least the bleeding and cramping had almost stopped.

∼

When the kids were positioned on the couch with a plate of cheese and crackers in front of them, Charlie watching videos on his iPad and Ruby reading a book, I perched on the arm of the sofa next to them.

"Have you thought any more about what you'd like to do for your birthday, Rubes?" I reached out to the pat the soft, shiny hair on the top of her head. Charlie shuffled over so that his head was next to hers and I could pat his, too.

She didn't look up from her book. "Capybara party."

I paused. "You mentioned that. What do I need to find for a capybara party?"

She gestured expansively. "Capybara cake, capybara decorations…"

I swallowed. "Um okay. We've only got a couple of weeks so we'd better get moving on that one."

She nodded solemnly. "I've made a guest list. Auntie Amy is bringing Audrey and Simone."

I paused. "Is she? When did she tell you that?"

Whatever was going on between me and Amy, I had to stop it interfering with her relationship with the kids.

Ruby looked at me as if I had taken leave of my senses. "We messaged each other last night. She sent me some videos of capybaras in a swimming pool."

She had better not be planning to bring any capybara substitutes to swim in our pool.

"That reminds me," I cleared my throat. "Can you guys look at me for a minute?"

They both looked up. "What?" Charlie leant his head back on the top of the couch, stretching his neck.

"I need to let you know that the baby that I told you about, Amy's baby... things didn't work out there. I won't be having a baby for her."

Ruby's face fell. "What happened?"

I sucked air through my teeth while I tried to put it into words for her. "The baby wasn't well and sometimes when that happens, the pregnancy just comes to an end."

"So Aunty Amy's not having a baby?"

I folded my hands in my lap. "Well, not right now."

"That's sad."

I squeezed down beside her and pulled her into a hug. "You're right, it is."

Megan arrived as I was dishing up a makeshift dinner of baked beans on toast. She was wearing a tracksuit, her shoulder-length hair pulled back in a ponytail.

She grinned at the kids. "How's the mini-break?"

Charlie shrugged. "It could be worse."

She and I sat at the other end of the kitchen table from the children. "Thanks for coming to see us," I looked at her. "It's a long way from your place."

She shook her head. "Not at all, I'm sorry you're feeling so rattled. I hope it all turns out to be nothing."

I gestured to the kids with my head, trying to indicate that they didn't know the details. "Should we maybe watch a movie?"

Charlie leapt up. "I'll see what I can find."

Megan walked over to the TV, to help him decipher the menu but he was already logging in with my Netflix details. She looked at me across the top of his head and smiled. "The younger generation has it in their bones, don't they?"

I retrieved a bag of microwave popcorn from a carrier bag that

I'd left on the kitchen counter. As I waited for it to pop, I tapped my laptop to wake it up.

There was a message from Krista at the top of my inbox. It was short and to the point. "Please call."

I reached for my phone. There were no missed calls – why had she not tried me first?

I gestured to Megan that I was going outside. "Just calling Krista, won't be a minute."

The evening air was cool. I leant against the front door, selected Krista's name from my recent calls and listened as it rang.

When she answered, it sounded as though she had been running. There was some faint noise in the background that faded out as she must have pushed a door shut. "How are you getting on?"

I looked through the frosted glass to the outline of the children and Megan in the house. "We're okay. Hanging in there. We've found our spot and settled in."

She hesitated. "Look, I need to talk to you."

I waited.

She was speaking slowly, as if wanting to make sure I was listening. "We think we've worked out where the emails are coming from."

I swallowed. "Okay?"

"We're still getting IT to triple-check because it is quite unusual, but it seems like it might have been Megan, or at least someone using Megan's logins. Daryl is giving her a call now."

I paused. Time seemed to slow to half-speed. Daryl was Krista's boss. I put my hand on the glass, through which I could see Megan leaning over, passing something to Ruby. What was Krista saying? It couldn't be true, could it? From in the house, I could hear a phone ringing.

My mouth was dry and my voice was strangled. "Megan?"

Krista sighed. "I'm sorry."

"Are you sure?"

Krista clicked her tongue. "I still need to speak to her to get the full story but from some other writing we've found saved in her drive online, it seems like she might have been hoping to take over some of your job."

I grabbed at the door to pull it open. "But hold on. She's here."

"She's what?" Krista's voice lifted an octave. "Are you serious?"

I nodded pointlessly, unable to speak as I pushed the door open.

"You need to get her out of there, now."

I hung up the call and strode into the house. The kids looked up, surprised. I locked eye with Megan. "Can I speak to you outside? Now?"

She raised an eyebrow but followed me to the front door.

When I'd shut it behind us, I whirled around to face her. "It was you? You've been sending me the emails? You need to get out of here immediately."

She was walking backwards, in the direction of her car, her hands raised in an imitation of surrender. "I came over planning to apologise..."

I stared at her, my mouth open. "Are you serious? Get out of here! What have I ever done to you?"

She scowled. "Can't you see how hard it is for me? You get all the glory and I'm stuck here writing about boring council meetings that no one wants to read about."

"So you thought you'd terrify me and my kids? How could you? Are you insane?"

She looked as if she was going to say something but then turned on her heel and wrenched her car door open, collapsed into the driver's seat and yanked her car into reverse, before accelerating up the drive in a spray of loose metal.

I stared at the rear lights of her car, disappearing down the road. My heart thumped in my chest. Megan had told me many times she was thankful for her job – we all were, really, in an industry that seemed to be falling apart a little bit more each month. She had complained that her role was a bit boring in comparison to mine, but I thought that was just her being a bit self-deprecating. Was I that clueless? Had she been plotting to get rid of me all along?

I hurried back into the house and bolted the door behind us, trying to calm my breathing. From the windows on the other side of the living room, you could see a long way – along the bottom of the valley was the main highway north, where a steady stream of traffic crawled like ants. Logging trucks were followed by tiny hatchbacks and SUVs like mine. I slumped on to the sofa next to the children, who were captivated by their movie. The room was spinning.

How had I got here? Both Megan and Amy seemed to have decided that I had some sort of perfect life, or at least a better one than theirs. But it certainly wasn't from my point-of-view. A lot of the time, it felt like a grind, with a lot of demands for support from people who were slow to offer it in return.

I put my hands on either side of my head and pushed my hair back off my face to try to still my brain. The betrayal was hard to process. When I looked up, Ruby was watching me.

"Mum, what's going on?"

I forced a smile. "Nothing. We can go home if you'd like to. It turns out we didn't have to have a trip out here, after all."

Charlie whipped around, his eyebrows raised. "I thought you said we were staying here for a break."

I sighed. Poor kids, no wonder they looked bewildered. They couldn't even rely on their mum to tell them what was going on.

"Well, it's up to you. If you'd like to stay out here for the night, we can do it. But my boss has just told me that I don't have to write a review after all, so we can head back if you'd like to."

"And what about the stuff being done on the house?"

"Finished earlier than I expected, too."

As I waited for their answer, images of Megan kept flashing into my mind. What if she came back? But she knew where home was, too, so there was no safety benefit in either place. But she hadn't looked like someone who wanted to physically harm me.

"Let's stay here," Charlie finally decided. "It's kind of fun with the animals around. Ruby wants to go and pat a sheep before bed."

I coughed out a laugh. "Well then, as you wish. We'll go home tomorrow."

∼

When the kids were finally asleep, I returned to my laptop.

Krista had already emailed me. "Megan is being spoken to by the police tomorrow. Lawyer says she'll probably just getting a warning, but I think you can start to put this behind you."

I replied with a short message. "Is she going to keep working with us?"

Krista replied almost instantly. "Absolutely not. She's handed in her resignation, and I've accepted it. I would have terminated her if she hadn't. I won't be giving her a reference. She was clearly delusional. Utterly bizarre."

I hesitated. "Maybe we should have found her a role in our team? I didn't even know she wanted one."

A Teams message popped up from Krista. "I doubt it would have worked out. Your style is warm and engaging – perfect for the lifestyle round. She suits court and council reporting, getting straight to the point. I suspect it was possibly the name recognition from your column she was most envious of, and she could never have managed that. Can you imagine?"

I exhaled. "Maybe we wrote her off too quickly. Women of a certain age and all that ..."

Krista responded again. "Breanna, you're far too nice. Don't worry about it. She was awful to you. She's gone now. I cannot believe she turned up to see you there. That's crazy behaviour."

∼

"Sorry, what? Can you start from the beginning again?"

I'd propped my computer open on the coffee table so I could sit across from the screen in a weak imitation of having Brad in the house with me. I called him once the kids were asleep – at last – in the small bedroom with bunk beds off the other side of the room. I could hear Charlie snoring softly. Our conversations had been careful since our fight – he hadn't acknowledged what I said, and I'd been too overwhelmed with everything else to try again.

I took a deep breath. "The person who's been harassing me is Megan. I don't know why."

"And she put a letter in the letterbox? Why didn't you tell me about that earlier? I thought it was just the emails."

I bit my lip. "I went to the police and Krista had it in hand…" My voice trailed off. The truth was, it seemed pointless to tell him the details. What would he have done?

"And they've fired her? Are the police pressing charges?"

I shrugged. "She's quit. I don't know if we really want to go through all the hassle of pressing charges. I'd rather just drop it. It's better for everyone that way."

He scowled. "She's crazy. I don't think you should let her off that easily. Are you sure you're safe?"

I spread my hands out in front of me and stared at the palms. "Apparently my life is perfect. Did you know that? Because I sure as hell didn't. You know, from my perspective, I thought I was struggling along trying to keep it together for the kids, trying to manage my work life, trying to save my marriage. But hey apparently all that's wonderful."

He fell silent. "It's not that bad, is it?"

I half-laughed. "Which bit?"

"Our marriage doesn't need saving, does it? We'll get through it."

He was staring at me.

I shrugged. "I love you, but I wasn't joking the other day when I said this is getting a bit impossible. On the kids, too."

"Is Amy helping you? Your Mum?"

As if. "Amy's angry at me. Mum is acting bewildered by the whole thing."

"She's angry?"

I spread hands, palms up on the table. "She's lashing out, I guess. She's angry and I'm the easiest target. It'll pass."

"Typical. Honestly, that woman needs to grow up and take some responsibility for her own choices. I'm sure she drove Andy away by blaming him for their problems."

I closed my eyes. The last thing I needed was to be told off by him. "Yeah, maybe."

His voice softened. "I'm sorry. I know you love her. But that is ridiculous. You did your bit for her. More than most people would have done. You have to put your own needs first for a change."

I looked out the window. "I know. I'm trying. Hadn't you noticed?"

"I didn't mean to make you upset," Brad was leaning forward, into the screen.

I looked back at him briefly before lowering my gaze to the coffee table. "But you know, on top of all this I've got to work out getting the house sprayed for bugs before the winter, I've got to sort the school holidays and Ruby's birthday is upon us. I need to somehow put together a capybara party, all by myself. I'd never even heard of a capybara until six months ago."

"It's not like it's all a picnic for me over here either." His voice was sharp.

I scowled at him. "It doesn't have to be a competition all the time, you know. It's not who has it harder, it's that it's really hard for both of us. All the time."

I was jittery with annoyance.

"But you know, if it was a competition, when's the last time you got interrupted 12 times in the space of 20 minutes while you were trying to get something done, to give the kids snacks or fix a drink or find something that's needed for school tomorrow? It's pretty damn hard to work in those circumstances."

He frowned. "We couldn't have Ruby going to all those dance classes and gymnastics if I wasn't over here earning good money. We wouldn't have as much in savings for them for the future."

I let my hands drop to my sides. It was so tiring. "I'm sure we'd find a way. Do you think the kids are going to finish school and think how happy they are that they didn't have a father because now they don't have a student loan? I doubt it."

He sat back. "They have a dad."

"Other people manage to find good jobs that don't mean they have to be away from their families for 11 months of the year."

He stared at me, the muscles in his jaw working.

"Although I suspect that's part of the appeal, if we're honest, isn't it?" I spat the words at him.

He put his head in his hands. We sat in silence. Part of me wanted to apologise but a bigger part was relieved I hadn't dropped it.

"Do you really think that?" He looked up at me.

I shrugged. "Is it not? You get to sail home and be the exciting fun one for a couple of weeks at a time and then leave me again to do the boring stuff."

He shook his head slowly. "I wish I was there to do the boring stuff. I wish I could be with you at the end of the day when the kids are in bed. I hate finding out what's going on via video calls. It makes me feel useless."

"What do you think it does to the kids?"

He really had no idea. This call was meant to make me feel better about everything that was happening but instead I just felt angry at him as well as devastated by Amy and betrayed by Megan.

We looked at each other. Would this be so stilted and weird if he was in the room? Probably not, because I could wander off and seethe on my own in the bedroom and then come back to find him. As we were, we had to schedule our talks and stew on them the rest of the time.

There was a cough from the bedroom. I paused.

"Mum?" A scuffling signalled Ruby's arrival at the bedroom door.

I shot Brad a quick glance. "I've got to go."

I pushed the laptop shut. Ruby looked at me questioningly. "Was that Dad?"

I put my arm around her to steer her back to bed. "Don't worry. We were finished anyway."

CHAPTER FIFTEEN
AMY

I lay flat on my back on the couch, my feet extending beyond the arm rest at the far end. A mustard knitted throw that Mum had got me for Christmas was half-pulled across my chest. How long had I been lying like this?

It was mid-afternoon, easily. The headache that drummed on the inside of my skull reminded me that I shouldn't have had the bottle of wine I'd found in the fridge when I got home from the pub.

I picked up my phone and let it drop to the ground again. There was a message from Simone. It made me want to scream. Here she was, this beautiful woman wanting to spend time with me, caring about me, but all I could do was lie around and stew on how my life had completely fallen apart.

You thought you were spending time with a motivated businesswoman about to become a mother for the first time? Surprise! Instead, you've got an unemployed girlfriend with nothing but an enormous pile of debt to show for it.

There was a knock on the door. I pulled the throw over my face. Whoever it was could try again another day. I could feel a dreadlock in the hair on one side of my head and I knew from the way I had been sleeping that there would be a large red wrinkle up one side of my face where I had been resting against the seam of the cushion. Even the courier didn't need to see me in this state, and he had seen a lot.

Fear squeezed my chest. Could it be the shop landlord? I'd ignored a couple of emails from her wanting to talk about the shop's lease but there was still time to run on that. Did she even know where I lived? It wouldn't be hard to figure it out.

I shifted my thoughts. The shop doors would be shut today and the beautiful racks of clothes untouched. Nat had just put out a new display of gorgeous olive-green sandals on top of the denim rack.

Would someone want to buy the business, and keep running it? No chance with the amount of debt it was carrying. I'd probably have to go bankrupt to get away from it all. I used to think the idea of bankruptcy was awful but now the prospect of a fresh start was kind of appealing.

The house was in a trust on the advice of my accountant so there was a chance I wouldn't end up homeless, so long as I found a way to keep paying the mortgage. Having a home to live in seemed such a small and ridiculous thing to be hoping for when I had started the year with dreams of what I wanted most in the world. But I'd definitely take it as opposed to a future of couch surfing – Breanna wouldn't be offering me a corner of a living room to sleep in any time soon.

The knock sounded on the door again. Whoever it was, they were persistent.

I lay very still as if any movement I made might be detected. Crumpet leapt on to my leg and stretched down to my toes, running his teeth along my toenails.

I looked at him. "That is so gross."

"Amy!" She sounded angry. "I know you're in there."

I wriggled to my feet. The mirror above the fireplace on the wall opposite confirmed the worst – I looked a sight. One side of my hair was standing completely on end. The other was glued to my face with saliva from falling asleep on my side. Streaks of tears were still evident on my cheeks.

"Give me a second." My voice croaked as I tried to shout loud enough to be heard down the hallway to the front door.

I couldn't let Simone see me like this. Yesterday had been bad enough. Sure, you want people you love to see you at your worst at some point, but does that really need to be your absolute worst, and so soon?

I staggered into the bathroom and stared at myself in the mirror. I had to stop being so ridiculous. Make myself presentable and get on with it. As quickly as possible.

I swiped at my face with a makeup wipe until it looked relatively clear, then applied a fresh coat of mascara. The bags under my eyes would have to stay but a swipe of lip-gloss made me look at least partly human.

Simone was leaning against the doorframe, stabbing at her phone when I opened the door.

"At last," she looked at me.

I shrugged. "Sorry."

She gestured for me to go inside. "Can I come in?"

We wandered through to the lounge. The air was decidedly musty.

Simone cracked the French door on the other side of the kitchen and gestured towards my tiny slice of lawn, on which I had placed two white metal chairs. "Let's sit out here? I need to talk to you."

Her tone was cool, almost professional. My heartrate started to pick up. Had she come over to end things with me? Was I that much of a mess that it wasn't worth her time?

"Do you want a drink?" I cursed myself for stammering. Keep it cool. Maybe we can pretend none of this has happened and it's all just like it was before.

She seemed to soften. "Just a water."

"Where's Audrey?" My hands shook as I retrieved a glass from the cabinet and the jug of filtered water from my fridge, trying to drag the process out as much as I could.

"She's at a friend's. She wanted to come and see you, but I thought we should have this chat by ourselves."

"Oh," I tried to keep my voice light. "I would like to see her."

Simone nodded but said nothing. The light through the overhanging kowhai tree was dappled on her face, which had a sort of luminous glow. She was wearing a fitted t-shirt and yoga pants. There was an indent running down the muscle of her upper arm.

I settled into the chair opposite her and watched her as she took a sip of water.

She looked up at me, our eyes locking. "How are you holding up?"

I shrugged. "I'm alive."

She pressed her lips into a thin line. "That's good, but I don't think that's enough."

"It's enough for now."

She cleared her throat. "I saw Natalie in the street..."

I looked up at the tree above us. My bird friend was nowhere to be seen.

"Are you really closing the business?"

I leant back in my chair and looked at her. "It's not sustainable. It wasn't making enough money to continue. You know what it's like."

She nodded. "It's been a tough year, but things do seem to be getting better..."

I forced a fake smile. "You always think things are getting better. Remember you've got the benefit of people who have to keep coming in to buy their supplies or whatever. No one has to buy a pretty dress."

She frowned. "I don't think that's quite true, I have the online competition too."

I waved it away. "But people love you. They want your advice."

She looked at me. "The same used to be true for you."

"Used to be?" I studied her face.

She looked at her feet, tracing an unpolished toe in the grass. She'd kicked off her Birkenstocks when she walked in the front door. "Before you became so singularly focused. You have a good eye for what works for people, Amy. People rate your opinion. But lately..."

I let the words hang between us.

She cleared her throat. "Lately you've not really been interested in a lot else, and people can tell. We miss you."

I crossed my arms. "I'm sorry if my desire for a child has been boring. You'll be pleased to know I will be leaving it in the past."

She shook her head and reached for my hand. "That's not what I meant, and I think you know that. I am so sorry for your loss. I'm just saying that there's more to you..."

I looked away from her and studied the flowerbed. The small array of hot pink gerberas I'd planted were drooping. I couldn't even keep flowers alive reliably, why had I ever thought I'd be any good at raising a child?

"I'd better hope I can find that again, then, right?" It sounded more bitter than I intended but Simone smiled.

"You will. You know that business coach I was telling you about? He'd be willing to meet you to chat about how you could continue with the shop, if you wanted to. I could send you his number."

I shrugged. "Maybe. I'll think about it."

She reached for my hand and held it, her eyes locked on mine. "Whatever you decide to do, I'll do what I can to help. I don't know if you know, but your landlord is my landlord, too. I can talk to her about giving you a bit of grace."

I withdrew my hand slowly. "Why are you being so nice? I'm a basket case and remember I've spent the last year or whatever boring you all with my baby plans."

She pulled me back in again. "That's not true. You're amazing. You're funny, Audrey loves you, you're gorgeous," she hesitated as I looked down at my t-shirt, which had what might have been a coke stain on one side and leggings that were threatening to go into holes in the knee. "Even when you're dressed down. I'm thankful for every minute I get to spend with you."

She held my gaze and my breath seemed to get stuck in my throat.

"You're not so bad yourself." I cursed myself - what an inane thing to say – but she laughed.

"One other thing, though."

I groaned. "What is it?"

"You need to make it right with Breanna. The way you've been treating her is crazy. It's like you think have a right to her body – and I know you well enough to know that that's exactly the sort of mindset you hate from other people."

I looked at my feet. The bright pink nail polish had made me so happy when Audrey chose it in the nail salon. Now my big toe was chipped. It reminded me why I steered away from the really standout shades – where the chip was made it look from afar like part of my toe was missing.

Simone was right, I knew it. I'd behaved appallingly. Again, I'd been caught up so deeply in getting to my picture-perfect future that I'd mucked everything up in real life. "I know I've been mean. I just wanted to know that she felt some of it, too. Like I wasn't so alone."

Simone shuffled around so she was sitting next to me and put her arm around my shoulders. I leant into her. Her perfume, a sort of musky gardenia, wafted over me.

"I know. She definitely feels it, she really did want to help. She would do anything for you and I'm sure she's devastated by what happened."

I shrugged. "I guess. I get sick of being the sister nothing good happens to, you know?"

She patted my shoulder. "You have to stop saying that, or I might get a complex."

I smiled despite myself. She was right – there were some bright spots in my life. "Sorry."

"No one would offer to help like that unless they really wanted to. She loves you. It's not her fault that you think she's got the better deal."

"Overall, she has, though."

Simone pulled me closer. "Does she?"

"She's got the huge house, lots of money, two gorgeous kids, a job she doesn't even have to get out of her pyjamas for if she doesn't want to…"

"And she's got a husband who's away more than he's at home, she's juggling all that by herself. I reckon she's got things to be jealous of, too."

"Like what?" I sounded like a stubborn toddler, but I didn't care – anything to keep Simone saying nice things to me.

"You're creative, you've got great friends, you've got the freedom to do whatever you want any time you want to, you've got me…"

Her voice trailed off. "That is, assuming that you still want me around."

I grabbed her hand. "Of course I do. I just don't know what happens now. I thought I had it all planned out and now…"

She leaned in and kissed me quickly on the lips. "That's the great part, you get to figure it out."

She reached out to touch the pounamu I still had around my neck. "You'll still get to be a māmā, in your own way. You can put the energy out into the world in other forms."

I ducked my head. "I hope so."

"But first you need to call Breanna and make it right."

"Can I email?"

She frowned.

"I can express myself better if I have time to write it down."

She sighed and leant back in her chair, draining the last of her water. "I'm not going to tell you what to do. But if you're going to email, you need to repeat it in person afterwards."

I wriggled in my chair. They looked great and perfectly fit

with my vision for a sort of cottage garden vibe, but they were not the most comfortable things ever.

"Do you want something to eat?"

Simone shook her head. "Why don't you go and have a shower? You'll feel better if you get changed. Maybe we can go for a walk or something before I have to go and get Audrey."

I almost bristled. "I'm sorry that I'm in such a state."

She waved it away. "That's not what I meant. You've been through such a lot. But you don't have to stay there, wallowing in it. You get to choose and I'm bringing you back to us."

A tweet from the tree above caught my attention. My friendly bird was bopping along the branch. She seemed to make eye contact with me before flitting to another branch. Simone followed my gaze. "That bird's always there."

I pointed to the branch above. "I think her nest is just up there, but the other birds seem to have moved on. We can be empty-nesters together."

Simone winked at the bird. "I'll keep an eye on both of you ladies, then."

As I wandered towards my bedroom to collect a new set of clothes, I pulled out my phone to send a message to Breanna. Where to start? "I'm sorry I went a bit crazy," I started to type. "You don't owe me anything…"

Twenty minutes later, I was dressed in a fresh pair of wide-leg trousers and a white tank top. It was a look that was intended to give Amal Clooney vibes, but I had concerns that it was more "retiree on a bucket list cruise". But it was cool and with the humidity still far higher than should be allowed, I was going for comfort. I popped a bronze necklace over the top. The finished look was satisfactory, if not exactly showstopping.

Simone smiled as I returned to the garden. "Beautiful. Let's go for a walk around the block."

"The block" from my house was actually an expanse of probably about two kilometres, winding up a side street, down a larger road with a big park on one side and round to the busiest highway through town.

My street was quiet, even the neighbours across the road who always seemed to be out in the garden pottering with some sort of shrubbery were nowhere to be seen. Further down, the young guys who had half a car in the driveway were sitting in a paddling pool, drinking beers.

"That looks kind of appealing," I whispered to Simone we drew nearer.

She grinned at me. "Nothing to stop you getting a paddling pool. Can Crumpet swim?"

We rounded the corner and drew closer to the park. It was relatively small, with a cluster of trees at one end that provide a bit of shade to sit under, and a playground at the other. Sometimes when I drove home past the park, I'd averted my eyes from the playground because it was too painful to see little kids playing with their parents when I'd been going from one pregnancy disappointment to another.

This time I kept my gaze steady. There were only a handful of people at the playground, a woman with a boy who looked to be about five who was sitting on the wooden car at the far side, and an older couple watching a slightly younger girl. Closest to us, a man who looked a bit like Brad was pushing a girl a little younger than Ruby on the swing. She was soaring into the air, shrieking at the peak of each movement.

I took a deep breath and let it out slowly. Simone reached for my hand and squeezed it. "I bet that woman's looking at you, thinking she wishes she was as put together and stylish as you. She's probably not had a minute to herself in a week. And that guy probably was up all night dealing with a tummy bug or something."

I smiled. "You don't have to try to make me feel better. I get it."

We watched for another minute before I turned to her. "I feel like I should do something for Breanna."

Simone grimaced. "What kind of thing are you thinking?"

I half-laughed. She was probably imagining some sort of weird plot. "I'm going to get Brad to come home."

"Is that what she wants?"

I nodded quickly. "Absolutely. It's what they all need."

Simone looked at me out of the corner of her eye. "Okay. Just be careful. No making things harder for your sister."

A car went past, bass thumping from its speakers. Simone took my hand in hers, interlacing our fingers. "Let's go and get an ice-cream."

There was a petrol station around the corner that would have a decent selection. As we prepared to cross the road, Simone stopped. A couple was standing on the other side of the road, preparing to cross towards us.

I swore under my breath. "Just what I need."

Andy was dressed in a pair of cargo shorts, of the type I had tried to wean him off for years, and a baggy Pearl Jam t-shirt. Next to him was a small woman with dark hair in a pixie cut. It was a look I'd always wanted to try but never had the cheekbones or the confidence for.

He raised his hand in greeting as he drew nearer, then reached in to kiss me on the cheek. "Hey, it's lovely to see you."

I hesitated. That was a warmer greeting than I was expecting.

"Where are you off to?"

I cleared my throat. "Just out for a walk, needed a change of scenery."

He nodded, a bit too vigorously as if trying to prove to someone – probably the woman next to him – that he was happy to see me. "Oh cool, we're just heading out for a drink at that new café that opened on the corner."

I hesitated. His apartment at the waterfront was much closer, there was no reason to be in this part of town. "Bit of a scenic route?"

He half-laughed. "I swung past Lucia's to pick her up on the way."

She smiled as I turned to her. "Nice to meet you, I'm Amy."

Her eyes widened but her smile remained fixed. "Andy's told me about you."

Simone extended her hand in greeting. "I'm Simone, I'm Amy's girlfriend."

I whipped around to look at her. Her face was unreadable, but she put a hand on my lower back and pulled me closer.

Andy coughed in a way that sounded a bit like he was choking but Lucia just took her hand and clasped it. "I'm Lucia, I'm Andy's... friend." She hesitated before settling on the word.

I had to bite back my smile as I locked eyes with Andy – wasn't the relationship with Lucia meant to be more serious than that? "Would you like to join us?"

I shook my head quickly. "No, I won't crash your outing."

Andy was still watching my face, as if he was trying to decipher something.

Simone slid her hand into mine and intertwined our fingers. "We'll be off – have a nice afternoon."

Lucia smiled as we walked away, Andy still watching over his shoulder.

When we were out of earshot, I turned to her. "You called yourself my girlfriend."

She laughed. "Is that okay?"

Was it okay? What would that make us? What would it mean for Audrey?

"Yes, it's okay" the words came out in a rush. "I don't know what I'm doing though. I don't even know if I know who I am anymore."

She laughed again. "It's okay. I'm looking forward to meeting all the versions of you that you can come up with."

A message from Andy popped up on my phone. "Slowing things down a bit with Lucia. Great to see you. Wouldn't have picked it."

Simone was looking at me questioningly.

"Just Andy, trying to control things as usual. Sounds like he's mucked it up with Lucia."

Simone sighed. "Poor guy, trying to replace someone like you."

I laughed. "Hardly."

CHAPTER SIXTEEN
AMY

Breanna agreed to see me the next morning. The day was slightly cooler, and dew had formed on the windscreen of my car. The end of summer might be approaching.

I drove down my street and through the town's largest intersection, then up past the hospital to Breanna's house. Every time I visited, one of her neighbours had a new pool, or another huge new house had popped up on one of the mass of sections that had been created by sectioning off old farmland and avocado. They all looked a bit the same, now that I thought about it, and you could bet inside they were full of the same white marble countertops, bleached fake wood floors (why always plural, when someone was talking about interior decorating?) and cream-on-cream paintwork. My little bungalow in town was dripping with character in comparison.

I pulled up to Breanna's front gate and turned off the car. Taking a couple of minutes to calm my breath, I studied the trees that lined the road. They weren't natives – instead, something imported. Brian had been good at trees. I pulled open my phone to send a message to Brad. "Do you know Ruby's favourite colour?"

I waited a couple of seconds. "Does she know your favourite song?"

He replied a minute later. "What are you talking about?"

I sighed. "I need to speak to you. But I have something important I have to do first."

Breanna opened the front door slowly and stood holding it, not stepping aside to let me in.

"Can I come in and talk to you?"

My heart was beating too fast, and it was hard to meet her eyes. If this was what being an adult and taking responsibility was like, I was not a fan.

She gestured for me to follow her into the house. I traipsed behind her through into the "good" lounge, where we took seats on her cream couches. As I settled in the corner, a pillow next to me shifted, exposing a bright red stain.

Breanna clocked it. "Blackcurrant juice. How many times have I told them not to drink on the couch?"

I smiled. "Ruby always assures me she's a very tidy eater."

Breanna rolled her eyes. "I'm sure. Now, what can I do for you?"

I twisted my hands over each other. "Nothing. You can't do anything for me. I wanted to apologise for the way I treated you. It was unforgivable. I don't know what came over me. Grief, I guess."

Breanna settled on the couch next to me. "Thanks."

I flicked a glance at her. "That's it?"

She leant back against the cushions. "I appreciate you apologising. You were so hard on me. I don't really know what else to say."

I picked up a polished shell from the coffee table and turned it over in my hands. The soft pink reminded me of a childhood holiday we had taken to Fiji. "You know I've always been jealous of you. I was temporarily insane, and it all came out."

Breanna raised an eyebrow. "I honestly have no idea why you would be."

"Well, starting with Brian – you two were so tight…"

She cocked her head to the side. "You always say that, but he loved you madly, too. Remember how he wore that jacket you made for him at school every Christmas?"

I smiled. It was a creation from when I first started sewing and he must have been having someone re-stitch it for him in between wears because there was no way it would have lasted 10 years otherwise. It barely fitted across his shoulders and finished well above his waist. It had a line of sequins around the collar, and he told me he loved it.

I put the shell down. "Yeah. I know. I just felt like the outsider. I kind of always have."

Breanna exhaled hard enough to make my hair move. "Amy, everyone feels like the outsider some of the time."

I studied her face. "But compared to you…"

Breanna spluttered with laughter. "Why does everyone think things are so good for for me? I've not got a friend to my name who would turn up when I needed them these past few weeks, everyone expects me to look after them and even my husband doesn't come home. I don't even know if I want him to, anymore."

She dropped her face in her hands and her shoulders shook. I put my arm around her, not quite sure what to do. "I didn't mean to make you cry. I didn't realise…"

She brushed me away. "I know you didn't. You didn't think. No one ever does – I guess they're too used to having me do it for them."

A sick feeling burbled in my stomach. "I'm so sorry I wasn't here for you. That I haven't been a better sister. I'm going to do better."

She didn't respond. I leant against her, inhaling her expensive perfume. I had to do better. I could start with the next thing on my to do list.

It wasn't until the evening of the following day that Brad finally sent a message, agreeing to take a call. My head was still spinning from the conversation with Breanna. Did she really feel she had no friends? She was always greeting people when we walked around town together, and she went to what seemed like endless kids' birthday parties. I tried to send her a message whenever I thought of her during the day. I had to keep myself in check, though – there was a risk I could push it too far and become a bit weird and overwhelming about it all. Again.

I settled on the sofa to pull up my laptop to talk to Brad. Had we ever actually had a call, just us, before? I'd only really been there when the kids were talking to him and sometimes waved in the background if he called when Breanna was with me.

He flicked his eyebrows up in greeting when the call connected.

"I won't keep you for long," I was talking too fast, but I had to get it out while I had it straight in my mind. "You need to come back, Brad. The kids are growing up so fast and you're missing out. They're missing out."

He blew air out through his teeth. "I don't know if this is any of your business, Amy."

I waved him away. "I'm their aunt and I love them. I shouldn't know them better than you do, though."

He folded his arms and stared at the camera. "I'm earning good money here. We'll be able to send them to a great private school for high school and get them set up for life. I'm trying to give my family everything I can."

I bit my lip. "Breanna and I didn't go to private school, and we turned out fine. Money isn't what they want, Brad."

He scoffed. "Tell that to the kid who wants the latest console. Or the girl who takes up horse riding on a whim."

I sighed. "They'd rather have you. Breanna and I were talking about our childhood. What you remember – it's not that you had the latest gadgets or whatever, it's that your parents were there for you. That they knew you. I think I underestimated how much Dad in particular really knew me. Don't be the one to muck it up with Ruby and Charlie, they're amazing."

He was looking at the table now, avoiding eye contact. "I hear you, Amy."

"Do you know what Charlie's favourite game is, anyway?"

He frowned. "Does that matter? It's the one with the...."

I cut him off. "Do you know what Ruby's best friend's name is?"

"Olivia."

I shook my head. "Olivia moved to Wellington last year."

He pushed back from the table in frustration. "Okay, stop. I get what you're saying. Can we leave it there please? This is for me and Breanna to work out."

"Breanna needs you, too."

He raised an eyebrow. "I'm not sure about that."

I balled my hand into a fist. "Don't be ridiculous. She might be angry with you but only because she loves you and she wants you around more, not less. I don't know if you realise how alone she is. I didn't."

He steepled his fingers and rested his chin against them. "Let's leave it there, Amy. I've got the message, okay? Just let me work out how to handle it."

I glared at him. "You'd better do something quickly."

CHAPTER SEVENTEEN
BREANNA

Even though Megan had been dealt with, it was taking a while for my column to come naturally again.

I stared at a letter from a woman who wanted to know what she should do about a sister who wanted her to postpone her wedding until after she had had breast augmentation. I started to write a paragraph telling her to take a firm line, then deleted it. Maybe there was more to the surgery? I added a caveat.

The next problem in my inbox was from someone whose mother-in-law was trying to sabotage her attempts to throw a 50th birthday party for her husband. At least I didn't have that to worry about – Brad's parents were lovely but almost completely absent, occasionally writing us emails from their home in Perth and dropping in for a visit every year or two.

At 11am, I closed the page I was working on and collected my things. I was meant to be meeting my mother, her new boyfriend and Amy for a coffee at a café on the corner.

No one else was there when I arrived but I took a seat in the corner. From the window, I could see the carpark. There had once been a garden centre next door, but it had been sold and replaced by a pizza restaurant, an Indian restaurant and a vape shop. How vape shops managed to be the only thing flourishing in a tough economy, I had no idea. They were like the cockroaches of the retail world. If only Amy had been into vapes instead of clothing, she might have had quite a different business.

Mum's little car turned into the carpark and I watched her nose into a spot, clamber from her car and pick her way across the potholed concrete to the café. A man followed a couple of steps behind. She was wearing sandals with little heels, and a matching skirt and blouse. It made my jeans and a t-shirt look dressed down. She and Amy had always been much better at putting outfits together than I had been, always looking for a top in just the right shade or a skirt that would be a perfect match for a new pair of shoes.

She was in the door of the café a minute later and made her way to me. "Have you ordered?"

I nodded. As I'd walked in, the owner had spotted me and raised a hand in acknowledgement. I ordered the same thing every time I came in and no doubt it would arrive any minute.

She indicated the man next to her as they took seats opposite me. He was late-70s, almost bald and dressed in a plain white polo with khakis. "This is Reg. Reg, this is my daughter, Breanna."

Amy appeared behind them, slung her bag on to the back of the other remaining chair and slid into it. She waved to Reg. "I'm Amy."

Mum looked from me to Amy. "You're all okay?"

I nodded and Amy shrugged. "We'll get there." We hadn't communicated since her apology at my house the day before. It had been a big step for her – usually she tried to make everything other people's fault – but I was still wounded. I filled our four water glasses from a pitcher that had been placed on the table by a passing waiter and quickly changed the subject. "Tell us about how you and Reg met."

Reg looked relieved. Mum launched into a story of meeting at pickleball, bonding over the garden and going out for lunch. She'd never been much of a gardener when we were younger.

"And what about you? Any dates?" She turned to Amy.

I fixed her with a stare. "Have you not told her?"

Mum looked at me. "Told me what?"

Amy cleared her throat. "I am seeing someone, actually, her name is Simone."

Mum picked up her water glass and then put it down again. "Her?"

Amy said nothing but nodded. Mum looked at Reg, then me, then back to Amy.

Reg smiled. It was a sincere, kind smile. "That's nice."

Amy smiled. "It is. She's lovely."

A waitress slid a coffee in front of me.

Mum cleared her throat. "I don't know if I'd ever considered what it would be like to have a daughter who is a lesbian." She pronounced the word carefully.

Amy and I locked eyes and I had to clamp my lips together to avoid a giggle. Only Mum could make this about her.

"I don't think it matters, really," Amy shrugged.

Mum was silent for a few minutes, then turned to me. "I've a favour to ask you."

I groaned inwardly. "Okay?"

"Reg and I are planning a trip to the islands and I was wondering whether you'd be able to drop us to the airport in Auckland and pick us up."

I opened my mouth, then shut it again, suppressing my instinct to agree instantly. That was a two-hour drive. Each way.

"When are you flying?"

She tapped her fingers on the table, thinking. "I think we need to be at the airport around 10."

"In the morning?"

"Evening."

I shook my head. "What about the kids? Are you thinking I'd bring them to Auckland with us?"

She leant back in her seat. "I just thought, I usually ask you…"

Amy waved. "I'm here, I could do it."

Mum pondered this idea. "I suppose you could. Do you mind?"

Reg put his hand on her shoulder. "We can look at other options, you know…"

"I'd like to," Amy interrupted, looking from one of them to the other.

"I'll just go and order some drinks. The usual for everyone?" I looked around the table.

Mum nodded. "Long black for Reg."

There was a line at the counter, but it was moving, slowly. I stood behind a short woman wearing a striped green top. As she turned to point to a piece of cake in the cabinet, I recognised her profile and recoiled. "What are you doing here?"

Megan turned around, her face going slack when she spotted me.

"I'm not here to cause any problems," she took a step away from me. "I'm just meeting a friend."

"You know this is my local."

She put her hands up in a gesture of surrender. "It's a coincidence, I didn't even think."

I glared at her.

She cleared her throat. "But since you're here, can we talk, very briefly?"

I raised an eyebrow. "About what?"

"Order and I'll meet you outside. I need two minutes, maximum."

I ordered the coffees and followed her through the sliding glass door to the front of the café. She was leaning against a big plant pot, looking at her shoes.

She looked up as I got nearer. "I couldn't email because you blocked me."

Could she blame me? "What did you expect? I didn't deserve any of that. I trusted you. I can't believe you came out to see us out there, when we were hiding from *you*."

She nodded. "I was struggling and I took it out on you. I don't know what came over me."

I frowned. She made it sound as if stalking people was a normal reaction to having a difficult time. "I tried to be your friend, to support you at work. What did I do to make you want to scare me like that?"

She went silent as an elderly couple walked past us and into the café. When they were out of earshot, she spoke again. "You did nothing to deserve it. You're always so sweet. You just seemed to have everything together, and it was going so well for you while I was just going backwards. I thought if you left your job and were out of the picture…"

I sighed. This again.

"I was terrified for my kids. I thought someone was going to come and break in and I'd have to fight them off on my own."

She lowered her head. "I am really sorry."

When I didn't respond, she pulled her bag strap a little higher on to her shoulder. "I just wanted to clear the air between us."

My heart rate had picked up. "We're not going to be friends, Megan. This isn't just some misunderstanding."

She looked as if she was going to say something but stopped herself. "I'll get my order to go. You don't have to see me again."

I turned and headed back into the café, where my family was waiting. Amy turned to me as I took my seat again. "What was that?"

I glared at the door where Megan had been. "No one."

CHAPTER EIGHTEEN
BREANNA

There are few people who can operate with as singular a focus as an eight-year-old getting ready for her birthday. In the week leading up to the day, Ruby had supplied, in intricate detail, a full list of the food she wanted to have at her party: Fairy bread, cupcakes with mauve piped flower icing, burger rings - but not rashuns, cupcakes with tiny capybara toppers that we found online.

There was also a list of the friends who were to be invited, which fluctuated according to who was currently the best friend of whom and who was sitting on which table in class. Mum and Reg had talked about coming. Amy. Simone and Aubrey would definitely be there. I lay in bed, staring at the ceiling. It was before dawn but I always woke early on the kids' birthdays. It was a mix of excitement on their behalf and anxiety that I might mess something up for them.

There was a pile of presents in my wardrobe, wrapped in matching purple paper. Almost everything on Ruby's list had been produced – with the exception of a pet capybara. It was easier than Charlie's birthday. He'd ask for a phone and a laptop, as well as a new bike and hoverboard. Ruby just wanted some more soft toys, not that she needed any more, and some clothes for school.

There was a rustling on the other side of my bedroom door, and someone hissed something. The kids were awake. "Come in, you two."

The door inched open, and Ruby peered around. "Is it morning?'

I shot a look at my watch. It was almost 6am. "Close enough."

She grinned and skipped to the side of my bed, almost vaulting into it, and snuggling in beside me. I had started sleeping right in the middle of the bed. What was the point of having a side when there was no one to take the other most of the time?

"Can we call Dad?"

I quickly did the mental calculation – it was roughly the middle of the night where he was. "I think we might need to wait til a bit later on."

I gestured to Charlie, who had followed Ruby into my bedroom but was sitting on the end of the bed. "Do you want to go and grab Ruby's presents? They're in the bottom of my wardrobe."

He ducked into the walk-in closet and started to slide the presents behind him along the floor. "Is there anything for me in here?"

His voice was muffled by the clothes hanging around his head.

I wriggled to sit up. "It's Ruby's birthday, remember."

He threw a present on to the bed, and it landed with a thunk next to us.

"Can I open it?" Ruby looked to me for approval.

I nodded. "Of course."

She tore through her gifts in about four-and-a-half minutes flat. At the end of the process, the bed was littered with discarded wrapping paper and the plastic covering that her clothes arrived in. She was clutching an enormous Squishmallow. Where she was going to find space on her bed for it, I had no idea.

"What's that one's name?"

She consulted its label. "It says Spencer. I think I'm going to call it Diamond, though."

"Oh, like Ruby."

She nodded.

"Have we got everything sorted for your friends?"

They were due at 11am, so we still had ample time to get any additional food prepared. Ruby looked at the corner of the ceiling as she turned the thought over in her mind. "Do we have enough bread for the fairy bread?"

I pulled her in for a hug. "We do indeed. Do you want to do sausage rolls?"

She nodded. "The ones with cheese. And can we get sushi?"

"We can get some delivered, yep."

Charlie was rolling around the end of the bed. "What about hot dogs?"

I looked at them both. "I don't know if we can eat sushi and hot dogs, can we?"

"Don't underestimate us, Mum," Charlie gave me a mock salute. "We can do anything we set our minds to, remember? That's what you said."

"Very funny. Let's go and get some breakfast. Is it pancakes for the birthday breakfast?"

Ruby nodded again.

"We're going to have to roll to bed at the end of the day."

After breakfast, I checked my watch again. I cleared my throat. "It's probably okay to call Dad now."

Ruby leapt from her seat and bolted for the iPad lying on the kitchen counter.

Charlie jostled behind her to get a look at the screen. She pressed a couple of buttons and the cheerful blips sounded as the call tried to connect. After a couple of minutes, I held my hand out for the iPad. "Doesn't look like that's going to work right now. Let's try him a little bit later."

Ruby's mouth was downturned. "I wanted to show him my presents."

I sighed. "I know. I'm sure he's excited about seeing them, too. He must be busy with something."

It had better be important. He knew there were some days that he could not go AWOL and the kids' birthdays were top of that list.

"Let's get some flowers from the garden to make the place look nice for your friends," I gestured to the flowerbed outside the front window, where some alstroemeria were turning their faces towards the sun.

Ruby pouted but took the kitchen scissors from me and went for the door. I pulled a vase from beneath the counter and placed it on the dining table. How much time could I spend stalling until she really noticed Brad's absence? If I was so much as three minutes late to pick one of them up from something, I would hear about it for hours. The bar applied to Brad was continually so much lower, it was like simply by existing he managed to tick all the boxes.

Ruby returned and thrust the flowers into the vase, before turning back to the iPad. "It's still not connecting," she turned to me as if I was personally doing something that was stopping her from speaking to her father. "What do I do?"

I shrugged. "I don't think there's a lot we can do at the moment. I'll send him a text to let him know that we're trying to get hold of him and hopefully he'll be finished whatever he's doing and will be back and ready to talk to us very soon."

He had better be, honestly. I sent him a text: Where are you? Ruby's birthday. You haven't forgotten???

∼

Three hours later, we still hadn't managed to reach Brad, but Ruby's attention had shifted to her impending party. She had swapped her pyjamas for a deep purple sundress and fixed a floral headband in her hair. She stood in the hall, watching the front door, as if willing her friends to appear in the driveway. When she was still, I could catch glimpses of what I assumed she might look like when she was an adult, a more serious curve in her cheek, an all-knowing expression – though if I was honest, she had been making me think she was not new to any of this from about the second day she was alive. One eyebrow raised, she looked at me. "Why are they late?"

I slid my arm around her shoulder. "They're not actually, you're just a little bit early. Shall we check we've got all the plates we need?"

An online order of purple paper plates with capybaras around the rim had arrived earlier in the week. I had bought two sets of 10 just in case – I was sure we had only invited 10 girls but on the off chance another turned up, or a sibling, as had happened in earlier years, I did not want to spark a debate about who had to eat off a boring plain white paper plate. I was still burnt from the time at Charlie's party a few years earlier when Amy, tasked with finding the paper cups, had decided it would be completely fine to only have enough Thomas the Tank Engine cups for half the party.

Ruby had scheduled her party down to 10-minute intervals. Friends would arrive. We would open presents. We would have a pinata (shaped like a capybara). We would play pass the parcel. Then we'd have some food and cake and hope everyone felt like going home.

How many kids' parents would stick around? It was hard to predict. When the kids were younger, you were forced to meet and talk while they ate sand in the sandpit together or smushed slime into the carpet. Now we usually just waved and commiserated about how exhausted everyone was.

There were footsteps on the path outside the front door and hushed voices. Ruby bounced on her tiptoes. "I'll open the door."

I smiled. "Of course, bring them through to the lounge."

It was her friend Kaylee, a tiny girl with a mass of blonde curls. She'd pulled her hair back off her face with a sparkly headband in the same hot pink as her dress.

"Come in, you look lovely," I gestured for her to follow Ruby.

Her mother passed a soft, brightly wrapped present to me. Undoubtedly another Squishmallow.

"Thanks very much," I kept my voice light. "I don't think the party will be too long but do you want me to text you when we're finishing up?"

Her mother was saved in my phone as Kaylee's Mum, and it was far too late in our acquaintance for me to do anything about trying to work out her real name. She nodded. "That would be great."

She shouted a farewell to Kaylee, who did not respond.

As she turned to head for the front gate, another pair opened it and traipsed along the path to the front door. I vaguely recognised the girl from Ruby's class but drew a blank on the name. Her mother, who I knew was called Awhina because she worked at the hair salon I sometimes went to, smiled as she handed her over. "How's it all going? Do you need a hand with anything?"

I hesitated, pushing down my reflexive refusal. "Come have a cup of coffee if you like? I could do with some adult company."

She smiled. "Sure, sounds great."

We hovered around the edge of the room, clutching our drinks, as the rest of the girls filed in. They soon formed a circle around Ruby on the lounge floor. Like an emperor being brought gifts by her subjects, she slowly worked her way through them. They had clearly all been shopping in the same stuffed toy aisles.

The front door creaked open and I leant back to look down the hall and check who was coming in. Amy was holding the door open for Simone, and her daughter, Audrey.

"Come and join the girls, sweets," I gestured to her.

Amy and Simone filed in quietly and stood beside me. Audrey

settled cross-legged into the circle on the floor and handed over a small parcel wrapped in tissue paper.

Amy stood beside me, so our shoulders were almost touching. "What do you want me to do?"

I pointed to the kitchen. "Come and help me make some more fairy bread. It's always the first to go. Can Simone help Awhina keep an eye on this?"

In the kitchen, we set up a production line, passing white bread to spread to hundreds-and-thousands. At first, we worked in silence, remnants of awkwardness still hanging between us. We'd been apart in the past and it always took time to pull back together.

Eventually, she broke the silence. "I've been thinking I might go back to university and train to be an art teacher, maybe."

"That sounds good." I could picture her being a teacher. "You'd be one of those cool ones everyone likes."

"I just need to find somewhere to live to save on rent if I'm going back to being a broke student..." she trailed off.

I looked up quickly, but she was smiling. "I'm joking. If I did that I might live with Simone for a while. I'm not expecting to move in here."

I raised my eyebrows. "Must being going well, then."

She blushed. "I haven't scared her off yet with everything that's happened, so I don't know what would."

Simone stuck her head around the door. "The girls are heading out to the pinata, if that's okay?"

I brushed my hands on a cloth that was sitting on the bench next to me. "Sorry, I'll just be a second."

Simone shook her head. "Don't worry, we've got it, you two do what you need to in here."

"Oh, thanks."

She disappeared back into the lounge and we could hear her corralling the girls on to the balcony where the pinata was hanging.

"She's great." I tidied the bread into a perfectly balanced stack.

Amy smiled. "I told you."

There was a steady stream of thuds as the girls took aim outside. I coached myself through a couple of calming breaths – there was no chance of them hitting the windows or the paintwork of the house, was there? Eventually there was a shriek and a splatter of sweets hitting the wooden deck.

A few minutes later, the girls were back inside, and Amy and I returned to the lounge, where they had got into formation for a round of pass the parcel. I'd spent an hour wrapping the parcel the night before, hiding gifts in each layer. Simone took over music duty, setting a Taylor Swift song playing.

"Where's Mum?" Amy leant over to tuck a stray piece of hair behind Audrey's ear as the game began.

I checked my watch. "I'm not sure whether she's going to make it after all. I guess a children's party probably isn't really her scene. She was away yesterday with Reg and she wasn't sure when she'd be back. They're coming for dinner tonight."

"Lucky you."

I smiled. "He's okay. Maybe he'll sort her out."

Amy raised an eyebrow. "Perhaps."

Bits of wrapping paper covered the lounge floor as the game progressed. I reached for a rubbish bag to collect them, but Amy put her hand out to stop me. One of the girls picked up some paper, rolled it into a ball and threw it at another.

Amy smiled. "Worry about it later."

"We must be nearly at the end," Simone stopped the music again. The parcel was a fraction of its original size. "I'm going to turn my back so I can't see who's getting these last layers."

I nodded in her direction. "I'm glad she knows what's going on."

Awhina, hovering over two of the girls, laughed. "I know, this kind of thing gives me hives."

Amy gestured outside. "We can take the ones who want to swim out to the pool after this, if you like."

The music stopped as Kaylee took the parcel from Ruby and

the girls all shuffled closer. She ripped off the final paper layer to reveal the prize – a bubble kit.

"You're so lucky," Ruby almost frowned.

I poked her gently. "Says you, with your pile of presents."

Kaylee held up the bubble mixture. "Can we go outside and blow bubbles?"

"Sure, head out through the kitchen."

The girls filed out, sparkly headbands catching the light and layers of their party dresses blowing in the breeze.

A hand clasped my shoulder, and a familiar voice whispered in my ear. "They look like they're having fun."

I whirled around. "What on Earth are you doing here?"

Brad grinned. "I thought I'd make it a surprise."

Behind him, his suitcases were propped against the couch. He pulled me towards him and I wrapped my arms around his middle, breathing in the smell of his aftershave. It was still the one I had bought him for Christmas. Should I push him away? Had he turned up to try to convince me to change my mind about carrying on with the long-distance life?

"Turning up for one party doesn't make it okay," my voice was muffled in his shirt.

He kissed my forehead, leaving his lips resting against my skin. "I know."

I shook my head. "I meant what I said. I can't do this."

He rested his cheek on the top of my head. "I know. I'm home."

I pulled back and looked up at him. He had a smattering of stubble on his chin and his shirt was crumpled from his flight. "But for how long?"

He kissed my forehead, then my nose and finally my lips. "As long as you'll have me."

I pushed him back so that my arms were outstretched, my hands on his arms. "What?"

He shrugged. "I quit. You're right. It's not fair on you. I don't want to see the kids growing up over FaceTime and I definitely don't want my wife to forget about me or give up on me."

I was aware I was gaping at him, but I couldn't get my face to cooperate. "But...what will you do?"

He laughed. "Don't worry, I've got a few offers around here. But first up I'm going to enjoy hanging out with my family for a bit. I think I've got quite a bit to catch up on."

Charlie ambled back into the kitchen from the garden. He had bubble mixture dripping down his arms. Without looking towards me, he opened the pantry door. "Mum... we need something to make some more bubble mixture."

Brad cleared his throat, and Charlie stumbled back out of the pantry. "Dad!"

He launched himself at his father and clung to him.

Amy followed him into the kitchen. "Is everything alright in here?"

She stopped when she saw Brad. "Are my eyes deceiving me? I was starting to think you'd become just a figment of our imaginations."

Brad rolled his eyes at her, one arm still around Charlie and the other encircling my waist. "It's nice to see you, Amy."

"Ruby's in the garden," I said.

Brad ducked his head in acknowledgement. "I'd better see the birthday girl."

We walked like some sort of expanded three-legged race through the kitchen and out into the back garden, none of us wanting to let go of the others.

Ruby was surrounded by her friends, speckled sunlight coming through the leaves of the trees that bordered the garden and playing on her face.

She sprung to her feet when she spotted us. "Dad!"

I shifted out of his grasp so that she could throw herself at him.

"Happy birthday, darling," he buried his face in her hair as she wrapped her arms and legs around him.

"This is the best birthday ever," she pulled back and looked up at him.

Amy caught my eye. "Maybe it is all going to be okay, after all."

I nodded, watching Simone reach for her hand. "It's funny how things work out."

"I still think you're the lucky one, though," she hissed. But she was smiling.

THE END

ABOUT THE AUTHOR

To learn more about Susan Jane Edmunds and discover more Next Chapter authors, visit our website at www.nextchapter.pub.

Publisher contact information
Next Chapter
2-5-6 SANNO
SANNO BRIDGE
143-0023 Ota-Ku
Tokyo, Japan
https://nextchapter.pub

Printed in Dunstable, United Kingdom

79147592R00143